"Everybody wins when a classic form, such as the private-eye novel, meets up with a class act, such as Dave White. In this remarkable debut novel, White manages the neat trick of respecting the genre's traditions while daring to nudge it toward something new and unexpected. And Jackson Donne is a wonderful character, someone with whom readers will happily share many beers in the Olde Towne Tavern for years to come. Lots of promise here—in Donne and White. I'm rooting for both of them."

—Laura Lippman, Edgar Award–winning author of *Every Secret Thing*

"Every now and then you find a debut novel that carries the clear promise of big things to come. *When One Man Dies* is one of those. Fast and funny, with plenty of classic action but a setting and character that are entirely new . . . Dave White is creating a winner with Jackson Donne. Always good to get in on the ground floor."

—Michael Koryta, Edgar-nominated author of *A Welcome Grave*

"Jackson Donne takes his place alongside the grim and battered PIs of yore— your Archers, your Spades—uncovering painful truths and doling out what passes in this tarnished world for justice. Bracing stuff."

—Charles Ardai, Edgar Award–winning author and founder of Hard Case Crime

"When I read my first Dave White story, I knew that he was going to be huge someday—like, Robert Parker huge. *When One Man Dies* is the first bold step in fulfilling that promise. It's the great American private-eye novel reborn for the twenty-first century, with a fast-moving, spare style that punches you in the gut at the same time it squeezes your heart."

—Duane Swierczynski, author of *The Blonde* and *The Wheelman*

"*When One Man Dies* barrels straight out of the old school and swerves onto the highway that will take detective fiction where it's going next. Dave White has one hand on the wheel, the other on the gear shift, and his foot on the floor."

—Sean Doolittle, author of *The Cleanup* and *Rain Dogs*

"Every new crew of crime writers has one standout, and true to form here comes Dave White, an author who made his bones in short story form before most writers ever find their legs. *When One Man Dies* steps him up as a made man in the genre . . . an awesome debut . . . forgetaboutit."

—Charlie Stella, author of *Cheapskates* and *Charlie Opera*

WHEN ONE MAN DIES

a NOVEL

DAVE WHITE

THREE RIVERS PRESS
NEW YORK

Copyright © 2007 by Dave White

All rights reserved.
Published in the United States by Three Rivers Press, an imprint of the Crown Publishing Group, a division of Random House, Inc., New York.
www.crownpublishing.com

Three Rivers Press and the Tugboat design are registered trademarks of Random House, Inc.

Library of Congress Cataloging-in-Publication Data

White, Dave, 1979–
When one man dies : a novel / Dave White.— 1st ed.
1. Private investigators—New Jersey—Fiction. 2. Ex–police officers—Fiction.
3. New Jersey—Fiction. I. Title.
PS3623.H5727W47 2007
813'.6—dc22   2007001240
ISBN 978-0-307-38278-8

Printed in the United States of America

Design by Maria Elias

10 9 8 7 6 5 4 3 2 1

First Edition

To Mom, Dad, and Tom
For their love and support

acknowLeDgments

There are so many people I need to thank. To Allan Guthrie and Jason Pinter for taking this book and making it so much better than it was.

Sarah Weinman, who put up with more whining from me than anyone should, then still forced me to get my butt into gear and get this done.

My family and friends for always believing, sometimes more than I did.

Kevin Burton Smith, Victoria Esposito-Shea, and Gerald So over at the *Thrilling Detective* website for accepting my first stories and pretty much being the ones who got me into this mess.

The faculty, staff, and administration at Christopher Columbus Middle School for their constant support.

Lisa and Nick Poggi, who told me the best bad joke ever and then let me use it in this book.

Ray Banks, Laura Lippman, Duane Swierczynski, Pat Lambe, Charlie Stella, Bryon Quertermous, John Rickards, Christin Kuretich, and Jim Winter, who told me I sucked when I sucked, who told me I was great when I was good, and for dragging me—kicking and screaming—into this world of writers and becoming great friends and great inspirations.

Thanks everybody.

When one man dies, one chapter is not torn out of the book,
but translated into a better language.

—John Donne, *Devotions Upon Emergent Occasions*

1

I've killed three men in my life. One the police know about, two that I've kept to myself. For the fourth time in three months, I had blood on my hands, and all the forgotten images of the dead were swirling back to me.

This time, however, I wasn't doing the killing. I was in the middle of Easton Ave., trying to pump life back into a man I used to drink with for hours on end.

He was bleeding from the nose and mouth. He wasn't breathing. I could feel his ribs crunch with every compress of my hands on his chest.

I couldn't yet hear the ambulances and Robert Wood Johnson Hospital was right down the street.

I yelled, "Someone call nine-one-one!"

But I knew it was too late, and Gerry was gone. Dead bodies look different from live ones. I should know.

* *

The Olde Towne Tavern was pretty crowded for a late Monday afternoon. Standing in the back, under a dimming Budweiser neon light, two college kids played pool. To my left, leaning against the stained wooden wall, two guys discussed baseball and the greatest American rock and roll band at the same time. It was impressive. A young couple sat at a dirty table finishing their lunch. Gerry sat next to me, and bought me a Heineken. He had his cup of coffee, and the breath to go with it.

We were celebrating.

"Accepted, huh? Gonna be a freshman at twenty-seven years old?"

"Twenty-eight."

"Whatever. It's still old to go to college. But I'm proud of ya. Can't keep this private eye stuff up all your life."

"Hey, I have to pay tuition somehow." Not that I was getting many cases lately. When your face is plastered all over the news and most of it isn't good, the clients aren't exactly knocking down your door.

I decided to come to the tavern for lunch today after getting my mail. I pulled out one of those big envelopes that high school seniors pray for. Opening it up, I found a letter that began, "Dear Mr. Donne, We are pleased to announce your acceptance to Rutgers University . . ." Best news I'd had in two months.

I drank my beer and Gerry blathered. Eventually, my burger would show, I could eat and get out of here. Gerry's a nice guy, but grating when he starts to get a rant on.

"Never went to college myself. Had a war to fight. Fucking Korea."

"I remember, Gerry."

Gerry talked about two things. Korea and his former life as an actor.

"So, tell me about this college thing. What are you going to do? When are you going to start?"

I finished my beer, still waiting for Artie to bring me my burger.

"Probably start next fall. In September, once I get all of the tests out of the way."

Gerry shook his head.

"You have to take an entrance exam. See what classes you can take," I said.

"Then what? You take your classes? Get a B.S. Ha! Get a B.S. in BS." He slapped himself on the leg, let out a short chuckle.

I gave him a smile. "Probably be an English major."

"How's that going to help you? What can you do with an English degree?"

"We'll see."

He plunked ten bucks on the bar as Artie finally brought my burger.

"Well, Jackson," Gerry said, "I best be going. Gotta get home."

I heard the door swing open behind me and he was gone. I poured some ketchup on my burger as Artie flipped a switch behind the bar. The Stones popped on over the speakers, "Beast of Burden."

"That guy doesn't shut up. Been coming here since I bought the place," Artie said with a grin. "I love that guy."

I took a bite of my burger.

In New Jersey, especially a busy town like New Brunswick, there is a lot of traffic. Brakes squeal all the time. So I chewed and swallowed, listening to the Stones, until I heard the crunch. Like metal hitting something hard. Artie and I made eye contact just before the screaming started.

I dropped the burger, bolted out the door.

It was a warm day for mid-April, most people walking around in T-shirts and jeans. The sun heated my skin and stabbed into my eyes as I made the adjustment from the darkness of the bar to the bright afternoon. People stood on the sidewalk, staring. Some young coed screamed. No one was moving.

In the middle of the road Gerry lay in a prone position. Blood streaked down his face. His eyes were closed. I couldn't tell if he was breathing.

Traffic had stopped in Gerry's direction, one car about twenty feet from him. It didn't have a dent in it.

"I can't believe the guy just drove off," someone was saying.

I raced into the street, I knelt next to Gerry, my knees digging into the asphalt.

"Someone call nine-one-one!" I yelled.

It had been too long since I'd trained in CPR. Four years since I was a cop, too long since I'd had to do anything remotely like this. I'd been surrounded by too much death over the past few months, and not enough ways to save life. I hoped muscle memory would kick in.

Pressing my fingers to Gerry's neck, I tried for a pulse. I didn't feel anything. Then I turned my head, put my ear to his nose and mouth. He wasn't breathing. Gerry was in trouble.

I opened his mouth, shut his nose, and breathed twice into his mouth. His blood pasted my face, and something told me I was doing the procedure wrong. I didn't care. His chest went up and then let the air out. No other reaction.

Down Easton Ave., horns were honking. The sun beat on my neck, but it wasn't the reason I was sweating.

I put both my hands on his chest and pumped five times. I didn't know if the number was right. I didn't know if anything was right. I was going on instinct.

I exhaled once more into his mouth.

I finally heard the sirens, the sound of ambulances, police, and fire. Someone must have called 911. When you call, they send everybody.

I pounded on Gerry's chest until I felt someone wrap a hand around my arm and tug at me. I whirled and saw Artie staring at me.

"Let it be, man," he said.

I tried to turn back to Gerry. Artie pulled harder.

"Let it be."

I let him tug my arm, and I finally got to my feet. I knew I wasn't going to be able to help Gerry anymore.

An ambulance swung around toward us off Somerset. Its siren was louder than the screeching tires.

Gerry's chest didn't rise or fall.

CHAPTER 2

after about ten minutes, Artie couldn't take it anymore. He turned and went back inside the bar, mumbling something about having customers to serve. Those customers were all standing outside with me, pint glasses in hand, watching the cops and EMS work. Not much talking going on. In fact, the only sounds were the whispering of the cops asking witnesses questions and a few horns honking down the street.

I stood and watched the EMS guys. They were doing what I had been doing, but nothing was working. One of them, a guy with a goatee and shaved head, was just watching. The other, a woman with a short bowl-cut hairdo and no makeup, was pumping Gerry's chest. They were both shaking their heads. Finally, the bald guy and the driver got the stretcher, as the woman kept pumping. Two more pumps, and she stopped, wiping her brow. Making eye contact with her partner, she backed away and they lifted Gerry onto the stretcher. Checked his pulse one more time. Wheeled him into the ambulance, which pulled away without sirens. Gerry's blood stained the street, a crusty dark red mark. The odor of asphalt and car exhaust permeated the air.

EMS workers can't pronounce someone dead on the spot. They have to do everything they can to keep the patient alive. Even if the person is dead they have to put on the act. From what I could see, these guys didn't try too hard.

Down the street, the cops were talking to a crying woman. They had one of those small, spiral notebooks out and were taking notes in blue pencil. A cop was nodding as the woman spoke, probably doing his best to be understanding through all her blubbering. Once the beat cops determined this was a hit-and-run, the plainclothes detectives would show up. If they heard I was here, they'd want to talk to me. I turned to one of the regulars and told him I'd be inside if the cops wanted to chat.

"Yeah," he said, taking a sip from his glass. "You might want to wash up. Look like a goddamn vampire."

First thing I did was hit the bathroom. Artie did his best to keep it clean, but it still smelled like someone had puked. The walls were a pale yellow, the toilet was white and chipped. The sink only ran cold water, and the mirror was cracked. I looked at the blood congealing on my face and hands and thought that even if I washed it off, I'd probably still feel its mark. I scrubbed harder.

By the time I returned, Artie had changed the music. The Band's "The Weight" was playing while he wiped down the bar. I wondered if he felt the same way about the bar as I felt about the blood on my face: if he cleaned it, then all trace of Gerry would be gone.

"I love this song," he said. I took a stool across from him at the bar. He got me another bottle of Heineken, popped the top, and put it in front of me.

I took a sip, listened to the music. I hadn't heard the song in years. Let the laid-back rhythm sink in. "Good song."

We listened to it play out.

When I finished my beer, Artie got me another. I let it sit. Something that sounded like Lou Reed came on. I wanted to ask who was singing, what the title of the song was, something to delay the inevitable, make some sort of small talk—even if I could guess all the song's information. But Artie didn't wait.

"So, what do you think?"

I picked up the beer, looked at it. Put it back down. "About the song?"

"No."

"Oh," I said. "It didn't look good."

He shook his head. "Haven't seen anything like that since 'Nam. One of us should have gone with the ambulance."

"We're not family," I said. "It wasn't our place."

"We were the closest thing he had. You know that."

"Fuck," I said. I hated when Artie was right.

I took the first sip of my fourth beer of the day. It wasn't even five o'clock.

This was the worst part. Waiting for the inevitable news you prayed wasn't going to come. Most people try to talk around it, sit with a knot in their stomachs and pray. I hated that. Instead, I laid it all out on the table.

"He's not going to make it. He wasn't breathing. I don't think EMS got him to start. He's dead."

"You don't know that for . . ." Artie made eye contact with me. "Yeah, you're probably right. Did the cops find the car?"

My beer was half-gone, and my stomach started to feel a bit light. I wished I had gotten a chance to eat the burger. "I don't know. I don't think so."

This time it was Artie's turn to put it out for all to hear. "Do you think it was an accident?"

He could wait while I finished off the beer.

Truth was, I didn't know. Gerry did have some enemies. Six months ago, the manager of a theater Gerry used to act at paid his landlord to try and evict him. That way she could drum up some press about starving actors to bring in theatergoers who felt bad. I stepped in and talked to her and the landlord. When I was done, he kept his home. Last I heard, she'd sold the theater, moved out of state.

Artie put another Heineken in front of me. I didn't touch it.

He said, "Are you going to look into it?"

"The police will." Sweat dripped off the beer bottle onto the bar. "They're already out there asking questions."

"I don't trust the cops. They'll look at it as a hit-and-run accident. If they find the car, good for them, they'll talk to whoever did it. Maybe put some sort of manslaughter charge on it."

"Maybe it is just manslaughter."

The beer looked lonely just sitting there. Artie had taken the empties away. The one green bottle made the bar look unprofessional and asymmetrical. I picked it up. Took a swig. The beer was still cold, tasted bitter going down. For the fifth, it should have been easier to drink.

Artie said, "If it is, I want to find out from you. And if it's not, I'd like you to take care of that."

"Are you trying to hire me?"

"That's what it sounds like." He mopped the condensation off the bar.

The rest of the beer went down a bit easier. I had a full buzz going on now.

"The cops can handle it. I don't want to do this. I want to focus on getting this college shit straightened out."

"You said you'd have to pay your way somehow."

"I can do some insurance work. They're still calling me."

I spun the empty bottle on the bar. Artie caught it, took it away.

The bar door swung open, one of the regulars stuck his head in. "Cops are gonna be in to ask questions in a few, guys."

Artie looked at me, said, "I don't trust the cops, Jackson. But I do trust you."

"Why do you care about this at all?"

"Why are you trying to act like you don't care? You know Gerry came in here every day. Even after he stopped drinking. Even after his son died. He has no one else. We're as close to family as it's going to get. I think we owe it to him."

I couldn't argue with that. "All right. I'll look into it. But first, get me another beer."

Artie reached behind the bar. "I want to pay your standard rate. Draw up a contract and everything."

"Fine," I said, not willing to argue anymore.

3

CHAPTER

BILL MARTIN STOOD ON THE CURB WATCHING THE
officers work the crowd. He puffed on a cigarette, which he knew he'd
catch hell for, but didn't care. He missed the days when Leo Carver
was still in charge. He could do whatever the hell he wanted then.

The body of the old man was long gone, but the chalk outline
was there. The street was closed off, and he could hear the horns of
cars being forced to detour. A hit-and-run could only make this town
more congested.

Martin got called in late, after the officers had started questioning witnesses and letting them leave the scene. Back when they origi-
nally thought it was an accident. It wasn't until more than one witness
said they thought the car aimed at the victim that he was summoned.

He hadn't worked a homicide in a long time. In a town like this,
only detectives and uniforms, usually the cops in good standing, got
the homicides. Martin was stuck with robberies.

But it'd been an unusual week in New Brunswick, with two drive-by shootings and a college kid pushed down a frat stairway. So Martin was the only detective left on duty when this call came in. He was glad it got him out of the office.

He wasn't sure what the crime-scene guys would find here. There were some drops of blood splattered along the pavement, but that was about it. Maybe some paint chips from the offending car? Like that would help. Pounding the pavement, getting descriptions, that's what would help. Maybe someone had been quick enough to catch a plate number.

Martin did a quick scan of the faces in the crowd, the dumbfounded looks. There wasn't anyone quick enough.

He waved over Officer Franklin, the first one on the scene. The short guy, hat tilted wrong, sweat pouring off his brow. He didn't make eye contact.

"Yes, Detective?"

Martin grinned, loved intimidating the rookies. "You talk to everyone here?"

"Most of them."

"Start letting some witnesses go?"

"Yeah," Franklin said. "After we talked to them, we told them to go home."

"Make a list of the people you talked to? Contact information?"

"Yes, sir."

Martin waited. Figured Franklin would get the hint and give him the list. But Franklin stared at something on the sidewalk.

Martin cleared his throat and Franklin's head snapped up.

"The list?" Martin said.

"Oh. Right. Of course." Franklin fiddled with his pockets and pulled out a piece of paper folded into fourths. Real professional.

Martin took the paper, lit another cigarette, and looked over the names. It was the third name that jumped out at him as if it'd been outlined in neon. It was a name he hadn't uttered in years, but thought about every day. Memories clouded his thought process. He barely re-membered the hit-and-run.

All he saw was the name that nearly ended his career. And he knew which witness he'd be speaking with first.

Jackson Donne.

4

CHAPTER

By the time I got back to my office, after being interviewed by three different patrolmen, a dull throb radiated behind my eyes. I sat behind my desk massaging my temples, eyes closed. I called Lester Russell. I used my office line to call his cell, got his voice mail. I left a message for him to call me back.

There was a knock at my office door. Probably Artie checking in. I splashed some water on my face, came back from the bathroom, and opened the door. It wasn't Artie.

It was a woman.

She looked at me between strands of brown hair that fell over her gunmetal eyes.

"You Jackson Donne?" She pronounced it "Doan."

I corrected her and said, "That's me. Can I help you?"

"I'd like to hire you."

I stepped away from the doorjamb. Said, "Come on in."

She walked past me, wearing a white New Jersey Devils T-shirt and jeans with a tear in the ass. She was wearing white underwear. She also had a wedding ring on her finger.

She took a seat in the chair set up for prospective clients, facing my desk. I circled around and joined her, crossing my hands on my desk, like a perfect student. Ready to listen.

"What can I help you with, ma'am?"

She pulled her long hair back into a ponytail. "Please, my mother's a ma'am. Call me Jen."

"Okay, Jen." I returned the smile. Mine probably was a little more natural. "What can I do for you?"

She played with the ring on her finger. "I think my husband is cheating on me."

"I see."

She twisted the ring to the tip of her nail, pressed it back on. "He comes home late. He doesn't call. He smells like alcohol and perfume."

"How long have you been married?"

"About a year."

"What does he do for a living?"

"He's a bouncer."

"Why do you think he's cheating on you? To my knowledge, all bouncers smell that way and stay out late. It's in the job description."

She shook her head. "Don't patronize me. It's just something I feel. And I need to know."

Time to give her the speech. "Jen, I'm sure it's just that. A feeling. A lot of women come in here with the feeling, and I follow their husbands around for days and find nothing. Save your money. You don't want to know anyway. It'll just mess up your life."

I don't know why I decided to give her the speech. I needed the money. I could take the case on, follow her husband around at night, and still have time to dig into the Gerry thing. But this woman looked shell-shocked, and I didn't want to screw her over.

She stared me straight in the eye. "You ever get a thought in your head and you couldn't get it out? It just keeps gnawing at you? That's what's happening here. I have to know, no matter what the consequences. It's been bothering me, in my head for the past few days. I can't get it out. I'm losing sleep. I can talk to my husband, but I can't just flat out ask him. I have the money. What do you care? Why won't you just allow me to hire you?"

"Because I don't like seeing people get hurt."

"I appreciate that you have a heart. But I want to do this. I'm a grown woman."

I opened the desk drawer. Pulled out a contract. "You've convinced me."

"So," she said, "how do we do this?"

"Well, first things first, Jen. I need to know your full name, your husband's full name, where he works. A place I can catch him to tail him, that sort of thing."

"My name is Jen Hanover. My husband's name is Rex, same last name. I have a picture."

"That'll help," I said, writing the information down.

She went into her purse and dug out a wallet-sized photo. Handed it across the desk to me. I took it, gave it a once-over.

Rex Hanover was a thickset guy, wearing a tight black T-shirt with a logo in script writing over a breast pocket. His arms bulged in the sleeves, and he wore black jeans. Looked like a bouncer, close-cut hair, strong cheek bones. Tan.

"Where does he work?"

"At Billy's in Morristown? It's a club or a bar. Off Two Eighty-seven."

"You have directions?"

"Just a business card." She dug that out and handed it to me as well.

"I'll MapQuest it," I said.

"He's working every night this week. I've never known anyone who does that. I go to work during the day, come home about seven, and he's just heading out. He doesn't get home till three, sometimes four in the morning."

"Let me ask you something. When he gets home, does he smell like cigarette smoke?"

She thought about it, eyes rolled up toward the ceiling. "No. He doesn't smoke. Well, on the weekends he smells that way. But not during the week. So many people to watch outside, he still gets that smoke smell, even with the no smoking law."

"Maybe it's just not that busy during the week," I said, not wanting to push her expectations either way.

She shifted in her seat, as if she was searching for something to say.

Finally she came up with, "He used to smell that way even during the weekdays."

"Any idea who he might be having an affair with? If he's having an affair."

She shook her head.

"What's your address?"

She gave me an address in Morristown.

"Why come down here?"

She scratched her nose. "My husband knows a lot of people. If he knew I hired a private investigator up there, if word got out, I'd be in trouble. He doesn't know people in this area."

I nodded. "Okay, we're almost done. I charge seventy-five bucks an hour plus expenses. I also require a retainer. Say five hundred?"

She nodded, took out her checkbook.

We finished the paperwork, shook hands, and she headed toward the door. I told her I'd let her know as soon as I had any information.

After she left, my cell phone rang. Lester Russell, the caller ID said.

"What's up, Jackson? You aren't in prison again, are you?"

"Think I'd have my cell phone with me?"

"Good point. Why are you calling me when I'm in trial? You knew I wouldn't get back to you until now."

"Out already?" I said as I looked at my watch. Close to four.

"I only have a few minutes."

"I need a favor."

"Of course you do."

I told him about Gerry. Told him I wanted some information from the cops.

"Jeez," Lester said. "I'll make a few calls. See what I can find out. But not until the trial is out this afternoon."

"Thanks, Lester."

He sighed. "I can't keep doing this stuff for you. I'm a lawyer, not a snitch, not an informant. I think it's time you made nice with the boys in blue."

"There are two sides to that coin," I said.

CHAPTER 5

BILL MARTIN NODDED AT THE WOMAN COMING down the stairs. She didn't seem to notice him. That was fine.

He flicked his last cigarette of the pack onto the ground, crushed it with his shoe, and hiked to Donne's office. The glass door was opaque and had his name inscribed in black lettering. Beneath it said PRIVATE INVESTIGATOR. Should have said *Traitor*.

Or even better, *Asshole*.

Martin didn't bother to knock.

Donne was hanging up the phone. He looked up and froze.

"How's it going, kid?" Martin asked.

"Bill."

Martin took the chair in front of the desk, flipping it around so he could sit with his arms resting on the back.

"I've heard," Donne said, "that sitting that way means you're intimidated by women."

He fired back. "If you knew what I've done, you wouldn't bring that up. I'll tell you someday."

"Why are you here?"

"You were at the tavern today, right? Saw what happened with Gerry?"

"You're investigating the case." He wasn't asking a question.

Martin shrugged. "So, what did you see? What happened?"

"I don't think I'm going to talk to you about this."

Martin allowed himself a wry smile. Getting Donne to talk to him was half the reason Martin was looking forward to this. It was a challenge. Finding a way to screw Donne over in the process was the other half.

"I guess reminding you that you were my partner is out of the question, so how about helping me find the killer of someone you drank with."

Donne shifted in his seat. "I don't need your help."

"Jesus Christ. You're investigating the case, aren't you?"

Donne stayed silent, now motionless.

"Listen, the best thing you can do for this guy is leave it to me. I'm a cop. You know the resources we have at our disposal. What are you going to do, pound the fucking pavement and hope someone tells you who did it?"

"Come on, Bill. You never believed in that CSI shit."

"I just want to find out who killed Gerry Figuroa."

The air smelled musty, as if Donne hadn't cleaned or even aired out his office in months. How did Donne get clients to sit here and explain their problems? Place stank to shit.

"I don't know anything," Donne said. "I sat in the bar, I heard tires squeal. By the time I got outside, the car was gone and Gerry was dead."

"That's your story?" Martin felt heat in his stomach. Rage building. His cheeks flushed.

"That's all I'm telling you."

"My old partner, and he won't help me find his friend's killer."

"It was a hit-and-run. Could have been an accident."

"Hit-and-run," Martin said. "Still a murder in my book, kid."

"Since when did they let you work homicides?"

Martin's cheeks probably turned cherry red, he was so pissed. "You always were an asshole, Donne."

"If it wasn't for me, you'd be in jail."

"If it wasn't for you, things would still be the way they were."

Donne stood. "I think you should go."

"Probably right." Martin found a business card and dropped it on the desk. "I have a new number. You change your mind, want to tell me what happened, call me."

"Sure."

Martin stepped out of the office. Once on the street, he smiled. This was going to work out just fine.

Not only did he get a chance to solve a murder, he was going to get a chance to fuck Donne over as well.

Yeah, this was going to work out perfectly.

6

CHAPTER

THREE HEINEKENS AND A FEW HOURS LATER, my watch read ten after eight. I had my MapQuest directions and a picture of Rex Hanover in the car, so I decided not to stop at my apartment. I already had everything I needed. I headed up route 287. Traffic was light and 287 takes you through a section of the state the opposite of Newark and the turnpike. While the turnpike is full of smog and rusted metal, the Morristown-Madison area is very wealthy, with large houses spaced out among trees, mountains, and parks. The smog and factories of northeast New Jersey were only a scant twenty miles away, but felt like hundreds.

I took the exit for Madison Avenue as per my directions and saw Billy's on my right. I parked the car in a supermarket parking lot next door, took my picture, and went inside. Apparently it was too early for a cover charge, but the bouncer at the door, who was two inches shorter than me and probably twenty pounds heavier, told me to tuck in my shirt. "Dress code," he mumbled. His name tag read JEFF.

21

I did as he said, not wanting to make waves, and then found a seat at the nearly empty bar. The bartender, a thin woman with huge breasts and long black hair, asked, "What can I do for you, hon?"

I debated several answers before simply saying, "Heineken." The buzz was wearing off from the three I'd had earlier.

By the time she put the bottle in front of me, I was holding the picture of Hanover out. "You know this guy?"

"Four-fifty for the beer," she said, and took the picture from me. Examined it close to her face.

I put six on the bar.

"This is Rex," she said, taking the money, dropping the picture. "He works here."

I drank some of the beer. "He here tonight?"

She looked toward the door. "Is he in trouble?"

She ran her hand through her hair. There was another guy, younger than me, at the other end of the bar, staring at her ass. When he saw me notice him, he winked.

"He's not in trouble, I just want to ask him a few questions."

"You a cop?"

I didn't answer the cop question. It was just as well she assumed I was a cop.

She waited a moment, then said, "I don't see him. He's usually in only on the weekends. Sometimes Wednesdays. Well, if I see him, who should I say is looking for him?"

"Don't mention I was here." I dropped a twenty on the bar. Finished my beer.

"Not a problem." She smiled, picking up the bill.

I got up and went back out to my car. Four beers and it wasn't even eight-thirty. I figured it was best I stayed out of the bar, even if that meant I had to sit in my car and think.

The night air was crisp, and I shivered as I unlocked the door. Behind me I heard footsteps. I turned to see a large man heading toward me, wearing a black Billy's shirt. His hair was blond, crew cut, eyes bright blue. Up his right biceps was a long scar.

"You the cop?" he asked.

"Maybe," I said. Acting tough to a bouncer usually gets you tossed out of the bar. But what the hell, we were already outside.

"Why are you looking for Rex?"

"I need to ask him a couple of questions."

He was standing about three feet away, towering over me, his arms crossed.

"He in trouble?"

"Should he be?"

He suppressed a smile and said, "Damn. That guy gets scheduled for every Tuesday night. Then he calls up and switches with me."

"Why?"

"Doesn't say. Just tells me he's going to this chick's apartment in Madison. It's up on Elm Street over by the university. Original name, Elm Street Apartments."

"Why did he tell you this?"

The bouncer's face went red. "He takes my shift on Thursday nights."

"Ah, do you go to the same place?"

The bouncer shut his mouth.

"Why don't you go on Tuesdays and he can go on Thursdays?"

The bouncer didn't say anything.

"Listen," I said. "I don't give a shit about you. Just him."

"The chick I like is only there on Thursdays and Sundays."

I nodded. "What apartment?"

"Thirty-seven C."

"Thanks," I said. "What made you tell me?"

"I don't know. When Rex called me, he didn't sound happy. Something in his voice. Something wrong. I don't trust the guy. Got a fucking temper like you wouldn't believe. I saw him take this drunk one day, toss him into the parking lot, kick him in the head until we had to pull him off. I'm worried."

"What's your name?"

He hesitated.

"In case I need to contact you."

He sighed. "Eddie Fredricks."

I opened my car door. "Do me a favor, Eddie."

He raised his eyebrows.

"Rex shows up tonight, don't mention me."

I gave him my card, told him to call me if he thought of anything else. We shook hands and he went back toward Billy's.

I started my car, pulled out onto Madison Avenue. I forgot to get directions. I'd stop at the next gas station.

*   *

I found the Elm Street Apartments, just across from Drew University, a small, private university in Madison. Brick buildings, quaint and relaxed, surrounded by a tall metal fence. I parked, sat for a few minutes. I wasn't sure that Rex was in there, I didn't know if I'd missed him, but if I just went up and knocked on the door I would blow my cover. Ah, the catch-22s of being a private investigator. One thing I did know, sitting here and doing nothing would only lead to boredom. So I dialed information, found the number for the nearest pizza place that delivered, and ordered a large pepperoni. I'd have to wait forty minutes.

After thirty-five minutes of thumb twiddling, I got out of my car, crossed the street, and got a better view of the apartment door.

A few minutes later the delivery guy pulled up. He stepped out of his dented, gray Corolla, carried the pizza to the apartment door. He rang the doorbell. He checked his watch as the door opened. Rex Hanover, bulging biceps, crew cut, and all, filled the doorway. The delivery guy was looking at his receipt and Hanover was shaking his head, probably saying he didn't order a pizza. The delivery guy said a few words and Hanover shook his head some more. The delivery guy slumped his shoulders and turned back toward his car. The door to 37C closed behind him. The guy got back in his Corolla, his tires squealing as he pulled off the curb.

Hanover was in there, but I wasn't sure with whom. If I went on what Eddie said it was probably a woman. My next hope would be to catch Hanover saying good-bye on his way out. Hopefully it'd be a woman, or hell, even a guy, and Hanover would give the person a kiss, I'd take a picture and collect an easy paycheck. But as another hour passed, my hope for an easy evening and an easy paycheck slipped away.

I decided standing on Elm was more comfortable than sitting. About eleven-forty, my bladder was throbbing, trying to get rid of the Heineken my liver hadn't soaked up. I took a leak through the fence, not worrying about onlookers. A car hadn't passed on the street in twenty-five minutes. When I zipped up and turned back, 37C's door was open. Hanover stepped out of the doorway. He didn't turn around to kiss anyone good-bye, no one was standing in the doorway, but he had a huge rolled-up carpet dragging behind him. Carpets are heavy, but the way he pulled it, struggled with it, my stomach flipped. He dragged it like it was a deadweight.

I found my camera and scooted out of sight around the corner behind one of the brick posts of the fencing surrounding the university. I snapped two photos of Hanover with the carpet. Hanover moved slowly but confidently, as if no one was watching him and if they were, he didn't give a damn. He would drag the carpet a few feet, then stop, and then drag it another few feet. He pulled the carpet all the way across Elm. I took another set of photos. I hoped the streetlights would be enough in the darkness, because I didn't want to risk using the flash.

A breeze was picking up, and cool sweat pooled on my neck. Hanover pulled the carpet in front of the high iron gate that opened to the university's road. He dropped the carpet there, as if he wanted it to be found, turned, and walked back across the street, wiping his forehead. He returned to the apartment. I snapped a picture of him going around the corner to the rear of the building, and another of him behind the wheel of a maroon Honda CR-V pulling out of the driveway, making sure I had the license plate in my viewfinder.

The car turned right onto Elm and disappeared down the road. I waited a few seconds, my knees stiff and my stomach tight. I knew I was going to go over to the rolled carpet and open it. I had an idea of what I was going to find. Once the CR-V was out of sight, I walked toward the carpet. The closer I got, I could see it wasn't rolled that tightly, and it was already starting to unravel.

By the time I was half a block away, I could see an arm peeking out from beneath the lime green fabric.

7

"Hands in the fucking air!"

I raised my hands sky-high. Said, "My name's Jackson Donne. I'm a pri—"

"Shut the fuck up! Keep your hands up!"

Two cops had hopped out of a patrol car and apparently seen the arm protruding from the carpet first. The guns were unholstered immediately and trained on me. It wasn't the most pleasant feeling, two gun barrels pointed in my direction.

"Against the fence. Assume the position," the taller one said.

I did as I was told, saying, "I have a camera in my pocket and a Glock under my jacket."

The cop frisked me down, took the Glock, took the camera.

"What are you doing with this?" he asked. I wasn't sure if he meant the gun or the camera.

"I'm a private investigator. I was hired to follow someone, and he dropped the carpet off in front of the university here."

"Hands behind your back."

I followed his instructions and allowed him to handcuff me.

"I have ID in my wallet," I said.

He took my wallet and opened it. "Okay. You are who you say you are. You'll still have to wait for the detectives to get here."

He ushered me into the back of the car. Both cops went to take a closer look at the carpet. One of them looked like he was about to be sick. I peered harder and could see the face of a woman, someone I'd never seen before.

❋ ❋

I must have sat in the cop car for nearly an hour, watching an ambulance pull up, unmarked cop cars, photographers, an ME, and every other initial you could think of. Two detectives came over, one man, one woman, eyed me up. With the window closed, I couldn't hear what they said when they turned to the two cops who had first happened on the scene. All I knew was the cops got into the car and pulled out on the street.

"What's going on?" I asked.

"The detectives want to talk to you, but they want to do it at the station," one of the uniforms said.

"Am I under arrest?"

"Not that I'm aware."

"Do I have a choice about this?"

The cruiser stopped at a red light.

I nodded at the unspoken answer. In the back of the car, sitting at the red light, I lawyered up and didn't say another word until I saw him.

❋ ❋

Lester Russell showed up two hours later in a wrinkled shirt and tie. He was still rubbing sleep out of his eyes with his left hand, and held a cup of coffee with the other. His briefcase rested on the table I was sitting behind. There was another chair, empty, next to the table.

"Have you charged my client?"

Russell was talking to the two detectives I'd seen on the scene earlier in the evening. I'd since learned the woman was named Daniels and the male, Blanchett. They stood across from me looking at Russell.

"No," Daniels said. "We just thought it'd be easier to get some answers out of him down here rather than out on the street."

"According to my client, you didn't even give him the option."

Blanchett shrugged. "He was already cuffed. We figured, what the hell?"

He smiled, tried to play it off as a joke, but Russell jumped all over it.

"We can sue. That's all sorts of illegal."

"Listen, Mr. Russell—" Daniels said, giving Blanchett the evil eye.

"Don't 'Listen' me, Detective. I'm taking my client out of here."

Blanchett swore. He was probably in his midthirties, but the bags under his brown eyes aged him. His blonde hair was uncombed and hung over his forehead, with a cowlick in the back, as if he'd spent all day running his hands through it. He wore black pants and a white shirt. He opened his collar and loosened a red tie, which was frayed around the end.

Daniels said, "If you take him out of here now, it's just going to make us more suspicious. We can arrest him. Illegal concealed weapons charge. That won't go over too well. We just want to ask him a few questions, get some answers, and we'll overlook the gun. We understand you're a private investigator, Mr. Donne?"

Looking at me now, I saw she had black hair pulled back into a bun, and wore a crisp gray suit with pants. Her skin was dark, like caramel, and her eyes matched. High cheekbones, thin lips, she was more a model than a cop. It surprised me. Most cops wear the job on their face, in their clothes, in the way they hold themselves. She was professional.

Daniels waited for me to speak. I didn't say a word.

"Not only can we give you a hard time about the gun, we can take away your license."

She kept looking at me. Blanchett rubbed his face. I stared at his frayed tie. Like he didn't take care of his clothes. Like he had nothing else, no time to buy clothes, no time for anything but the job.

"Let me consult my lawyer for a minute."

Daniels nodded.

"In private?"

Daniels sighed. Blanchett swore. Again.

"Can't believe this, Donne. You're being stupid," he said. "Ten minutes."

Daniels nodded toward the door, and Blanchett followed her out of the room. He slammed the door behind him. Russell looked at his watch.

There was only silence in the room as Russell waited for me to speak. When I pushed my chair back, the squeak off the tiles echoed from the ceiling.

"I want to talk to them," I said.

"Not a good idea," Russell said, pulling out the other seat and sitting.

"Why not? They have my camera, all they have to do is develop the film and they'll see who did it. They'll know it's not me. It's going to be suspicious if I don't tell them what's on it."

"They might find a way to use it against you."

"Why?"

"Because they're cops. That's what they do. What if this guy—this Rex guy—runs? If they can't find him, these guys will turn back to you. I guarantee Daniels or Blanchett is on the phone with the New Brunswick Police Department right now getting background on you. You know the New Brunswick cops aren't saying good things."

"More reason for me to be honest. If I'm up-front with them, they can stop wasting their time on me and find Hanover."

Russell leaned back in his chair. Letting his client talk to the police probably went against everything he stood for. "Suit yourself," he said. He looked at his watch again. "They'll be back in three minutes."

"Okay."

Russell took his briefcase off the desk, put it on the floor next to his chair. "That thing with your friend. The one who got hit by the car."

"Gerry. Yeah."

"I'm sorry about that. I didn't have a chance to say so on the phone."

"Thanks." I told him about Martin.

Russell nodded. "They put him on that case, huh? Jesus."

"No kidding."

"Stay out of it." Russell opened his briefcase, closed it again, as if his hands needed to be doing something. "If Martin's involved, stay out of the whole damn thing."

I didn't say anything. If Russell didn't know any more about it than I had already told him, and I got myself into trouble, he could plan a defense better. Not that I was planning on getting into trouble. One night in an interrogation room was plenty for me.

Russell could tell my answer anyway. "You play him wrong, he'll put you away. My professional suggestion is let the police do their job."

I didn't get a chance to respond. The door opened, Blanchett and Daniels came through. Blanchett had now taken his tie off, and his sleeves were rolled up. The missing tie said a lot about him. With all the swearing, the frustration he let show through, I respected him more than Daniels. He cared about the job.

Daniels's suit was neatly pressed, nothing out of place. She cared more about appearances, to me. She was great to look at, long legs, great hips, breasts pushing against her shirt and the jacket, but there was something about her. She put up a professional front; something came between her and me. Blanchett, the frayed tie, the out-of-place hair, he put it all in the job. All in the solution. He let it get to him; Daniels didn't.

They looked at me expectantly.

"I want to talk," I said.

"You're going to confess?" Blanchett asked.

"I'm going to tell you who did it and what's on my camera."

Daniels looked at Blanchett. He looked like he wanted to high-five her.

"Are you cold, Mr. Donne? I am. Mind if I turn up the heat?" She moved toward a thermostat on the wall near the door.

"You want to tape-record me, go ahead. Just don't play games." She smiled, reached out, and turned the thermostat.

"So what's on your camera, Mr. Donne?" Blanchett asked.

"There's a photo of a man named Rex Hanover. He's dragging the carpet, the one that has the body in it, across the street to the university steps. He came from one of the apartments opposite."

"Rex Hanover? Gimme a break." Daniels this time.

"As far as I was told."

"Why were you there?" she asked.

"My client thought he was cheating on her. She wanted me to find out how Hanover was spending his nights."

"Who's your client?"

I hesitated. It was a natural instinct of mine to protect my client, to use discretion, even though it was inevitable the police would find out now.

"If your client wanted to find out if Hanover was cheating on her, we can narrow it down quickly. You know that," Blanchett said. "So save us the trouble. It's either a wife or a girlfriend. Just give us the name."

"Jen. His wife."

Daniels was writing in a small notebook. "How did you find Rex?" she asked.

"I went to his job. Someone was covering for him. The guy told me Rex was sleeping around and was spending the night with his girlfriend."

"Where'd Hanover work?" Blanchett asked.

"Billy's. The bar?"

"I know it well. What did Hanover do? Bartend?"

"He was a bouncer. When you see the pictures, you'll see the size of this guy. He was huge."

"Gotta be to carry a body across the street," Daniels said.

"He dragged it," I said. I wanted to be consistent. I wanted to keep my story straight and not give them a chance to say I was contradicting myself.

Daniels smiled like she did when I told her it was okay to record me. "Okay," she said, "we're almost done here. But we're going to have to keep your camera as evidence."

I'd figured as much. I was giving them Hanover on a platter. They asked me a few more questions—where Hanover lived, what I knew about the victim, things of that nature. They then found variations of the same questions to ask. I was consistent.

All in all I got out pretty early. Lester Russell offered to give me a ride to my car. The clock on his dashboard said it was just after three in the morning.

.

8

CHAPTER

BILL MARTIN expected GERRY FIGUROA'S HOUSE to smell worse than Donne's office. Old men who lived on their own were rarely clean, and, he suspected, their ability to smell probably went even before hearing did.

Climbing the stairs to the top floor of the two-family, he was surprised. The fresh scent of lemon wafted in the air, and everything was pretty much in place. As if Figuroa was rarely even here. He'd shown the landlord his badge to get in. Now, he could hear the landlord's TV playing an old episode of *Sanford and Son*. Three-thirty in the morning and he was watching reruns. *Go to bed*, Martin thought. *Get a real job*.

It wasn't necessary to make the old man's floor a crime scene. It was a hit-and-run, but Martin liked the idea of coming up here and getting a feel for the victim. To see how he lived. He liked knowing who he was investigating.

And making it a crime scene would keep Donne from getting up here. And the idea of that little pissant being completely frustrated at the front door made Martin chuckle a bit to himself.

He checked the kitchen first, wanting to know what the man ate, if anything. The fridge was bare; only a bottle of milk, some eggs, and a half-eaten leftover sandwich. He looked at the oven. It was spotless and looked like it had just been delivered from Fortunoff. He went through the drawers one by one: plates, glasses, paper towels, silverware, trays. Underneath the kitchen sink he saw a ton of coffee filters and even more boxes of matches.

At that moment, the feeling from the old days returned. He knew what he'd find elsewhere in the house.

He did a quick sweep, looking for specific items. They wouldn't be hidden. Unless you had a trained eye, they wouldn't strike you as odd. Good thing Martin had a trained eye.

In the closet near the bathroom, he found twenty bottles of Sudafed. Above that, tons of batteries. There was more to Gerry Figuroa than met the eye.

He called the station and told them to send some crime-scene guys down here. They'd have to tape it off, collect evidence, and take fingerprints. He hated to wake the crime scene guys up in the middle of the night, but hell, this was important. When he hung up the phone, he allowed himself another chuckle.

This case was going to put him back on the map.

CHAPTER 9

I DIDN'T HAVE TIME TO GO HOME. I WANTED TO
talk to Jen Hanover before the police did. She was my client, and she
deserved to hear the news from me, not two detectives who were
thinking about arresting her husband. I found her address and tried to
navigate the streets of Madison, following street signs toward Morristown. At nearly four in the morning, with few gas stations open, few
streetlights on, it was hard to read the signs.

I drove around in circles for nearly half an hour before finding
the street. I drove down Washington Street slowly eyeing the cross
streets. That turned out to be unnecessary, and I found the house by
watching Blanchett and Daniels make their way to a small house,
ranch style, and ring the doorbell.

Jen Hanover answered the door after a few minutes. She was
wearing a long New York Giants T-shirt that I assumed she used as a
nightgown. She yawned as she opened the door.

I put the car in park and watched the detectives go inside. I decided to wait until they left before talking to Jen. A second encounter with the cops in one night was too much. Plus, I wanted to know what the police told her without me around. It was possible they'd give the wife more information than they gave me, a lowly witness. And if Rex was there I didn't want to be involved in an arrest anyway.

Though, if I'd committed a murder, left the body out in the open, the last place I'd go was directly home.

I sat in the car, engine and battery off, leaning my head against the headrest. My body was tense, not tired as I expected it to be. Adrenaline rushed through me, and there was no threat of my falling asleep. But sitting alone, on the dark street, my mind wandered a bit. After five minutes, neither Daniels nor Blanchett was dragging Rex Hanover out of the house in cuffs. I assumed my guess that he wasn't at the house was correct and they were now questioning my client.

I thought about Daniels, her ass swaying out of the interrogation room in perfect rhythm with her steps. She was confident, almost arrogant, as if she were better than the job. Every time Blanchett forced a question or a joke, she shot him a look like he was an idiot, not worth being in the same room as her.

But the frayed tie, the disheveled look told me otherwise. I only owned one suit. I didn't wear it much. I only wore a suit to impress the clients who held the kind of cash that could pay my rent two months in advance. One of the few times I did wear it, I ended up being attacked by a jealous husband.

A few years ago, I had stopped by the Olde Towne Tavern for a drink before meeting a client at his mansion in Old Bridge. Artie served my drink with a message. There was a man who had been raving about beating the shit out of me. He'd come in an hour earlier, downed four shots of Jack, and started to talk.

"This Jackson Donne asshole has ruined my life. Fucker took pictures of me coming out of the fucking Rahway Motel on Route One with a broad I'd met just three hours before I took her back to the hotel. What kind of world is this where a man can't bring some chick to a hotel room?" Artie assured me he was completely drunk. But, he warned, I should probably stay away.

I ignored Artie and ordered a beer, seeing the guy across the bar, head in his hand, about to pass out. Sipping my beer, I chatted with Gerry about the Yankees. They didn't have enough pitching, he offered. I thought their offense could overcome that. As Gerry was about to respond, the drunk, all dressed in leather like a biker, popped his head up and saw me across the room. One beer was all I was going to stay for.

The guy, I don't even remember his name, came at me in a drunken rage, pulling a switchblade. I tried to sidestep his first stab and did so, but the second one caught me in the sports jacket, tearing a hole right through it. As he withdrew the knife, I hit him with a right cross. It sent him sprawling toward the floor. Two of the other regulars grabbed him and held him, taking his knife. The cops showed up a few minutes later and took him away, Artie told me. By then I'd already gone to see my client, jacket on.

I never had the jacket fixed. In fact, if a client asks about the hole, I tell them the story.

※　※

It was nearly five in the morning when both detectives stepped through the screen door. Blanchett headed back to the car, while Daniels turned to shake Jen's hand. Probably thanking her for her help. That surprised me, the smile on Daniels's face. Did she care what Jen thought, about the information she'd given? She didn't act that way with me, didn't seem to care. She only wanted answers to the questions, and didn't get flustered when I didn't give them.

I was getting caught up in appearances, thinking about visual clues that I couldn't be sure about. Lack of sleep was getting to me. I was thinking too much. When the detectives pulled away, their brake lights disappearing two blocks down the street, I finally stepped out of my car and approached the front door. I rang the bell, hoping that Jen hadn't gone back to bed.

She answered, tears in her eyes and a tissue clutched in her hand. Her cheeks were red, and she was breathing deeply. We stood in silence, the screen door a barrier between us. A bird was singing somewhere, starting to wake up, and the realization that I wouldn't get home until after sunup hit me. I tried to fight exhaustion but yawned.

"I thought you'd wait until later this morning," she said, finally.

I said, "I wanted to get here before the police did."

"Too late."

"I saw."

Through the door I could hear music playing. Something soft, a piano background, violins, sweeping music. It was a song I didn't recognize, and it was too soft for me to hear who was singing. Jen didn't offer to open the door.

"What are you listening to?" I asked.

"Lou Reed. It's called 'Perfect Day.' " She wiped her eyes with the crumpled tissue. "Rex played it in his car our first date. We played it again our wedding night. It's our song."

"He's not here, is he?"

"No." Jen started to cry again. Between the tears, she said, "What happened tonight? What happened?"

"Can I come in? Let's talk. Please, I want to help." Help with what, I didn't know.

She pushed the door open, allowing me to step inside. The house smelled like steam. I couldn't exactly explain it, but it was something out of my childhood, the way my home always smelled when my mother made tea or soup. The house looked nothing like my home when I was a kid, but for a moment I was transported. Definitely needed to get some sleep.

Shaking my head, I looked around. The room Jen led me to was spare, with two chairs, a TV, a coffee table with tabloid magazines spread out over it, and a small love seat. In one corner was a bookcase filled with CDs. A small lamp stood between that and an end table with a CD player on it. The Lou Reed song ended, and Etta James came on.

"It's the CD we gave out as a table gift at our wedding," Jen said, before I could ask. "Sit. Do you want a drink?"

I shook my head.

"Please. I need one, and I don't want to drink alone."

"What are you drinking?"

"Scotch and soda?"

The scotch would knock me out, go right to my head. I said yes anyway.

Jen went through a door to what I assumed was the kitchen and I heard glasses rattle around.

The room, the house still smelled. My mind traveled back to the night my father walked out on my mother and me. He never gave a reason, never left a note. My mother said he woke up in the middle of the night and left. He didn't come back. She probably kept something from me that night; he must have said something to her. When my sister and I woke up she was sitting on the couch, crying.

Jen came back with the drinks and placed one in front of me. The taste was bitter and made me cringe. Not a big scotch drinker, it really didn't go down smooth.

"What did the police tell you?"

She took almost half the drink in her mouth. Swallowed and didn't even flinch. "They asked if I knew where Rex was. They asked a lot of questions. Said he was wanted for questioning. They wouldn't say if he was all right. Is he all right?"

"I don't know. Did he call here, did you hear from him?"

Etta James ended. Sam Cooke now, "We're Having a Party."

"What happened?" Jen said. "You're acting like the police. I hired you. I want to know what happened. I asked them the same thing and they wouldn't tell me. I don't know what's going on. My God, my stomach is in knots."

She finished off her drink. I told her what she wanted to know. By the time I was done, she was sobbing again. Now my stomach was in knots. Still couldn't clear the smell from my nostrils. The feeling of déjà vu.

I drank my scotch, let her cry. Over her shoulder was a window, venetian blinds closed. There was a hint of light against the blinds. The sun was coming up.

"He called," she said. "Just said he had to go away for a while, but he'd be back. He's done this a few times before."

"He has?"

"It's the reason I came to you in the first place. Sometimes he goes to work, calls me, and tells me he has to go away."

"Why didn't you tell me this before?"

"I didn't think it was too important." Her crying had slowed. "Tonight. When he called tonight, I was mad. I swore at him. He told me he couldn't talk long, hung up on me. Bastard."

"Did you tell the police he called?"

No tissue now, she wiped her face with the back of her hand. "No. They wouldn't tell me what happened. They wouldn't tell me anything. So I didn't tell them."

"Mrs. Hanover, your husband murdered someone."

She took a deep breath. "No. He didn't."

The music changed again. Sam Cooke to Van Morrison, "Into the Mystic."

"My husband didn't kill anyone."

"Mrs. Hanover—Jen—I took pictures of him."

"You have him on camera? Actually murdering someone?"

"I have him with the body."

"You didn't see him kill anyone?"

"No."

Jen nodded. "I don't believe Rex could ever kill anyone."

"You should have told the police he called. They need to find him. Did he say where he was going?"

"No."

"You should have told them."

"I don't want the police to find him."

I downed the last of my scotch.

"I want you to find him," she said.

"Mrs. Hanover. Please."

"Find him, Mr. Donne. Bring him home to me. Once you find him, we'll both see that he's not a murderer. This has to be a

misunderstanding. I can believe he cheated on me. I can understand that. But my husband is not a murderer."

I didn't say anything.

Sitting across from me, Jen leaned forward. Took my right hand
in both of hers.

"Will you help me?"

I took air in through my nose. The smell—again I was back in my
childhood home, my mother crying on the couch. My father had disappeared. We never heard from him again. I remembered how helpless I
felt, an eight-year-old boy who could only hug his mother. A helpless
eight-year-old.

"I'll help you find your husband," I said.

Jen Hanover smiled, stood up, and gave me a hug. I patted her
shoulder, and felt the weight of the past day get a little heavier on my
shoulders.

CHAPTER 10

tHE SUN WAS BARELY COLORINᏀ tHE sky, ᴀɴᴅ tHE
sound of traffic was still light. It wasn't even six. That meant the man
he was looking for was still around. He always was this time of
morning.

Jesus Sanchez made his way around the corner and froze. Bill
Martin saw and nodded at him. Sanchez paled.

"Yo, what the fuck you doin' here, man? Didn't think you were
into this shit anymore."

Martin extended his hand; Sanchez ignored it.

"I said, what the fuck are you doin' here?"

"Need to ask you a few questions."

"Yo, you ain't a narc anymore."

"I need to know who the big guy is these days," Martin said.

"Fuck if it ain't me."

Martin laughed. "You've never been a big seller. You never will
be. Answer my question."

Being out here felt great. You didn't get this working small-time robberies in New Brunswick. Martin loved moments like this, just fucking with a witness or informant until you got what you wanted. Working petty shit stolen from a frat house was boring. This was great.

"Shit, man. You don't gotta be like that. Michael Burgess, yo. Check in on him."

"Never heard of him." Martin dropped his cigarette on the ground.

"Yeah, you been away awhile," Jesus said. "You still talk to your boy? You know, Jackson."

"Who's Michael Burgess?" Martin fumbled for another cigarette.

"Man, that guy, he didn't give you up, did he? But yeah, you still holdin' a grudge like he fucked you."

Maybe working this case wasn't exactly as Martin had hoped.

"Tell me about Burgess."

"Man, you ever tell him about what happened? What you did?"

Memories rushed back to Martin, moments he'd long ago buried.

"No," Martin said. "I never told him."

"What you smiling for? You know I ain't gonna tell you shit. I don't have to."

"I can find out about Burgess without you." He inhaled some smoke. "You just gave me an idea. See ya around, Jesus."

"Man, what are you talkin' about?"

"You still see Donne?"

"Nah. Every once in a while walking up and down this block. But we don't talk no more."

"You decide to get friendly, don't tell him you saw me."

"Man, fuck you."

Martin turned and walked back to the police station.

CHAPTER

the ringing phone was like a jolt of electricity
through my body. I snapped out of bed, still in a sleepy daze, and
knocked the alarm clock off my nightstand. The ringing kept up and I
reached for the phone.

The clock, which landed faceup, said it was ten. I'd only gotten
to bed around seven-fifteen. Jen had given me a list of Rex's friends,
their phone numbers and addresses, and then let me go. I spent the
next hour and a half sitting on 287 in morning rush-hour traffic, listening to bad talk radio and fighting to keep my eyes open. I stumbled
into my apartment, stripped to my boxers, and passed out on the bed.
I hadn't even had time to dream when the phone started ringing.

"Hello," I mumbled into the receiver, rolling onto my back.

"This is Ellen Schwartz, admissions office at Rutgers University."

"Yes? How can I help you?"

"I'm sorry, Mr. Donne. Did I wake you?"

"Don't worry about it," I said. I could hear some disapproval in her voice, so I added, "I worked the night shift last night."

"I'm sorry to disturb you."

"Not a problem."

I tried not to yawn into the receiver.

"Mr. Donne, we're calling to schedule your entrance exam. You're a late admit, so we're afraid the letter wouldn't reach in time. We're holding the exam on May seventeenth. A Saturday."

"Okay."

"Will you be able to attend? It's a six-hour exam, two hours for language arts, two hours for math, and two hours for a foreign language."

"Foreign language?"

"It's for placement in your classes. If you can test out of the intro courses, you'll have to take fewer credits."

I found my daily planner in the drawer in the nightstand. I flipped to May 17.

"Terrific. I should be free that day."

"Good. Report to the lecture room in Scott Hall at eight in the morning. We'll sort things out from there." She hung up.

I closed my eyes for what felt like another minute. My blinds were closed, but the sun still found a way to force some beams into the room. The phone rang again. I opened my eyes; now it was eleven. I decided I wasn't going to get much more sleep.

I answered the phone, rubbing my eyes with my free hand.

"It's Artie."

"What's up?"

"Were you sleeping? Jesus, it's eleven in the morning."

"Yeah, I know."

"Holy shit. What happened? You okay?"

I leaned back. "Yeah, I'm okay. Just spent the night with the Madison Police Department."

"Did it have to do with Gerry?"

"No."

"What were you doing, then?"

"You at the bar?" I asked.

"Yeah. Tracy's on her way, too."

"Who?" Maybe I'd missed something while I was sleeping. I had no idea who Tracy was.

"Tracy Boland? Gerry's niece? You don't remember her?"

"No." But the memory of her face flashed before my eyes.

"Be here in twenty minutes. Maybe by then you'll remember."

* *

It was more like thirty-five. I nearly fell asleep again in the shower, but I turned the water to cold and was instantly awake. Finally, dressed in clean jeans, sneakers, and a plain red T-shirt, I entered the Olde Towne Tavern. Artie was behind the bar, looking like he hadn't slept in days.

As I came through the door, he said, "You look like shit."

"Right back at you."

He forced a smile. The TV was perched over Artie's shoulder above the bar, tuned to a news station. The words *Special Report* rolled across the screen.

I nodded toward the tube. "What's going on up there?"

"They raised that terror level thing again." Artie didn't even look at the screen.

"Any particular reason?"

Artie found two mugs behind the counter and blew into them. "Best way to get the dust out," Gerry used to say. Artie poured some steaming coffee, went digging. Came up with some half and half and sugar. "Nonspecific credible threats."

"The government at work. Damn fine as usual."

Artie found a fifth of Jack Daniel's. Poured some into one of the half-full mugs and nodded at me. "Want a nip?"

I shook my head.

"Suit yourself." He pushed my mug toward me.

"So, you gonna tell me why you spent last night with the Madison cops? Did it have to do with Gerry?" Artie took a sip, flinched, tasting the bitter end of the whiskey.

I looked around. "Tracy didn't show up?"

"She'll be here."

I tapped a rhythm on the bar top. "You really want to know about last night?"

Artie nodded. I told him about the Hanovers, the body in the carpet, and my interrogation. Then I told him about staying up and drinking scotch with Hanover's wife. Artie stopped me there.

"You took another job?"

"It's how I make a living."

"Fuck that. What about your friend? Your dead friend?"

"What's the problem here, Artie?"

Artie downed the rest of his drink. The bar had a mist to it. The smell of musk and wood chips was thick, and it seemed like they had a physical form as dust motes floated between Artie and me, making his image cloudy.

"The problem is you spent last night in a police station caught up in a murder investigation. You should be trying to find out what happened to Gerry. Your friend and my friend."

I finished my coffee, rested the mug on the bar. "I intend to do both."

"Yeah? How do you 'intend' to do that?" The words melted from his mouth. "You'll spend all your time searching for someone who's missing. Meanwhile your friend is dead, and it doesn't matter who killed him."

"Did you drink before I got here, Artie?"

"Fuck you. I can be pissed without drinking." He threw the towel he used to clean the bar at me. "Asshole."

I leaned across the bar, grabbed Artie by the shirt, and pulled him close to me. We were nose to nose. "Don't ever tell me that I don't care about Gerry. I'll find out what happened to him. But Bill Martin's watching my ass and he'll make it hard for me to do anything. If I'm working two cases, it'll give me some leeway. Now, Mr. Bartender, maybe you need to lay off the booze."

I pushed Artie away from me. He stumbled and then gained his balance. Coughed into his hand and seemed to regain some of his composure. "I remember when I used to have to tell you that," he said. His words slurred a little, but at least he was thinking straight.

Behind me, sunlight flooded into the place. I turned to see a woman in the doorway. She moved carefully, as if she was working a crime scene and didn't want to disturb anything. She crossed the room to the bar and had a seat on the stool next to me. Dropped a copy of the *Star-Ledger* on the table.

She gave both of us a tight smile. "I'm interrupting something?" She pointed her thumb over her shoulder. "I can come back."

"Nah," Artie said. "You're fine. Jackson, you remember Tracy Boland."

I said yes.

"Cool."

"You want anything?" he asked.

"This early?"

"Have something. Make Artie useful."

"He speaks," she said. "How are you, Jackson?"

"I've been better," I said.

"Well, you look a lot better than the last time I saw you."

Last time she saw me, I was coked out of my mind. So was she.

"Thanks," I said. "Have you started making the arrangements for Gerry?"

Artie put a cup in front of her. I hoped it wasn't filled with Jack.

"Working on it," she said. "I'm hoping to have the wake on Wednesday."

"Where?"

"Place on Milltown Road in East Brunswick. What was the name of that home, Artie?"

Artie laughed. "Why? It's not like he'll show up."

I kept quiet, let Artie have his moment. Tracy arched her eyebrows at me. I ignored her and flipped the paper open. There was an article about last night's murder. According to the third paragraph, the dead woman's name was Diane Peterson.

Artie must have rethought what he said, because he opened his mouth again. His voice was sullen. "Rinaldi's Funeral Home."

"That's right. Rinaldi's. I have an appointment with the funeral director this afternoon," Tracy said.

"What time?"

"Four o'clock."

I checked my watch. It was nearing noon. If I headed back to my office to make some phone calls regarding the Hanovers, I could be done in time to give Tracy a ride.

"Artie, you opening the bar tonight?"

He nodded.

"Cool. Tracy, do you want me to give you a ride to the home?"

"Yeah, that would be great. Thanks."

"It's a date, then," I said.

"Yeah." She laughed. "A date."

"Sounds good. Meet you at Gerry's quarter after three?"

"I'll see you then."

cHapteR

My office was as oRganizeD as it couLD Be.
There was a filing cabinet with alphabetized copies of the contracts of
my former clients pushed into the corner near the window. There
were two chairs facing the desk, high wooden backs to the door with
the glass window. To the left of the desk, pushed against the far wall
was an end table on top of which was the all-important coffeemaker,
filters, Styrofoam cups, and sugar. Next to that was a minifridge
where I kept cream, milk, and a few beers for special occasions or
boredom.

Early afternoon, sitting behind the desk, I flipped through
Hanover's address book. Best to go in alphabetical order. While dial-
ing I half listened to classic rock on the radio. The first two numbers
turned up answering machines, and I left polite messages explaining
who had hired me and what I was doing. The police had probably already been to a few of these, if Jen Hanover had given them some of

the same information, and if that was the case, I didn't have to worry about being discreet. If Jen hadn't given them the numbers, the cops wouldn't track down these people for a while.

My guess was the cops would talk to all the bouncers at Hanover's bar, see what they could come up with. They'd also identify the corpse and talk to the people close to the dead girl. I would do the same thing if I could find out who the girl was. What I wanted was a hit, someone who had talked to Hanover, someone who had seen him just after the murder. It was like building a pyramid or a house, you start with the foundation and keep adding. With any luck, I'd get to the top, finish it off, and end up with Hanover's location.

The third call was an actual voice. The address book said Michael Burgess. The voice was gruff, like someone who had spent the morning yelling. The moment I identified myself, he hung up So much for Mr. Burgess. I'd have to take some time and visit him personally if nothing else clicked. Then again, there was only a phone number in the book. No address.

I tried four more numbers. All answering machines. That didn't surprise me. It was midafternoon and most people had day jobs. I left messages, sat and waited. No one called back.

At three o'clock, it was time to pick up Tracy.

I left my office, down the steps toward George Street. Two guys the size of houses were coming in my direction. They filled the stairway by walking next to each other. One of them wore jeans, a black button-down shirt, leather jacket, and his hair parted to the right. The other had sweatpants, an Oakland Athletics sweatshirt, a goatee, and a shaved head. They didn't look like they were apartment hunting.

"Excuse me, sir. Do you know which floor a Mr.—" The guy with hair looked at an index card in his hand. "Where a Mr. Jackson Donne's office is?" He pronounced my name "Doan"—the second time in as many days.

"Well, actually, I'm Jackson Donne," I said. Might as well find out what this was about.

Hair smiled and said, "Can we see you in your office? We'd like to discuss something discreetly."

Baldy nodded and crossed his arms. I couldn't squeeze by these guys if I tried. I couldn't squeeze a dime past these guys.

I made a show of looking at my watch. "I do have another appointment."

"We won't take long." Hair smiled like he was posing for a photo. "It's urgent."

"Follow me, then." I turned and made my way back to the office. I didn't like turning my back on these guys, but if they were going to hurt me, they'd do it in my office, where the odds of someone walking in on them lessened. That is, if they were professionals.

They didn't assault me, waited quietly as I unlocked the door, opened it, and let them in.

I followed them in, made my way around my desk.

I offered the two chairs to them.

Hair decided to sit, but Baldy wanted to stand. Probably felt more intimidating that way.

Hair began. "Mr. Donne, I understand that you are looking for information on Rex Hanover."

"May I ask who you are?"

"We are associates of a friend of Mr. Hanover."

The only people who would know I was involved were probably people I called in the address book. That narrowed the number of suspects down to ten, most likely. Jen, though she hired me, so it wasn't probable, Artie, or any of the other people I left messages for. I suppose word could have traveled quickly among others I hadn't spoken with yet, but somehow I doubted it.

"Ah. Not going to tell me who that friend is?"

Hair shook his head.

"Okay. And if I am looking for Mr. Hanover?"

"Who hired you?"

I picked up a pencil from my desk and twirled it in my fingers. "My turn to plead the fifth."

Hair nodded. Baldy continued to try and look mean. It's tough to look mean in sweatpants and a bright green sweatshirt, but Baldy was doing his best.

"Well, either way, I'm here to ask you to stop."

"Why's that?"

"The police are looking into his disappearance, aren't they?"

"Yeah, but I'm giving it that personal touch."

Hair shifted in his chair. Crossed his left foot over his right knee.

"The police are not something to worry too much about. They'll find what we want them to find and will shut the case, but a person on their own? My associate is concerned that you might uncover some things by mistake that he wouldn't want uncovered."

I leaned across my desk. "So you're saying you control the Madison Police Department?"

"What I'm saying, Mr. Donne," he said, "is that we're willing to make you an offer."

He reached into his jacket with his left hand. I tensed. He came out with a stack of money, rubber band wrapped around it. The money landed on my desk, under my nose.

"Five thousand dollars cash," Hair said. "Don't look into Hanover's disappearance anymore."

"And if I refuse?"

He looked at his watch. "You have an important appointment to keep. If you say no, Maurice and I will have to try other methods of persuasion. And I also have a schedule to keep."

"Don't like to be late to the next leg breaking."

He laughed.

I looked at the money on the desk. "I think I'll take the money."

"Wise choice." Hair stood and shook my hand. "It was a pleasure doing business with you."

"Yeah," I said.

Baldy and Hair let themselves out of my office, leaving me alone with five thousand dollars cash. I picked the money up and smelled it. Not that bad a smell. I flipped through the cash, counting the twenties bundled together. All there.

I picked up the phone and called Tracy's cell phone and told her I'd meet her at Gerry's in ten minutes.

The money was going to come in handy. I could use it to pay for dinners for the next few months. I could buy plenty of beer with it if I wanted. But the best option was to spend it on the expenses I would pile up on my continuing search for Rex Hanover.

CHAPTER **13**

BILL MARTIN SAT IN HIS office, TIE LOOSENED at the neck, jacket off, not sure what the fuck to do. Five years ago he would have gone back to the corner on Easton Ave. and beaten the shit out of Jesus Sanchez. Pounded him into a pulp until Jesus broke and told him who Michael Burgess was, how to get in touch with him.

Now, with Leo Carver rotting in Rahway penitentiary and the new blood upstairs watching his every move, Martin had nothing. Pounding the pavement, making phone calls to old contacts only went so far when you hadn't talked to them in years.

He rubbed his eyes and coughed. They didn't even let you smoke in here anymore.

Bill Martin grabbed his jacket and went down to the street. Lighting a cigarette, he noticed two other detectives—Bob Richardson and Paul Cramden—smoking as well. All good cops look the same when they're busy: wrinkled jackets, loosened ties. It was the ones that were too clean-cut you had to watch out for. They'd stab you in the back to look good in front of the bosses.

Just like these two.

"How's it going, Bill?" Richardson asked. "Heard you got the hit-and-run over on Easton."

"About time I got something interesting."

Cramden sauntered over. "Any leads yet?"

Time to be careful. Martin could say too much and then be paranoid he'd lose the case. But, fuck it, these guys may know people.

"The name Michael Burgess keeps coming up."

Richardson squinted. "You into drugs with this one, Bill?"

"I don't know what I'm into," he answered. "It's just a name that popped up."

He was damn well involved in drugs with this one, with all that shit he found in Figuroa's house. Absently, he wondered if Donne knew about that. Damn, it would be fun to tell him.

But, no, he had other plans. Other secrets.

"Yeah, Bill," Cramden said, "Burgess is a big drug name. In fact, if he was around and you were a narc, that would be the guy to take down."

"He's big, huh?"

"Where the hell you been, Bill? You've never heard of Burgess?"

"Don't hear about much working frat robberies."

"Guess not." Richardson put his hand on Martin's shoulder. "Listen, if Burgess is involved, you've hit on something."

Martin tensed just a bit and Richardson probably felt it. The hand jerked away. If these two detectives knew Martin was starting to scratch at something big, they might stab him in the back, too.

He'd let that happen to him once. Not again.

"You know how to get in touch with this guy?" Martin asked.

"Nah," Cramden said. "But you're smart, I'm sure you'll find him."

Martin dropped his cigarette butt into the trash. "Thanks, Paul. You're a big help."

Richardson shot Cramden a look. Then turned back to Martin. "Bill, there are a few guys who messed with Burgess a couple of months ago. Had to talk to him about something. Harry Lance and Mike Johnson. Ask them."

Martin thanked them.

"No problem, Bill. You deserve to get back on the horse."

Martin nodded and turned his back to go up again.

"Oh, shit. Bill, wait. Did you hear?"

Martin looked at the two detectives. "Hear what?"

"That asshole, what's his name . . . Jackson Donne, he got taken in by a few cops in Madison last night. Got caught up with a dead body by Drew University."

CHAPTER 14

"Have you been inside yet?" I asked Tracy, standing outside Gerry's house.

She was staring at the front door, hands in her jeans pockets. "No," she said. "Not yet."

"Do you want to take a look?"

"How long does it take to get to the funeral home?"

A breeze cooled the air, making the temperature perfect for a light jacket. Off to the west, some dark, thick clouds hung. April showers were probably about to roll in. But for the moment, above us the skies were still clear, a few birds circling, squawking and singing.

"About twenty minutes. Depending on traffic on Eighteen."

Tracy stood, eyes closed. It seemed she was either making a decision or trying to build up some courage.

I waited, putting my hands in my pockets. My Glock rested in the shoulder holster pressing against my arm. After this afternoon's visit, I wasn't going anywhere unarmed.

"We can be a few minutes late," she said after a deep breath. "Can we go up? Do you have a key?"

"I know the landlord."

We walked onto the wooden porch, and I rang James's doorbell. He answered. I told him what we wanted.

James said, "The cops told me not to let anyone up there."

"We have to feed the cat."

"There's no cat. The police said—"

I pulled sixty bucks of the two hundred I'd taken from the stack of five thousand. Gave it to James. It was real easy to throw around.

"You're not going to let the cat starve, are you?"

He unlocked the door and let us in. We had to duck under crime-scene tape.

Climbing the stairs, I got the same smell of lemon as the last time I was there, just a bit stronger. Tracy pushed the door open.

"I'm going to check the kitchen. I want to make sure he was eating right." The words were laced with sarcasm, and I had the feeling she really wanted to look for bottles.

I was confident she wouldn't find any.

I decided to make a sweep of the apartment. I started with the bathroom, which was crowded, small, claustrophobic. The color, a deep brown, made the walls seem closer than they actually were. There was a sink, a toilet against one wall, with about three feet between the end of the fixtures and the wall. The opposite wall held a radiator and a tall closet. A walk-in shower took up the wall opposite the door. I pushed the door closed and relieved myself.

Next, I washed my hands and checked the medicine cabinet. Nothing unusual: two bottles of Sudafed, a bottle of Advil, toothpaste, nail clipper, shaving cream, and a razor. Crouching, I checked behind the toilet and the sink. Nothing but floor tiles. I pulled open the shower and found a leaky faucet and a wet floor. Soap and shampoo rested on a shelf. Finally, I turned and opened the closet. What I saw made me catch my breath, though I wasn't sure why.

The bottom shelf of the closet had a stack of bath towels. The shelf above it was filled with packages of lithium batteries, fifteen, twenty, maybe more. Very odd to be stored in a bathroom closet. On the shelf above that were about twenty bottles of Sudafed. Something started tickling the back of my brain, something from my days on the police force. Something I knew, something that if I wasn't out of practice would have registered with me immediately.

I closed the closet door and found Tracy waiting in the living room.

"Did you go through all the cabinets?" I asked.

"Yeah."

"Did you see anything unusual?"

"Is something wrong?"

"Nothing unusual?"

Tracy paused, as if thinking about it.

"He has a lot of matches. But I think that's to start the oven."

"Show me."

"What's wrong?" she asked, leading me into the kitchen.

"I'm not sure." It wasn't clear, but unless Gerry collected the items—which would be odd—something wasn't right.

I checked the oven in the kitchen and saw it was autostart. No matches needed. Tracy, meanwhile, found a closet under the sink. It was filled with red-and-blue boxes of matches, the wooden kind with the sulfur tip. Next to it were two boxes of coffee filters. My brain was cramping. I was missing something, some connection. Sudafed, sulfur matches, and lithium batteries.

"What's wrong?" Tracy asked. "Why does he have all these matches?"

I took a deep breath. Slowly it started to come together in my brain. I just had to talk it through.

"When I was on the police force, I was a narcotics cop. We used to go to workshops, where they'd teach us different ways to make different drugs. That way when we went to take someone down, a dealer, someone trying to make shit out of their bathtub, we knew what to look for."

"What does that have to do with matches?"

"Sulfur, pseudoephedrine, and lithium. Each ingredient is

tracked by the DEA, you can't buy it in large portions. You do that, the DEA will be at your door in no time. But you can find sulfur in matches, lithium in batteries, and pseudoephedrine is the active ingredient in Sudafed. I found Sudafed and a ton of batteries in the bathroom closet. Plenty of matches here."

Tracy took a step back, covered her mouth.

"These are the ingredients of crystal meth."

Tracy's face turned pale. She pushed past me and slammed the door to the bathroom. I could hear her crying, even as I tried not to listen. Deciding to give her privacy, I took the stairs out to the street. The air was cool and the faint breeze had picked up into a stiff wind. Heavy clouds hung overhead.

* *

The clouds had opened and rain poured, my windshield wipers fighting to keep up. Traffic on Route 18 had slowed to a crawl, and we hit all the lights red. Ahead of us, a trailer truck kicked up puddles of water, which splattered over the windshield. The storm had hit quickly, soaking the asphalt and shocking the rush-hour drivers.

Except for the rain tapping on the roof, the ride so far was silent, Tracy looking out the passenger window, me squinting to watch for brake lights. My Honda Prelude didn't handle too well in the rain, and I didn't want to push it. Questions about Gerry were just starting to come to the forefront of my mind, but I had to push them aside in order to focus on the road. It was slick and the first time I stepped on the brakes, I felt them lock and I had to struggle to control the car.

"Do you mind if I put on the radio?" Tracy asked.

"Go for it," I said, swinging into the left lane. Passing the trailer would make it easier to see, I hoped.

Tracy spun the dial on the radio and came across a hip-hop tune. She whispered the lyrics to herself as she turned back toward the passenger window.

I passed the trailer, pulled back into the right lane, and said, "You okay?"

"Are you sure about what you saw in there?"

I nodded. "We found meth labs all the time on the force."

"You know, when I was a kid, Gerry was the guy who gave me the drug talk. Not my dad, not my mom, but Uncle Gerry."

"What did he tell you?"

"You know, the usual stuff you tell a kid. The stuff that goes through your head the first time you smoke a joint in college. You'll get hooked, no one in their right mind does the stuff. It'll kill you. Your future will be screwed. The scary shit."

"Why did Gerry give you the talk?"

"My parents were always working. My mom was a teacher, my dad was in business. After school was over, when my mom was still working remedial or driving home, Gerry was still around before he went to act. Steve came home from first grade and was talking about some kid who said his dad smoked different kinds of cigarettes."

Steve was Gerry's son. He died of cancer a few years ago.

Tracy continued, "Gerry took the opportunity, jumped right into the conversation. Must have watched a public-service announcement just before he picked us up. He sounded like a commercial."

"I'm pretty sure your uncle did smoke pot at times."

Tracy laughed. "I'm sure he did, too, but he never let us know about it. He wanted Steve and me to be like brother and sister, not cousins, and he wanted a Norman Rockwell childhood for us."

"Did you get it?"

"Not a chance."

Most of East Brunswick was strip malls and traffic lights, and I seemed to hit every red light. In fact, I think everyone did. It gave motorists more time to decide whether or not to stop at the Borders, Dick's Sporting Goods, or Kohl's that lined the highway. The rain hadn't let up, but traffic was lighter as I crossed the last traffic light. I pressed the accelerator.

"I was thinking," she said.

"What about?"

"The landlord said the cops had been up to the apartment."

I knew what was coming. It had been bothering me as well. "Yeah. He did say that."

"If you know what ingredients go into crystal meth, wouldn't the police know as well?"

Martin sure as hell would. He went to the same workshops I did. "Yeah, they should."

"Why didn't the cops take all those ingredients in as evidence?"

"I don't know," I said. I put on my right blinker and took the next exit for Milltown Road. "Best I can figure is it's circumstantial. There was no proof that Gerry was actually making crystal meth."

"But you seem sure of yourself."

"I'm not. But Gerry never seemed like the guy who would collect batteries, matches, and Sudafed. He was never that sick."

"I don't think my uncle was like that, though."

I didn't think he was either, but something inside me, that old cop instinct, was screaming at me to look at the evidence. I had no tangible proof, but all the evidence was there. Making crystal meth was a big deal; it wasn't easy; and it could blow up on you at any moment. But someone confident, someone who knew what they were doing, could make a fortune selling the stuff.

Just a year ago Gerry was struggling to pay his rent. He even hired me to help him out. I tracked down a woman who owned a theater he used to work in. She was trying to force him out of house and home to drum up business. She figured if she could say this old actor was homeless or worse, she would drum up support for modern actors to keep them from finding the same fate. After clearing the case, I hadn't heard any complaints about money from him, and I saw him at the bar nearly every night. I couldn't prove anything, but I knew something bad was going on, and what we had found in the apartment seemed to support that idea.

I pulled into the funeral home parking lot, the rain still pounding down. I wondered if Gerry had enough money to pay for his own funeral. We exited the car and headed inside.

CHAPTER 15

BRUSHING the rain off my shoulders and running my hand through my soaked hair, I followed Tracy into Rinaldi's Funeral Home. The lobby was carpeted in red, and the wallpaper was mute beige. A few thick easy chairs, also dark, more a maroon, contrasted with the carpet. Perfect for a wake. A bronze coffee table sat across from the chairs, a few magazines resting on it. The lobby was clean and smelled antiseptic, a cross between lime and bleach, a scent I hadn't experienced in a while.

A short heavy man in a black double-breasted suit stepped out of a room I assumed was his office. To his right was a larger room where they held the actual wakes. The man's face was pale, except for deep red cheeks. He had dark hair slicked back. His clothes were neatly pressed, and his loafers reflected the artificial light from above. He smiled at Tracy.

"Ms. Boland, I assume?" He reached his hand out in her direction, taking hers and pumping it twice. He looked at me. "And you are?"

Tracy introduced me.

He took my hand loosely and shook it. "Mr. Donne. I am John Fleming, the funeral director."

"Nice to meet you."

"Ah," he said, looking at his watch. "I wish it was under better circumstances. You are about ten minutes late, Ms. Boland. I was beginning to worry." He tugged at his lapels, then brushed a piece of lint off his shoulder. "If you'd like to get started, we can go to my office."

Fleming turned on his heels and stepped through his office door. Tracy turned my way.

"If you don't mind, I'd like to handle this on my own."

Tracy disappeared into Fleming's office, the door swinging shut behind her. I took a few steps around the lobby and peeked into the funeral room. There wasn't a body or even a casket inside, but the room was set up with flowers and about ten rows of seats.

I walked around, the antiseptic smell growing stronger. The room's colors were the same as the lobby, same carpet, same walls. The chairs were maroon as well, though they were more like folding chairs than easy chairs. I stepped up to the small lift where the body would be kept, trying not to picture Gerry's body in a morgue; instead, trying to picture him lying at rest in a coffin tomorrow.

I never understood wakes, which were apparently for the living. Why keep a corpse, open casket, made up to look like some cheap plastic imitation of your loved one, lying at rest for four hours?

People came in and out, offered fake condolences for a while and said prayers, then left, hitting the local bar. It didn't do anything for me.

The antiseptic smell was unique to funeral homes, and it brought back the memory of Jeanne's wake. When Jeanne died, just two weeks after I had gotten out of rehab and six months before we were to be married, I wanted nothing to do with a wake. She had been cut down by a drunk driver as she drove herself home from a get-together with work friends. The driver had crossed the double yellow lines and smashed into her front fender, forcing her car off the road. By the time the fire department used the Jaws of Life, she was long dead. Her parents insisted I show at the wake and funeral, saying it would do me good to see her, to know how much her friends and relatives cared about her. I agreed.

Dressed in my best suit, then missing the puncture hole from the switchblade, I showed up, stone-cold sober. Jeanne was laid out in the black dress she wore to her first job interview. I had joked it was the reason they hired her. Around her neck was the silver locket I had given her for our second year together, and it rested open on her chest, revealing the small picture of the two of us together in a park. Memories of her flooded back to me, and I felt my knees wobble. Then I saw her face, the thick makeup washing out any sign of life. Her eyelids were stitched closed, and while people couldn't see the stitches, I always noticed them. It wasn't the woman I had spent the last three years with, the woman I slept with, the woman I shared secrets with. It wasn't the woman I loved. It was an imitation.

My vision clouded, my knees gave way, and I could feel myself falling. Jeanne's father caught me, sat me in a seat, much like the ones in the funeral home today, and got me water. I don't remember any more of the wake. The funeral the next afternoon, I remember it poured, much like it was doing now. I remember going to the bar afterward and going on a bender, waking up in my office days later, mouth dry and head pounding.

I had an empty feeling in my stomach now, and I sat in one of the chairs trying to clear my brain. Gerry's death wasn't the same as Jeanne's death. There were secrets, and they were gnawing at my insides. But the solutions weren't here; I wasn't going to find them. I sat and waited for Tracy to finish so I could drive her home. I was determined to find Hanover and find out who had run over Gerry. Then it was time to get on with my life, get away from the past. I didn't want to come to any more wakes for any more murder victims.

Tracy popped her head in the doorway and called my name, snapping me out of my daydream. Her hair and clothing had dried in the office, and she had redone her lipstick. She'd also run a comb through her hair.

Fleming stood in the background, his arms crossed in front of him. He tapped his foot.

"How'd it go?" I asked.

"Good. We're going to have the wake tomorrow, two to four, and seven to nine. Can we come back tomorrow? Drop off a suit for them to put on Gerry?"

There was a moment of silence during which I noticed a spot of mud on my left sneaker. I tried to wipe it off on the carpet.

Fleming jumped in. "That shouldn't be a problem. If you need to, you can drop the clothing off early tomorrow morning. Will that be acceptable?"

Tracy looked at me. "I just want someone to come with me."

"I should be able to take you. If not, Artie will."

"Okay," she said.

"I'm sure you will find the arrangement quite satisfactory, Ms. Boland. You will be pleased with all of your choices."

Fleming extended his hand and shook Tracy's. Then he shook mine, the same limp, pale handshake as before. The guy played the part of the funeral director well; I had to give him that.

We exited the funeral parlor, back into the easing rain and more rush-hour traffic.

Ten minutes into the car ride, Tracy said, "Feel like taking a walk?"

"It's raining."

She winked at me. "It'll stop."

"Where do you want to go?"

"Drop me at my car and follow me to Asbury."

＊ ＊

An hour or so later, she was right. The rain had stopped. The board-walk was empty and dark. Few streetlights illuminated the area, and only briefly did headlights flash behind me. Faintly, waves kissed the beach forty feet away. The smell of salt water filled the air, and though I couldn't see them, I could hear seagulls squawking above me. The breeze came off the ocean. It was colder here than in New Brunswick. High fifties, I'd say.

I had a windbreaker on, over a polo shirt, hiding my Glock. I zipped the windbreaker up about halfway, high enough to keep me a little warmer, low enough that I could still get to the gun. Two black guys in long football jerseys and sideways basketball caps sauntered past, giving me a look. I made eye contact. One of the guys called me a fag, and kept going. God forbid someone be polite in this neck of the woods.

There used to be a running merry-go-round on the boardwalk, and Skee-Ball and all the food you could imagine. But no more, they had long since closed down. Some of the painted advertisements were still there, the one I was standing next to, a faded clown smiling maniacally and thumbing over his shoulder toward the shore.

Tracy approached me, smiling.

"Nice night," she said, "I can only give you about an hour. Then I have to get to work."

"Where do you work?"

"I'm a musician."

We walked up the thick wooden boards and made a right, the beach to my left. The smell of the salt was stronger now, and sand blown by the wind onto the boardwalk crunched as we walked.

"Do you sing?"

"No, I play tenor saxophone. I have a gig at a bar in Sayreville tonight. Starts at ten."

"Cool. Not playing at the Stone Pony?"

She tilted her head, crossed her eyes, like saying "Come on." "I think only Springsteen plays there. Rehearses just before he plays twenty straight nights at Giants Stadium or whatever it is."

"Not a fan?"

"Please. I'd take Sinatra and Bon Jovi as New Jersey's signature musicians before I'd take Bruce."

"Bon Jovi?"

"Yeah."

We walked in silence for a few seconds. Tracy watched her feet.

She was right: even though it was a little cool, it was a nice night. The sky was clear, a half moon crested above the ocean, and the sea air always added something to an evening. I reminded myself, however, not to get sucked in by it. At any moment, my nerves screamed, I could be ambushed. What if the two thugs from my office had followed me?

"You really don't remember me, do you, Jackson?"

I looked at her.

She laughed. "I used to see this guy, Pablo. We hung out at Artie's bar. One night we had a fight. You were there."

"I remember."

Memories swirled at the edges of my brain. There was some familiarity to the story, but it was hazy. Four years ago, I was so coked up I hardly remember anything. Except for the few weeks when Jeanne and I were separated. Right before I proposed.

"Then why didn't you say so in the bar?"

"I didn't want to talk about it in front of Artie."

The memories started to come into focus. I could see Tracy's face, a little younger, drinking a mixed drink. Doing a line of coke with me. Kissing her.

"Tracy, I—"

"We never slept together."

"I know," I said. "But my fiancée thought we did."

She slowed a step. The buildings on our right were cracked and broken, rotting wood holding them up. It was quiet, not another soul around. To our left the waves crashed a little louder.

"I was the reason you two separated?"

I nodded. "Among other things."

"But you got back together?"

"When I cleaned up."

"I'm a different person now. I don't do coke anymore. I'm with a guy. I'm happy."

"I'm different, too," I said.

She nodded. "You know what's funny? That guy Pablo, he and I became best of friends. We broke up that night. But we're really close.

He married one of my best friends. What about you? The woman you were with?"

"Jeanne passed away."

The waves seemed to crash a bit harder, louder. Made it hard to hear.

"I'm sorry," Tracy said.

"Thanks."

I was suddenly aware of how easy it was to talk to Tracy. I was able to let myself go and give up information I usually kept close to the vest. Not to mention how easy she was to look at.

Then, "I should call Pablo. I haven't heard from him in a while."

"You mention him more than your boyfriend."

"Pablo's a good friend. I miss him."

We walked in silence for a few minutes. I had asked my questions. The waves continued to crash, hypnotic. We reached the end of the boardwalk and turned around, continuing to walk in silence.

Eventually she said, "I love it here at night. It's not as dangerous as they say. I come here alone before a gig, just to listen. It's like a concert of its own, the water crashing around like that. I find it inspiring."

"It is soothing."

She gave me one of those smiles you give a small child.

"So, where in Sayreville are you playing tonight? I might come and listen."

She sighed. "You won't appreciate it."

"You hardly know me."

We were back at the intersection. She walked away from me, toward what I assumed was her car. Unlocked the door, pulled it open. Turned back to me.

"Thanks for walking with me. If you are really going to listen, it's a place called Jacob's Jazz. I don't know the name of the road it's on, but you can Google it. That's how I found it."

"I'm glad we met up," I said.

She closed the car door and drove off into the darkened streets.

I exhaled a deep breath, turning over in my brain some new information, thankful that I hadn't been shot at.

16

It took Bill Martin hours to get through to the Madison police detectives. He would dial, get put on hold, and hang up in frustration. Finally, a Detective Blanchett got on the phone. He sounded exhausted, but gave Martin the rundown on Donne.

"Did you arrest him?" Martin asked.

"No. We couldn't hold him on anything," Blanchett said. "To be honest, I don't think he did anything. Just wrong person to follow, wrong time." A pause. "Why are you interested?"

Martin expected the question.

"Guy's a scumbag. He fucked up our whole department a few years ago. I wouldn't be surprised he was caught up in a murder or two."

"Oh. He doesn't have the best record as a PI either, does he? Been involved in a lot of shit."

"Follows him around. Too bad you couldn't put him away."

"Sorry I can't help you out."

Martin laughed and said, "Maybe next time."

Hanging up, he thought, I'm glad he got out. Leave him to me.

When he came back to his office with a cup of coffee, Jesus Sanchez was sitting at his desk.

"How'd you get in here?" Martin asked. Get the fuck out of my seat, he thought.

"What you mean?" Jesus balanced a pen on his outstretched index finger. "I just walked in. How you think?"

Martin shook his head. Just what he needed. He finally gets an important case, and this known drug dealer just strolls right into his office. He could almost hear Kevin Haskell yelling for his demotion.

"This is a hell of an office you got here. I only got some litter and empty boxes at mine." Jesus laughed like he was one of Johnny Carson's writers. "Then again, my office be a street corner."

Straightening his tie, Martin thought it was a good time to look professional. Christ, what if someone wanted to check on him?

"What do you want?" he asked.

"Man, it's time I help you out. I talked to Michael Burgess." The pen fell from Jesus's finger to the ground. He bent to pick it up.

Martin didn't want to wait, moved around the desk, grabbed Jesus by the collar, and yanked him up.

"Yo, man, what the fuck?"

"Worry about the pen later." Martin was nose to nose with Jesus, but he kept his voice calm. Talking as if he were a happy telemarketer. "Tell me what Burgess said."

"He said he would talk to you. Though I don't know why." Jesus pulled himself from Martin's grip and straightened his collar. "Must be my charming personality."

Jesus told him to expect a phone call from Burgess to set up particulars. He actually used the word particulars, which told Martin that Burgess must have told him to say that. Didn't matter. This case was finally getting somewhere.

"Thanks, Jesus." Martin patted him on the back.

Jesus stood to leave, made it to the door, when a thought hit Martin. As much as he hated to admit it, Donne was not a stupid man.

He would make connections. In fact, Martin wanted him to. He wanted to cross paths with Donne again. But he didn't want Donne ahead on the case.

"Just do me a favor. If Jackson Donne runs into you, you tell him none of this. You do not connect him with Burgess."

Jesus shrugged. "Whatever, yo."

As he left, Martin thought about it. He didn't trust Jesus any farther than he could throw him. The guy was an informant and a drug dealer, plain and simple. He'd bend to anybody.

Martin had to talk to Donne himself. Before Donne even thought about going to Jesus.

17

CHAPTER

JACOB'S JAZZ WAS ON a small street off Route 535. I didn't Google it; I called information and they gave me the address. A small bar, smoky and loud, with a ton of people standing in the back and sitting at small tables. I grabbed an empty stool at the bar as a small guy in thick black-framed glasses stepped away.

After ordering a Brooklyn lager, I turned to see Tracy fiddling with her saxophone as her bass player soloed. The drummer, stationed directly behind Tracy, was using brushes, the song slow, melodic, even with the solo going on. A guitar player strummed chords. Tracy was the only woman onstage. When the bass player finished, he got a round of applause from the audience as Tracy picked up the melody again. I didn't recognize the song.

I swiveled on the seat, looking around the crowd. Most of the patrons were black, dressed in shirts and ties, applauding at solos, cheering. It was a festive crowd, drinks spilling, people snapping fingers, bobbing their heads to the music, talking into each other's ears, and smiling. Over the bar, one TV showed the first inning of the Yankees game on the West Coast.

The song ended, the crowd erupted into applause, but not rock concert applause; there was only clapping. Tracy nodded, then gestured toward the rest of the band, giving them a moment in the spotlight. She was a natural, able to be at the center of the stage, but making sure everyone else with her got their share of the limelight. She took another bow, and freed the microphone from the stand, all while smiling.

My brain seemed to connect to her movements. I remembered her in the bar; she drank vodka cranberry. Always with one guy or another. I remembered doing lines with her. Seeing her brought the guilt of cheating back.

"Thank you," she said. The applause quieted. "Thank you very much. We're going to play one more before we take our first set break, but don't worry, we have two more sets for you. But before we end, I'm going to play a ballad written by a friend of mine. It's called 'Bernie's Song.'"

The drummer counted off and the ballad started. Slow, mournful, she played through the notes, and the crowd got into it, swaying with the music, smiling, eyes closed. I turned toward the bartender, called her over. I ordered Tracy a vodka cranberry, had it delivered to her while she played.

Tracy took a solo, running her fingers up and down the saxophone, knowing each place to touch for maximum effect. The solo started slowly, quietly, building toward a climax, her body moving in rhythm with the notes, swaying and bouncing. Her eyes were closed in concentration, and watching it was hypnotic. She drew me in, until it seemed there was no one else in the bar. I couldn't take my eyes off her. Her hair was pulled back in a tight ponytail, her face smooth and red as she breathed into the horn. Everything about her screamed intensity, nerves tight and ready to jump through her skin, an electric current connected between her and the instrument. She finished the solo with a jarring run through the notes, pulling the saxophone from her mouth dramatically, and the crowd erupted again. I joined them.

As the guitar player took his solo, she noticed the drink in front of her. She picked it up, took a sip, and then glanced around the crowd. I followed her eyes, and scanned in each direction she looked. They finally locked with mine. She smiled and winked at me. I smiled back and felt my face flush. I finished my beer, and I noticed my palms were sweating.

The song ended, faded out, and the crowd once again showed its approval. Tracy thanked the audience once more and placed her saxophone on a stand. She picked up her drink and walked in my direction, stopping only to accept compliments from various audience members.

Tracy said, "I didn't think you'd show up." She placed the drink on the bar, leaned on it as I sat.

The jukebox had started up in the time it took for her to walk over. Between the music and the crowd noise, I had to lean in close to hear anything. Tracy was wearing a perfume, just enough of it, that when I leaned in to talk I got a hint of orange.

"I appreciate good jazz."

"You saying I'm good?"

"I'm saying you're very good."

"We're a little out of time tonight." She smiled. "New drummer."

"Really? I couldn't tell."

The guitar player walked by and told Tracy he was going outside for a smoke and some fresh air. She said they were going back on in twenty minutes and to take his time. A few other members of the crowd walked by and looked Tracy up and down.

"Did you really come here to listen to jazz?"

I smiled.

"So, I have you to thank for the drink?"

"Yeah."

"Thank you."

"So, who's Bernie?"

She finished off the drink, and said, "Who?"

"The song you just played. 'Bernie's Song.' Who's Bernie?"

"I didn't write the song. A friend of mine did."

"Your boyfriend?"

"No. This guy's married. I think he said he wrote it for his brother-in-law. Maybe his father-in-law. Or his dog. I forget."

"What do you have in store for the next set?"

She finished her drink. "A little of this, a little of that."

She looked at her empty glass, rattled the ice around. "It's good to see you again, Jackson."

She walked away.

I ordered another beer and relaxed for a few moments. No sign of Hanover, nothing going on with my case. For the first time since Gerry died, I felt I could enjoy my drink. I liked people watching in a crowded bar, and this bar was interesting, because it was an older crowd. There weren't the drunken frat boys falling over women or puking in the corner. There weren't empty bottles spilling on the floor. The place had an air of class. Everyone was talking casually, smiling, laughing. No one screamed, no one threw anything. There wasn't even a bouncer, like the threat of someone getting cut off wasn't even a possibility in this place. I felt myself begin to relax, some of the tension that had been growing between my shoulder blades started to loosen.

A woman sitting across the bar caught my eye. She was next to a man who was standing with his back to the bar. She had a glass of white wine in her hand, caramel skin, and dark black hair that hung loose over her shoulder. She was talking, I guessed, to the man next to her, though she wasn't looking at him. She sat upright, drinking the wine with her pinky off the glass. She held the glass up in front of her, in the light glancing at the wine, like she knew what she was doing. A wine taster, I thought. Or maybe a wealthy lawyer, out on a free evening.

I finished my beer, tried once to make eye contact and failed. As I put my pint glass back on the bar, my cell phone buzzed. I pulled it out and looked at the caller ID. Artie. I got up from the bar, left a three-dollar tip, and moved out the door to the street. The bass player tossed his cigarette into the street. I nodded at him, then answered my phone.

"Artie," I said.

"Hey. Where are you?" He talked loudly, over the sound of the music, clinking glasses, and yelling frat boys at the Olde Towne Tavern.

The bass player checked his watch and went back inside.

"In Sayreville."

"What are you doing there?"

"Watching Tracy play."

"Oh."

I watched two cars drive by the bar before either of us said anything.

Artie finally broke the silence. He tried to sound casual, but I could sense his anxiousness. "How are things going with Gerry?"

The past surrounded me. Gerry telling jokes. Tracy sitting in the Olde Towne Tavern years ago. The evidence in Gerry's apartment. It wasn't the man I knew. It wasn't a man I wanted to know more about.

"I can't do it," I said. "I can't look into it."

"You can't—what the fuck, Jackson?"

"The police can do it. They'll do it better than I can."

For a while all I could hear was the ebb and flow of noise at the tavern. I didn't want to tell Artie what I'd found. It would ruin Gerry's memory.

"We're doing some good business tonight, and I'm going to use that to help Tracy pay for the funeral," Artie said. "Gerry's insurance won't cover the whole thing. So, by the time I get everyone out of here, clean up, and get home, I won't be back until at least four. No way I'll be up in time to help her deliver Gerry's suit to the funeral home. The least you could do is go with her tomorrow morning."

I took a deep breath. Behind me the music started up again, an upbeat tune, muddled by the concrete barrier between me and Tracy.

"Yeah," I said, "I'll be there."

CHAPTER 18

I DROVE DOWN THE STREET SLOWLY, LOOKING FOR parking, only to find Bill Martin standing outside my apartment building. Before I lived here, when I was still with Jeanne and we could afford living on the top floor of a two-family, Martin and I chased an informant into the building. He was running from us, refusing to betray a friend like we had wanted. When we caught him I remembered thinking that the informant shouldn't be hanging around an apartment building like this one. That it was well kept, nice, and, since no one was watching us with their doors open, the neighbors minded their own business.

Now, as I found a rare spot on the street and put the car into park, I doubted Martin wanted to find anyone other than me. I still had my Glock on me, but if I decided to leave it in the car, he'd see me. I did leave my phone in the car. It needed charging.

Through the windshield, Martin watched me undo my seat belt. I opened the car door and stepped out.

"Hey kid," he said, stepping away from the building toward my car. Hands in his pockets, he leaned on the hood. Like he hadn't a care in the world. Like meeting me here wasn't a big deal.

"What do you want, Martin?"

"No 'hello'?" He kept the smile on his face. Very casual. "Remember the days we used to just sit in the car and talk about music?"

"I remember you liked the Hollies."

"Yeah, great band."

"What do you want?" I asked.

He laughed. "I thought you'd tell me I'm lucky to still be on the force."

"I didn't think of that. You want to start over?"

"No. Not really. James told me you stopped by your buddy's place today."

"Had to feed the cat."

Martin curled his lip and nodded. "There is no cat. Did you take a look around when you were there?"

"I used the bathroom."

"Probably checked the closet, huh?"

"Uh-huh."

"So you saw what I saw."

"Why didn't you put it into evidence?"

"At the moment it's all circumstantial. You know, maybe he caught lots of colds. But your buddy doesn't seem like he was the cleanest guy. Had some baggage."

I didn't answer. It was warmer here than in Asbury or even Sayreville, and I wanted to unzip my jacket. However, I didn't want to risk showing off the Glock, give Martin a reason to put me away.

"Listen. I know you don't like me. I don't like you. Given the chance, you slip up, I'll put you away just for the hell of it. But let me do my job. Stay out of this," Martin said.

"As much as I think your sloppy handiwork will screw this up, don't worry. I'm not working the case."

Martin's eye opened wide. His body tensed like he was going to leap off the car and beat the shit out of me. It was real anger. I had seen it for years on the force. A smart-ass junkie or pimp or mugger would insult Martin, and he'd nearly take their head off. A couple of times those guys had come to the precinct in handcuffs and with black eyes and cut lips. But this time Martin was able to hold himself back. Didn't stop me from taking a step away, however.

After a deep breath, Martin stepped off the hood of my car. Leaned in toward my face. This time I held my ground. His breath smelled like onions and cinnamon Trident. "You fucked up years ago. You could have been a good cop. Now you're just a fuckup. It's about time you got smart and let me do my job."

"You're going to give out parking tickets?"

I thought I had pushed him far enough. His face turned beet red and he gritted his teeth together, baring them. I thought he was going to take a swing at me. I wanted him to. That would give me the opportunity to swing back, something I had wanted to do for years.

But he stepped away. Looked at my Honda. I heard him breathing hard, working the muscles of his mouth into a sneer. "One of these days, I'm gonna tell you something. Man, it's going to blow your mind."

"Yeah?" I said, not knowing what else to say.

He pointed to my car, and I could see a little glimmer of metal in the streetlight. "Looks like you might have kicked up a stone or something on the highway. You could try to buff the scratch out, or a dab of the right paint will take care of it."

"Thanks. I'll do that."

"I only ever wanted to help you, kid. No matter what you wanted."

"Sure you did."

"We'll get the guy who got your buddy. We're cops. We're the good guys."

He stepped into his car, parked on the corner, and started it up. As he pulled away, I realized I'd been warned off two different cases by two different people in one day. It was something to put on the résumé. Too bad Martin didn't come carrying cash. I would have taken it from him just as easily as I had from the hoods. I made it up to my apartment and found my bed.

✳   ✳

Six in the morning, someone was buzzing on the intercom. I stumbled out of bed, in boxers and a T-shirt, and found the speaker. I asked my visitor to identify himself.

"This is Detective Daniels, Mr. Donne. Detective Blanchett is with me. Can we come up?"

"Sure," I said. "Apartment Two Thirty-seven."

I hit the buzzer and went to find another shirt and a pair of jeans.

Minutes later, I was opening the door for the two detectives. Daniels had one of those Styrofoam trays with three cups of Dunkin' Donuts coffee in her hands. Blanchett looked like he hadn't gotten any sleep since I'd last seen him, bags under his eyes, unshaven. Daniels looked great. Her eyes were sparkling and aware, pressed suit, crisp and professional.

"Cream and sugar?" she said.

I nodded, thinking I probably looked more like Blanchett, groggy and out of sorts. Daniels took a large cup out of the tray and handed it to me.

"Do you mind if we sit?" Blanchett asked.

"Go for it. To what do I owe the honor?"

"We've got a couple of questions, and Daniels here thought it'd be nice if we came down to visit you. Ya know, instead of making *you* suffer through rush hour, she thought it'd be cool if we did."

"I appreciate that." What they really wanted was to come early and catch me asleep. Though Daniels did bring coffee. She couldn't be all bad.

Daniels said, "I'm glad someone does."

I popped the top on the coffee, took a long sip.

"What do you want to ask me about?"

Daniels leaned across after giving Blanchett his coffee. "Who was the girl Hanover carried out of the apartment two nights ago?"

"The paper said Diane Peterson."

"The papers did say that. Are you saying you don't know her?"

"Not a clue."

"Could be anybody?"

"Sure." I loved the rapid-fire approach, made me feel like I was just as smart as them, that I was able to answer questions as quickly as they asked them. Like I was a step ahead, knew what was coming.

"Come on, Donne. We looked you up, we talked to New Brunswick. We know what you did here," Blanchett piped in, proving that my lawyer was right about what they were doing when they were out of the room. "They don't like you down here. Let me tell you, the cop we talked to was hoping we'd arrest you for the murder. So give up the act and tell us what you know about the dead woman."

My stomach knotted a bit, and it wasn't from the coffee. Daniels and Blanchett were getting at something. If they were asking me who the woman was and expecting me to know, that meant they thought I *should* know. Maybe she was someone who had popped up in a crime before, most likely back when I was on the force. But where? Did it have to do with drugs? How much research had Blanchett and Daniels done since I'd last seen them? Maybe Blanchett really hadn't gotten any sleep, and Daniels looked so good because she was a freak of nature. I felt as if I was missing a huge piece of the puzzle, like I had walked in in the middle of a movie and was expected to give a recap of the first half.

"I really don't know anything about her," I said. "My job was to find out if Hanover was cheating on his wife. I did that."

"So you left it at that, then?" Daniels asked.

I nodded. I wondered if I'd be able to manipulate the conversation with my answers, direct them to telling more about the dead woman. Because they weren't about to volunteer the information, and I was getting really curious.

"Why did you visit with Jen Hanover after we went to see her?" Blanchett asked.

I hesitated too long before speaking. I tried to cover, saying, "I wanted to inform her of what I'd seen. She should know that I was doing my job. She was my client and I felt that I should be the one to tell her about her husband. I didn't know you had gotten there already."

Daniels said, "Come on. You didn't really think we'd leave that place unwatched, did you? If Hanover was going to run, we thought maybe he'd at least try to contact his wife. But it seems like he's smarter than that. We haven't seen him in the area, but we have the place staked out."

"Tap the phones?" I asked.

"Working on it," she said. "We don't get many murders in Madison, but we intend to solve the ones we do get."

"Better than some of the cops in this town," I said.

"Mr. Donne, what did you have to say to Jen Hanover?"

"I told you already." The last thing I wanted was to let these cops know I was working on the case. If they knew I was trying to get to Hanover before them, they'd shut me out completely.

"You're done working for her?"

"I told her that if she needed my help with anything, finding a lawyer, legal issues, to call me. I would help her with that. I also had a drink with her and gave her a chance to cry on my shoulder."

"You haven't heard from her since?" Blanchett said.

"No." That wasn't a lie, at the moment. But I was going to call Jen as soon as they got the hell out of my apartment, hopefully before the phones were tapped.

"And you don't know who the dead woman is, Mr. Donne?" Daniels said.

Trying to catch me off guard, come back to a topic I'd thought we left already. "No. I have no idea. Do you guys know?"

"Mr. Donne, we're asking the questions," Daniels said. She had to know she sounded like an episode of *Dragnet* when she said it.

"Call me Jackson," I said. "Mr. Donne was my father."

It was an old saying, and not true. I remembered again why I took the case from Jen. My mother sitting on the couch crying after my father had walked out on her. I never knew if he preferred to be called Mr. Donne. I never really knew anything about him.

"I'm Sarah," Daniels said. "And this is Harry. But we prefer to be called Detective. Or at the very least, Mr. and Ms."

Daniels was showing me a sign of respect. She trusted me enough to let me in on the personal sides of their lives. Just a little. The last bit, however, showed me she still intended to be professional.

"I still don't know anything about the woman."

"Thank you, Jackson. But if you know anything, if you're holding back on us—"

"I will call you," I said.

They weren't out the door three minutes when I picked up the phone and dialed Jen Hanover.

She sounded like she'd been up for a while. It bothered me that I was the only one sleeping. Everyone was a step ahead, it felt like.

"Have you heard from Rex?" I asked.

"No. Can you come down here?"

"Now? Is everything okay?"

There was silence between us, and all I could hear was a hiss on her line. I hoped it wasn't a phone tap.

"I need some help," she said.

CHAPTER 19

tHe pHONe RANɢ earLy IN tHe mORNINɢ. BILL
Martin didn't know what time it was. He just knew he had a Jameson
headache and a slight sense of failure. How the hell could Donne not
be working the case anymore? That was complete bullshit.

On the phone, a voice said, "If you want to meet with Mr.
Burgess, meet us at the corner store, Easton and Hazel. One hour."

Click.

Getting Donne back on the case was something to worry about
later.

* *

The corner store was a mess. Shelves weren't level and the soup cans
and small packets of macaroni were strewn everywhere. The air
smelled like old coffee and rotten fruit.

He stood and waited. Hearing the second hand on his watch tick.

Two thick guys came from the back room and said something to the Chinese cashier. The Chinaman locked the register and went out the front door.

Thick guy number one was bald, with a goatee, wearing track pants and a tank top with the words GOLD'S GYM emblazoned on it. He looked like a professional wrestler. If it came down to it, a quick shot with his boot heel to the instep would take him down easy, Martin figured.

The other guy was a bit trickier. Not a professional wrestler type, he looked more like a model. Button-down blue silk shirt, pressed khakis, steel-tipped loafers. He had a way about him. Slick, fast, like he'd stab you and not even blink. Martin would have to play it careful with this guy. Let him talk, eye him, find his weakness.

Again, *if* it came down to it.

The model spoke. "You Martin?"

Martin shrugged.

"All right, then, cop," the model said. "Assume the position."

Doing as he was told, Martin felt the wrestler's hands pat his waist. They moved up his sides, until they felt his shoulder holster and Beretta. The wrestler spun him around, reached into his jacket, pulled the gun, checked the clip, and handed the weapon to the model. The wrestler completed the frisking and stepped back.

"Most action I've gotten in months," Martin said. "Thanks."

"Fuck you," the wrestler said.

"You want to see Mr. Burgess, you're gonna keep your mouth shut," the model said.

Martin shut up.

"Good," the model said. "Follow us."

* *

The back room was immaculate compared to the shelves in the front. Boxes were neatly stacked, the floor looked like it'd just been waxed, and a big guy leaned against a spotless mirror, arms folded.

Martin didn't bother to size the big guy up. If the shit was going to go down now, he was a dead man. He couldn't take on the model, the wrestler, and the new guy all at once. Not to mention Michael Burgess, who he assumed was the guy sitting behind a desk to his left.

"Josh, Maurice, thank you," the guy behind the desk said. "Leave Detective Martin's gun on my desk and make sure business in the front is being run legitimately."

The model and the wrestler did as they were told.

"Have a seat, Detective. I'm Michael Burgess. I don't usually hold audience with police officers, but I'll make an exception in your case. I've done some homework and it seems you have an interesting past."

"My past has nothing to do with why I'm here." Martin sat in a creaky wooden chair. The back was splintered, and he could feel shards pressing through his shirt into his skin.

Burgess nodded. "Then why are you here?"

"Gerry Figuroa."

Burgess spread his hands as if the name meant nothing to him. Smart man.

"Old guy, killed in a hit-and-run a few days ago?"

The big guy hadn't moved. Never a good sign. He obviously thought he was quick enough to catch Martin even with his arms crossed. The guy looked Hispanic. He also looked like he'd been brought up in the military. Thick, but quick.

"I read about it in the papers. Why come to me about it?"

Martin realized then what a bad idea this was. The only way to get Burgess to talk was to tell him what evidence there was. Ultimately, that would give Burgess the upper hand. Martin didn't like that idea and knew then how out of practice he really was. Thank God evaluations didn't always involve "on the job" observations.

He thought about getting up and leaving, but didn't expect to get to the door alive. Best to play it straight.

"When I investigated Figuroa's house, I found he had a lot of suspicious items in his possession. Batteries, Sudafed, matches, coffee filters, that sort of thing."

Burgess looked at the big guy, then back at Martin, a bemused look on his face. "So, are you asking me if this man shopped in my store?"

"You and me both know what I'm asking."

"Tell me."

"Did Gerry Figuroa work for you?"

"Are you saying my work here is less than legal?" Burgess was practically busting a gut now. Like he was having trouble holding in his laughter.

Martin's face flushed. "I'm saying the entire city knows what you do."

"Which brings us back to your past, Detective Martin. I know why you were demoted. I know why, for a time, you were suspended. I know about Jackson Donne."

"What does that have to do with anything?" Martin didn't like this one bit.

"You were involved with drugs. You and your crew practically kept the drug industry in business back when New Brunswick had a narc squad. Until Donne turned you all in, you were the drug lords of this town."

"That's not me anymore. That's not why I'm here."

Burgess sat back. "I'm going to make you an offer. That's the only reason I agreed to see you. Gerry Figuroa's name is something I saw in an obituary page. Nothing more."

"What are you talking about?"

Every instinct told Martin to run. Get the hell out. Still, he stayed.

"I'm offering you a chance to work for me," Burgess said.

C H A P T E R

It was seven-thirty, traffic was moving slowly on 287, and I had just realized I had forgotten to charge my cell phone. An A.M. radio morning-show DJ was talking about having to pay for a missed doctor's appointment because she hadn't given a seventy-two-hour cancellation notice. The story was supposed to be humorous, an example of the cynical eye of the New Yorker or New Jerseyan, but all it did was remind me of my promise to help Tracy Boland this morning. No way I'd make it back in time. Especially if Jen Hanover was in trouble.

She hadn't said much else before I'd hung up. I asked her to call the police if she was in immediate danger and that I'd be there as quickly as possible. No idea what she needed help with, I got dressed and shot out the door with only my keys, my wallet, and my gun.

Traffic on 287 North was brutal. The traffic report which interrupted the DJ said there was an accident about ten miles ahead of me. I couldn't swerve, I couldn't drive aggressively. All I could do was sit and wait it out. There was too much going on, and the fear that Jen Hanover could be in trouble and there wasn't anything I could do about it didn't help matters. I hoped she would be smart and call the police. Her safety was more important than covering for her husband, or even seeing her husband before the police did. The image of my bald friend from yesterday hovering over her wouldn't leave my mind.

Miles of red in front of me, brake lights shining and reflecting in the early-morning sun caused me to grip the wheel tightly. I spun the radio dial trying to find a song or something relaxing and came up with nothing. I hated this feeling, the lack of control.

I thought of Bill Martin. When I was his partner, when he was training me to be his successor, he used to talk about this moment. The powerless feeling. He said it came often when you were a cop, but mostly, he said it came on the stakeout. Those moments when all you could do was sit in a car on the street and wait for your suspect to do something. Some cops dealt with it by eating and drinking. Some listened to music or an audiobook. Martin never felt either of those was productive. "Either give you a fat ass or a headache," he used to say. What Martin did was go over what he knew, make sure he had all the evidence correct, that he had the right guy. He said these moments when you had no control over what happened next normally came at the end of a case, and you'd figure it out if you took it slowly.

Except, as far as I knew, neither of the cases was anywhere near its conclusion. I had only snippets of information.

The traffic rolled a little and I was able to pick up speed, got the car to about thirty. At least we were moving. Nearly five minutes later I could see flashing lights, police cars, and flares in the right shoulder. A few cops were milling around on foot next to a twisted piece of metal. I didn't see an ambulance, but I also didn't see any civilians walking around. That told me the ambulance had come and gone already. Someone wasn't having a good morning.

Beyond the accident, the brake lights winked off. I floored the pedal, swerving in and out of traffic, trying to make up the time I had lost. The Morristown exit was still twenty miles away. I had a dead woman, I had two guys paying me off, and a wife in trouble. As far as I knew, as far as the phone book had told me, as far as Jen had told me, Rex didn't have relatives, didn't have anyone in New Jersey or New York to run to. What did it all add up to? Did it even add up? There was a sign telling me the Morristown exit was two miles away. I still had nothing. I hadn't reached any conclusions. All I had was a knot in the pit of my stomach to go along with my nerves and my sore neck.

Turning off the exit, I tried to find my way through the roads back to the Hanover home. The morning before I had gotten to the home on autopilot, half-asleep. The houses didn't look familiar, the streets all looked the same, and I was lost. The clock on my dashboard said eight-fifteen. If Jen was in trouble, serious trouble, and she was counting on me, she'd be dead by now. The radio went to a news update, and that's when how to find the house became clear.

"And now our top story, we'll hear from our reporter live in Morristown, New Jersey," the DJ said.

"Thanks, Susan. We're here outside the home of a man wanted by police for questioning. He is wanted in connection to a murder that occurred outside Drew University, just down the street here, in the next town over, Madison."

I turned off the radio and drove through the streets, circling, U-turning, looking up and down side streets, trying to find the circus. After about twenty minutes, I saw a blocked-off side street. Towering above a clutch of houses was a satellite dish attached to a news van.

I drove past the roadblock, a police cruiser sitting near it, lights flashing. Taking the next right, I parked on the street and got out. A strip of houses led to a dead end on the street. I climbed a fence, into a yard, and peered between the houses. The media was camped in front of a house. I had to cross three more yards, climbing another fence. If the police saw me, I'd be arrested immediately and I didn't need that. At the same time, I didn't want a throng of news reporters questioning me.

The lawn hadn't been cut in weeks. The grass was long, coming up over my sneakers, leading to a concrete patio with a picnic table on it. There was a spotless grill perpendicular to the house. I walked toward the patio and the glass sliding door. Through the door Jen Hanover sat at a kitchen table, dressed in a neat business suit, sipping coffee and reading the paper. If I hadn't heard the throng of reporters talking on cell phones, screaming about the position of their camera compared to other cameramen, it would look like a normal morning scene. I tapped gently on the glass.

Jen jumped before she looked up. She peered through the window at me, recognition crossing her face. She came to the door, slid it open.

"You scared the hell out of me," she said.

"Is everything okay?"

"I had to call in late to work. I'll probably lose my job. But I'm afraid to go out there. If I went out by myself they probably wouldn't let me out of my driveway."

"You're probably right."

"I didn't know who else to call. Have you dealt with reporters before?"

"It's best to avoid them. Do you have your blinds shut in the front room?"

"I didn't open them when I went to bed last night. I went out for the paper this morning and all the news vans were there."

"Did you say anything to them?"

"I said, 'No comment,' and slammed the door."

I laughed. "You're a natural."

She smiled, too. It brought a light to a face that looked exhausted. The light showed me what Rex saw in her. She probably hadn't done much sleeping these past few nights, sitting by the phone praying her husband would call. I wondered how much she really knew about him.

"Have you heard from Rex?" I asked.

She shook her head. "Not a word. Not a phone call. Nothing. Jesus Christ. I hope he's all right."

"It's probably better he doesn't call. The police are going to tap your phone," I said. "If they haven't done so already."

"You're probably right."

I shrugged. "I'm sure your husband is fine."

What was I saying? I watched this man carrying a dead body rolled in a carpet across the street. You don't do that if you haven't killed someone. But I was helping his wife cover his trail. Telling her it was better if he didn't call.

I've killed three men in my life. Two of whom the police don't know about. Two bookies who were trying to kill a client of mine. I cornered them in an abandoned hotel in Atlantic City, shot them both in cold blood. I drifted them out in the bay behind the building. Whether they deserved it or not was a question that woke me up in a sweat in the middle of the night. I could still smell the blood, see the look of fear on their faces. I hid their deaths from the law. Hid them from the police. Now I was helping a killer hide until I discovered him.

And the most frightening part: No matter how weak my knees were just thinking about it, I wasn't going to stop. I wanted to get to Hanover on my own. I had sat outside while he murdered a woman. I let it happen. It didn't matter to me that I didn't know it was going on. I was close enough to stop it and now I wanted to catch Hanover, let him talk to Jen one time, and turn him over to the police. If I was trying to make up for my past mistakes, so be it.

"Are you all right?"

"Yeah. I'm all right."

"Listen, I need a ride to work. Do you think—?"

"Say no more," I said. "We're going to have to go out the way I came in."

"Thank you. I get out at seven, but I'll call a friend. I didn't know how to deal with this."

"Stay out of view if you don't want to answer any questions."

She looked toward the front door. Though we couldn't see them, we could feel their presence. "I'll try."

She gathered her things, locked the front door, and we went back through the yard to my car. She had to climb the fences, too, but refused my help. My stomach was still tight, my knees still weak, but I did my best not to show it. We got in the car and pulled out into traffic.

We didn't talk much during the ten-minute ride, she only speaking to give me directions, and I to acknowledge I understood. I pulled up to a two-story office building. She leaned over and kissed me on the cheek before she exited the car.

CHAPTER 21

WHEN THE COPS DON'T LIKE YOU, IT PAYS TO HAVE
connections with the press. Outside of cops themselves, nobody has
more inside information about police work, people in the public spotlight, and dark dirty secrets, than newspaper writers. I don't know anyone with the big New York papers or networks, but I do know two local
reporters who work the crime beat. One, Albert Spater, used to write
for the *Record* and was currently between jobs. The other, Henry Steir,
wrote for the *Star-Ledger.* I counted on Steir being outside the Hanover
home.

I drove back and parked across the street from the blocked intersection. I could see the crowd milling about on the lawns, outside Jen
Hanover's home. It was after nine. Too early for the afternoon news,
too late for the morning shows. Unless something major happened
and they decided to go live, the TV field reporters weren't very busy
at the moment. Some were drinking coffee, others were writing in

notepads, probably what they wanted to tape for the twelve o'clock report. Most of them just looked bored.

The print reporters were a different animal. They stayed away from the TV people, huddled across the street. Most of them knew they were a dying breed, the days of the newspaper fading in their minds, but they stuck with it because they loved it. Instant media and information was causing newspaper reporters to work harder to find angles that TV didn't know about. The Internet and TV were instantaneous, and with so much put into the thirty-second sound bite, they could get by with just the facts. Newspapers had to work harder. Most of the reporters were on their cell phones, probably getting in touch with their contacts to see what little extra they could find out.

Like I assumed, Henry Steir was there. He was a little older than me, early thirties, just out of Columbia grad school. I don't know how he rose through the newspaper ranks so quickly. He had some high-profile stories over the past year. My best guess, he was an ass kisser.

I stood at the roadblock, trying to look like a casual observer. The last thing I wanted was to be caught on camera by someone taping a report for later in the day. There were a few other people, dog walkers and senior citizens, watching the media circus as well. The cop watching the block was standing next to the hood of the car, arms crossed, trying to stay alert. I doubt he expected any of us to rush the barrier.

My plan was to make eye contact with Henry and get him to saunter over. But he was busy watching the front door and didn't turn my way. I wasn't sure I'd get past the roadblock on good looks. Having Henry's number on my cell phone helped, but the guy's voice was louder than most people I knew—too much yelling questions at press conferences, he always said—and that might draw too much attention this way. And my phone was dead, anyway. It didn't look like I had any choice.

I walked up to the cop, knowing this was going to be a pain in the ass, for both of us.

"How you doing today?" I asked.

The cop looked me up and down. *Who's this asshole?* He was uniformed, my height, and fat. He had a thin brown mustache, a squint, two chins, and a name tag that read LIEBOWITZ. I had to refrain from making any doughnut jokes.

"What can I do for you?" he mumbled.

"Any chance I can get through?"

He finally got to earn his paycheck. "Not unless you're a resident of this street or you have press credentials."

I pointed toward Steir. "That's my boss over there. I forgot my press ID in his car. It's parked down the street. The red Nissan."

"You must be shit out of luck today, huh?"

"Not going to let me in?"

Liebowitz gave me a look, then checked out all the other observers, most of whom had gotten bored watching nothing happen and had started to leave. He sighed loudly, then said: "Go."

I stepped around the barrier and headed toward Steir at a near jog. I tried to keep my back to the TV people, making sure no one caught me on camera. The last thing I needed was my male model friend and his buddy catching me in front of the Hanover house while waiting for *Jeopardy* to start.

Steir hung up his cell phone, looked up, and saw me hustling his way.

"Jesus Christ!" he said. "What the hell are you doing here?"

"Shut the fuck up. Keep your voice down."

If he tried to hug me I was going to deck him. Then the gears in his head started to work. "You have something to do with this shit, don't you?"

I shook his hand. "Can we get a cup of coffee?"

"I can't leave. What if she comes out? Decides to give everyone the scoop?" He smiled. "Dumb as it sounds, some people do that. People are dumb."

"She won't."

"How the hell do you know?"

"She's not at home right now."

"Oh fuck, man." He could hardly control his glee. Steir tried to do three things at once: find a pen and notebook and grab the tape recorder out of his jacket pocket. He didn't really succeed at any of them, dropping his pen and accidentally hitting Rewind on the recorder instead of Play. His first question was, "What the hell do you have to do with this?"

"Put the tape recorder away. Take me for a cup of coffee before your snake-in-the-grass pals get suspicious and put me on camera."

"It'll be good publicity for the business."

"I didn't put my makeup on today."

He laughed, but still didn't budge.

"If they put me on camera, they'll get the scoop before you."

He put the tape recorder in his pocket and eyed up the networks. "I hate those fucks."

"I always thought you'd be jealous. They get the story out there first."

"Nah. I make more than they do. I hate 'em. But no way in hell am I jealous."

*   *

We found a Dunkin' Donuts in the center of town. I sat with a large coffee. Henry Steir had a medium and a corn muffin spread out on the table between us. Next to the food was an open notebook, a ballpoint pen, his cell phone, and a pager.

"What are you doing here?" he asked, midchew.

"I was following Rex Hanover the night of the murder."

"Who hired you?" He didn't have the tape recorder out, but he was scribbling faster than I could talk.

"I'm not going to get into that right now."

He sat back in his seat. "I thought we had a thing, Jackson."

"I'll give you the story."

"When?"

"When it's over."

"That's bullshit. When it's over, everyone else will have the story, too. It'll be everywhere."

"Yeah, but will they have an exclusive from the guy who found the body?"

"Bullshit."

"Not really. And you know I'll only talk to you."

"What about that guy from the *Record*?"

"He's not there anymore."

He got rid of half his coffee in one gulp, without wincing. "All right. If you aren't going to tell me anything yet, why are you here?"

"I want to know what you know."

He laughed. "Fuck." Took a chunk of the corn muffin. "I know less than you, probably."

"How did you guys know to go to the Hanovers'?"

"The cops released a statement last night. They told us about Diane's murder, told us Rex was on the run. I think they want to use us to find him." Wiped his mouth with a napkin.

"Who is the girl, Diane? The cops came asking me about her like I should know."

"You don't?"

I shook my head.

"So you want me to tell you?"

I nodded.

"What's in it for me?"

"I told you, the story."

"And?"

"I already bought you coffee and a muffin."

"Get me a refill?"

"When we're done."

"You're on."

"Isn't what you're doing to me unethical? Making me pay you for information that's going to be in the paper tomorrow anyway."

"You want to wait till tomorrow?"

Plus, he might keep things out of his article. And the TV would tell me her name, that's it. Whatever would fit in a shocking sound bite.

"Who is she, Henry?"

A line had formed at the counter, the small storefront suddenly busy. Probably a bunch of local workers on their coffee break. Some of them talked about the previous night's baseball games. The others discussed some reality TV show. Water cooler talk.

Steir flipped through his notebook. "Diane Peterson. Unmarried. Twenty-three, just out of college."

"What did she do for a living?"

"Substitute teacher." He turned the page. "Christ, the public is gonna love this. I've been on the phone with the Madison Board of Ed all day trying to get a statement."

"They give one?"

"Yeah. 'No comment.' "

"I'm not surprised."

"Neither am I. But that's it. She was a nobody girl. No one cared about her. She didn't make much money. What do substitutes make a day? Eighty, a hundred bucks, maybe? No one really knows anything about her."

"Did you talk to her landlord?"

"I gave him a call. He probably had a written response." Steir read off the notebook. " 'She was quiet. Always paid the rent on time. I didn't bother her. I didn't ask her about her life.' "

"The cops tell you anything about her?"

"Just enough to suck us in. The all-American innocent girl, murdered. Told us her job. That's it. They gave us a picture of Hanover, told us more about him."

"What did they say?"

"Where he lived. That he was married. That they had evidence he was worthy of an arrest. That he was on the run. They want us to flush him out. The networks show his picture on TV, if we're lucky he's on the front page, someone sees it and calls them. They come and make the arrest. All of America breathes a sigh of relief, another murderer off the street."

"You're not cynical, are you?"

"Nah, I'm too young to be cynical."

I had more questions about Diane, but not anything I wanted to ask Steir. He was smart enough on his own. I didn't want to direct him to answers before I was able to find them myself.

"You know what bothers me, Jackson?" He looked at his notes. "She's a substitute teacher. No family supporting her, but she's able to afford a place in Madison, just across from the university. Prime real estate. How?"

"I have no idea, Henry."

I looked at my watch. I had to be at the wake at two. It was already past ten. I still had to get back to New Brunswick, shower, and shave. Already I missed my appointment to pick up Tracy.

I stood up to leave.

"So, I'm going to get an exclusive?"

"You know I'm good for it."

"And?"

Ten minutes later, Henry Steir dropped me off at my car, holding another medium coffee in his right hand.

CHAPTER **22**

Back at the station, Bill Martin's hands trembled for the first time since Jackson Donne had been his partner. Toward the end, when he'd been paranoid about Donne every second of the day, just waiting for the kid to flip, his hands shook. Uncontrollably.

And now they were doing it again.

The way he figured it, agreeing to side with Burgess could work out in his favor. It would give him an in with the drug element. He'd have his ear to the ground, know what was going on before it happened. He'd be able to move up in the ranks on the force. Having the leading drug lord in New Brunswick as an informant. No one else would have that.

Burgess insinuated Martin would be working for him. Fuck that.

Martin picked up the phone and dialed the number they'd given him.

"I'm in," he said.

Placing the telephone on its cradle, he wondered: Is *this how it started last time?*

CHAPTER 23

THERE WEREN'T MANY CARS IN THE FUNERAL-HOME parking lot. Artie was parked about three spaces in, two other cars I didn't recognize sandwiching his. It was still early, only two-fifteen; the spaces would probably fill in later.

Inside, a man in black suit and tie greeted me. He was heavy, sweat dripping off his brow. He had a five o'clock shadow, greasy hair, looked like he hadn't showered recently. He smiled and asked whom I was here to view. After I told him, he directed me to a long room on the right. The same one I had sat in yesterday.

Tracy was sitting in the front right corner seat, clutching a tissue. There were rows set up, much like the day before. It looked as if nothing had been done except a casket had been lugged into the room, Gerry in it. I succeeded in avoiding the body when I entered.

Artie was standing near the American flag set up next to the casket, talking to two men I didn't recognize. Both older, graying hair, hunched in pinstripes, they may have been war buddies of Gerry's. In the last row sat Gerry's landlord, Devon James. He was the only person to make eye contact with me, nodding a greeting. I was glad he came. Tracy didn't turn around. If Artie saw me, he didn't acknowledge it.

Walking to the front, toward the casket, my body felt numb. My mind tried to force me back to Jeanne's wake, but I fought against it. Put my arm on Tracy's shoulder, leaned over, whispered a condolence in her ear. She looked up, eyes red, some mascara running. She smiled.

"You came. What happened?" She wrapped her arms around me. Stepping away, she looked me in the eye. "You promised. Where were you this morning?"

When I returned from my journey to Morristown, I charged my cell phone. I had missed seven calls. They were all from Artie and Tracy. After a minute, I had put the phone in my pocket.

"Let me say a prayer. I'll tell you after that."

She nodded, biting her lip, bringing the tissue to her eyes. I wondered how many times she'd done that already today. It was the first time she'd seen her uncle in years, and he was lifeless.

I walked toward the casket, taking in everything but the body. My mind wouldn't register it. The casket was finished wood, with two gold handles on the sides for the pallbearers. In front of that was a stoop to kneel on, padded in a color that matched the wood of the casket. A framed collage of pictures of Gerry, his military photo in the middle, stood on an easel. Behind it were a multitude of flowers— yellow, red, green—a bright flash contrasting with the otherwise drab room.

As I knelt in front of the casket, I finally looked at the body. Gerry was wearing a navy blue suit with a bright blue tie and white shirt. He looked peaceful and younger, like so many years had been shaved off. He had a natural expression, eyes closed, mouth shut, hair perfectly in place, combed to the side like he always wore it. I wanted to shake him, wake him up so we could get a drink and get the hell out of here. He would have hated the quiet of the room, no one laughing, no one drinking. I could nearly hear him bitching about it.

I bowed my head, and just before I closed my eyes, I noticed his hands. The same thing happened at Jeanne's wake, at every wake I'd ever been to. Folded over each other at his waist, I could see the makeup. That was always when it registered the person was dead, when I saw the hands. I wondered what the undertaker did with them, how careless they got with the hands. It looked like they were covered in petroleum jelly, trying to make them shine, and some of it hung off the thumb. Hands show life, they move, they twitch; Gerry's were doing nothing.

Someone had run Gerry over with a car. The police believed it was a homicide. My friend had asked me to look into it. He didn't trust the police to give full effort, and neither did I. Prayer wasn't in my playbook. It wasn't something I did regularly, and I wasn't even sure God existed. But I could feel Gerry's presence as I knelt. I closed my eyes. I promised to find who did this to him. I was going to find out what he had been hiding, and answer the questions his death raised. I didn't bother to say a prayer.

I felt a hand on my shoulder. I turned to face Artie. Behind him the two men he'd been talking to were finding seats.

"We need to talk," Artie said, keeping his voice low.

"Now?"

"Yeah." He started to walk away. "Come outside."

I followed him. As I passed the rows of chairs, I felt Tracy's hand touch mine. An offer of support, it seemed.

Out in the parking lot, the cars rumbled on 18, the sun's heat burned through my suit jacket. Five feet from me Artie stood, arms crossed, stiff, teeth clenched so tight his skin wrinkled at the jaw. He was pissed. And that pissed me off.

"Where the fuck were you this morning?" he asked.

"Do we really have to go through this?"

"Tracy called me in a panic. I didn't think we'd get the suit there in time. You said you were going to fucking be there." His hands went up in the air, waving frantically. "And then you don't pick up your cell phone. Why, because you said you'd find out who did this?"

I realized that if I snapped back, not only would it make a scene, it would fracture whatever the hell friendship Artie and I had.

"My cell phone was dead."

"Where did you go?"

"My client—from the other case—"

"Oh, Jesus Christ, here we go."

"What are you, my girlfriend?" I said. "My client was in fucking trouble. I didn't know what kind until I got to her, but I had to help her. I didn't want to let someone else die."

"Die? What the fuck are you—?"

"I didn't know what was going on. Gerry's death, fucking Bill Martin, the Madison cops, it's all been on my fucking mind the past few days. I don't know what to expect right now."

"But you promised . . ." He trailed off. The conviction in his voice faded.

"I told you, no. I'm sorry I didn't call this morning. Let's go back inside and get through this all later. Please, I owe Tracy an apology." Despite my new resolve to look into this again, I was not about to let Artie win this argument.

"What about me? I drove her."

"Quit whining."

"Fuck you." There was still anger in his voice, but he was trying to play it off with humor.

I let him have that.

The rest of the afternoon moved by like a glacier. I felt like I was out of place. This was the kind of wake I'd normally go to for half an hour, offer condolences, and then sneak out the back. But I felt required to stay, even though whoever did this to Gerry was out there. I stood and watched as, one after another, people shuffled in and gave Tracy a hug or a kiss. They would usually whisper in her ear and she'd smile or nod, and they'd move on to the casket. The minutes ticked by, and finally it was four.

We adjourned for a few hours. Artie and Tracy went to get something to eat, and I went back to my office and made a few more phone calls from Hanover's contact book. I got the feeling that either the police or the press had also gotten a copy of these contacts. Nearly everyone was screening their calls or hanging up on me when I identified myself. Damn. More footwork for me. I was going to have to visit these people at some point.

I went back for the evening session of the wake, arriving about ten minutes late. Artie and Tracy stood on opposite sides of the room. No one else was there. Even Gerry looked like he wanted to leave. The minutes and hours ticked by, and only one other person showed up, one of the older gentlemen who had been there that afternoon. Finally, at quarter to nine, I whispered in Tracy's ear that I had some business to take care of. She smiled, kissed me on the cheek, and said good-bye.

Truth was, I didn't really have business to attend to, but I had to get out of there. I'd spent the evening fighting off memories of Jeanne; all I really wanted was a drink. Tracy's performance of "Bernie's Song," her movements as she played were also in my head, doing battle with my nostalgia.

I saw Artie get into his car and pull out toward Route 18. He didn't look all that happy, and I was surprised he didn't wait for Tracy, who was lingering in the lobby. I could see her through the glass doors. I hated to think of her as option B, but I couldn't help it. I got out of the car and approached her.

She must have seen me coming, because she pushed the door open and stepped onto the sidewalk, a confused look on her face. "What are you still doing here? I thought you had some business. Did Artie—?"

"Artie didn't do anything," I said. "There was a chance I was going to have to go somewhere, but it didn't pan out. How come you didn't ride home with him?"

"He wasn't in the best mood. I told him I needed some time to myself and was going to call a cab."

"Did you?"

"Not yet. Do you smoke?"

"Not anymore."

She nodded. "I quit, too, but I could really use one now. I can't believe no one showed up tonight."

It was a typical New Jersey April evening. The sun had gone down and there was a chill in the air that was comfortable to sleep in. But to the skin and the brain it was warmth that hadn't been felt since early September. Spring was pushing its way through the haze of a cold winter and a rainy March. The scent of rain still hung in the air. Gave the night air a clean, refreshed feel. You could still smell the carbon monoxide from the cars on Route 18, and their horns carried through the air clearly. That's what I always noticed when spring came to New Jersey, you could hear and smell the traffic better.

"You feel like getting a drink?" I asked.

I think she was taken aback by my quick change of subject. Her eyes widened, and she didn't say anything.

"Come on, there's a sports bar on Eighteen. We can talk there."

✳   ✳

We got a table in Double Play, a bar on the northbound side of 18 in East Brunswick. The bar was crowded with Mets fans drinking dollar drafts of Yuengling and chewing on ten-cent wings. They were watching their team get their tails handed to them by the Phillies. The Yankees were still on the West Coast and hadn't started yet.

The best thing about the place was the Molson on tap, a brand of beer Artie had never invested in. I sat with a pint while Tracy sipped her bottle of Coors Light. She ordered a plate of mozzarella sticks. Tracy took one, broke it in half, and dipped it in the marinara sauce. I took one, dipped, and bit a chunk, the hot cheese nearly burning the roof of my mouth.

"Gerry didn't have many people here after Steve died. He kind of went into a shell. Hung out in his apartment and at the bar. That was it," I said, after a sip of Molson cooled my mouth.

"That's too bad. We used to see him all the time. Family was important to him. Sunday dinner. My aunt made a great pot roast. Mashed potatoes. It was like Christmas dinner every Sunday. In the summer we'd have them to our house for a barbecue."

"I never met Gerry's wife. He didn't talk about her much."

Tracy finished off her Coors and signaled the waiter for another round. I was only halfway into my Molson, but having a second glass on deck couldn't be all bad.

"How'd Gerry's wife die? Jesus, I don't even know her name," I said, realization striking me.

The Mets must have scored a run, because there was a spattering of applause from the bar. Tracy was taking another mozzarella stick, but wasn't talking much.

"What's the matter?"

"My aunt disappeared when I was eight or nine. Aunt Anne. According to Uncle Gerry, she went to the grocery store one day and never came back. Steve had to be taken out of school for a year, he was so upset. Gerry brought the police in, but no one demanded a ransom. The cops said maybe she just got sick of being married, wanted to start a new life."

"He never said anything."

"He alienated himself. Left the acting business, stopped talking to my family. My parents never spoke with him again. I went alone to Steve's funeral. They won't even think about coming to Gerry's."

I finished my pint just as the second was being placed in front of me.

"Listen," she said. "I don't want to talk about this. I can't. I just want to have a good time."

"Sounds good to me," I said.

I couldn't believe that Gerry would never mention his wife had gone missing, even if it was years earlier. He didn't say anything when Jeanne died. He never, ever mentioned it. And all Gerry did was tell stories. Stories about serving in Korea. Stories about being up onstage. Stories about watching old baseball players play games the right way, as opposed to today's home-run-happy superstars. Something didn't feel right.

But, then again, I'd been so inundated with information over the past few days, nothing felt right. Getting my mind off the wake, Rex Hanover, everything, would be worth it. Just sit back, have a few beers, and talk.

The bar was getting more crowded behind us, a few Yankees fans rolling in to take advantage of the beer and wings specials before their game started. We finished off the mozzarella sticks and drank.

"So, what's being a private investigator like?" Tracy asked.

She was now on her third beer, and I could see her loosening up. She had pulled her hair back into a ponytail, and the crow's-feet at her eyes were gone. Her cheeks were a little ruddy and a small smile formed. I liked the look.

There were several ways to go about answering her question. The stock answer, that it was boring, sitting outside random hotels on Route 1 waiting for sleazebag husbands to come out of rooms with prostitutes, just sitting in a car for hours at a time twiddling your thumbs. Or I could tell her the romanticized version: I'd solved murders, saved children, and stared down mobsters. Or my version: people die who shouldn't and you break people's hearts, showing them things they ask you to find. Things they don't really want to know. And it's not worth it, you're not really saving anyone, and it was time for me to leave the profession, once I paid my way through Rutgers. In all the activity, I'd almost forgotten about my upcoming enrollment at the school.

"While it might sound cool, sitting outside some of the hotels on the highways waiting to take pictures of sex scandals, it's not exactly my idea of an exciting job. A lot of sitting around and waiting, fighting off sleep in the middle of the night."

She put her elbow on the table and cocked her head, leaning it against her fist. "You've never killed anyone?"

I could tell by the glimmer in her eyes she was just kidding around. The smile looked like it was about to cave in to laughter. Two beers earlier and I'd have laughed at her statement and said no.

"Once."

"Oh my God. Really? What happened?" She was sitting up straight now, her arms crossed at the wrists on the edge of the table. She leaned forward a shade, as if to hear me better.

"I dated a woman a few times in February. She was a graduate student, just moved out here from Fresno. Her ex-boyfriend followed her. He wasn't what you'd call stable. At one point, he cornered her on his deck and threatened to slash her throat. I shot him."

"Oh," she said. She downed the rest of the beer. "Wow."

I finished my beer as well. "Sorry you asked?"

She reached across the table and covered my hand with hers. "Not at all. How'd that make you feel?"

I tried to recover and lift the serious mood with a joke. "You're a psychiatrist now?"

"Come on, I'm serious. Two months ago you killed a man. Sure, you did it to help someone, but that doesn't happen to everyone. Now a friend of yours is dead. I can't imagine how you feel."

I slipped my hand out from under hers, thinking I'd rather be talking about anything else. We could talk about jazz, we could talk about drinks, about baseball. We could talk about anything but death. "It's not something I like to talk about."

The waiter came back to our table, and we both ordered a fourth beer. I was feeling it in my bladder and excused myself.

In the bathroom, standing at the urinal, I took a deep breath. The conversation had been taken off to places I wasn't sure I wanted to go. Gerry's murder, I didn't really feel it. Not like Tracy felt it, seeing her childhood again, seeing a relative ripped from her, even though she wasn't as close to him anymore. I didn't feel it like Artie did, his best customer brought down, not by old age, but by some careless driver. I didn't feel a need for revenge. I didn't like having Artie watching my every move, using me to feed his sadness and anger, to at least find a reason why. But at the wake, I knew I wanted to find Gerry's killer. I just wanted to do my own thing, and stay as far away from pain as possible.

Returning to our table, I found the beers already there. Tracy's sat untouched. Condensation dripped off my glass, forming a small puddle around it.

"I'm sorry," she said.

I smiled. "Don't worry about it."

"No. I didn't mean to pry. I just thought—well, I thought maybe you wanted to talk about it. I know I would."

"It's not my favorite topic of conversation. That's all. Don't worry about it. I'm not mad."

We sat and drank, making small talk. Then I drove her back to the hotel, where she decided to stay for the night. Easier than going back to Asbury.

Pulling in front of the lobby, I turned toward her. "See you tomorrow morning." The funeral.

I leaned in to give her a kiss on the cheek. Before I realized it our lips had locked together. It was a long kiss, my eyes closed; I felt our tongues touch. My stomach fluttered a bit, and the buzz from the beer intensified. She put her hand on the side of my face. Our lips refused to part.

Finally, when we broke, she said, "I can't do this right now, Jackson."

A quick kiss. Her mouth was familiar to me.

"Are you sure?" I asked.

"I have a boyfriend. I—"

We kissed some more. As I pushed harder against her lips, she broke away.

"We have to stop," she said. She opened the door. "Listen, you don't have to come tomorrow."

"I want to."

"No. Work on the case. It'll probably be just me and Artie. Gerry would want you to be working on that case. That's more important. Find out who did this to him. Find out why he had that stuff in his closet."

She leaned in and we kissed again. "I've had too much to drink."

I watched her walk into the lobby. Despite myself, I smiled.

Ten minutes later, I unlocked the door to my apartment. The beer buzz was still strong, and I could taste Tracy's breath on my tongue. I noticed the smell of cigarettes in the air. The lights were off, but my blinds were open. I was positive they were closed when I left to go to the wake. If I hadn't had so much to drink, if my mind wasn't elsewhere, I would have caught it quicker. I would have been ready. Instead, I felt a sharp pain at the back of my neck.

The next thing I knew I was staring at my carpet. Shaking my head, I rolled over expecting to see the two guys who paid me off earlier.

I was surprised.

Hovering over me was Rex Hanover.

CHAPTER 24

It seemed like a good idea. a way to bring Donne back on the case. Get someone Donne used to trust and feed him important information. So, barely twenty-four hours later, after telling him not to talk to Donne, Bill Martin strolled along George Street looking for Jesus Sanchez.

The theaters had let out already, patrons finishing their drinks in bars around the city or driving home on the turnpike. Come to New Brunswick, dump your money here, get a few parking tickets to pay his salary, and head home. Keep the streets clean and make it look like this was a wholesome college town.

Fucking bullshit.

Ever since Johnson & Johnson moved in, this town was getting spic-and-span and it was all a front. Martin hated it. He would rather George Street still be overrun by porn and drugs and hookers. That was real. This new stuff—the theaters, the faggy bars—all fake. It made this town and its hierarchy too concerned about appearances.

Now Martin had to worry every time he talked to a drug dealer and declined to arrest him. It was exhausting, watching his back all the time.

He pulled up the lapels of his tweed sports coat, and kept going. He could see the C-Town sign up ahead, glowing in the dark street. Jesus Sanchez smoked a cigarette underneath it.

As Martin approached, the smell told him Jesus was smoking something other than a cigarette.

"How you be, Billy?"

"I need a favor."

"Shit, now I gotta listen to you, yo."

"Why's that?"

"I heard you be with Michael Burgess now."

Martin chuckled. "Word travels fast."

"You know what you doing, I got no doubt." Jesus patted him on the shoulder. "What do you need me to do?"

"Talk to Donne."

"But you tol' me—"

"Yeah, I know what I said. But times change."

A campus bus rumbled down the street. There used to be a porno shop right on this corner a decade ago. Glittering neon, bright lights. Now it was just a run-down grocery store. No matter how hard you try to keep up appearances, it just gets knocked down again.

"Times change in a day?"

"You know they do. You've seen it out here. One minute, some-one's alive, the next . . ."

Two drunk college girls ran down the street toward him, waving, trying to flag down the bus that just passed. They were unsuccessful and slowed into a giggling walk.

Jesus eyed them, reached into his pocket. Martin had seen that look before.

"Don't you dare," he said. "Not while I'm here."

"Shit, Bill, man's gotta make a livin'."

"Go talk to Donne. Feed him some information. He quit the case I wanted him to work. I want to get him back on."

"I thought you hated him."

"Just do what I said."

"All right, yo. What you want me to tell him?"

Martin relayed everything he'd planned out. Jesus nodded like he was actually paying attention. Martin knew the guy would only tell Donne half of what he was supposed to.

When he was finished, Jesus said, "Yo, I'll be there in the morning, when my shift's over."

"Jesus Christ. You don't work a shift," Martin said, turning his back and starting to walk away.

"Man's gotta make a living," Jesus said.

Isn't that the truth, Martin thought.

CHAPTER **25**

as I tried to sit up, Hanover connected with a right cross. I went back down, my eyes closing, stars flashing across the eyelids. Pushing my hands into the carpet, again it was time to get up. This time a boot to the ribs sent me to the floor. Air felt trapped in my lungs and inhaling became near impossible. I heard myself gasp, trying to catch my breath. *Learn your lesson. Stay down.*

I lay on my back, coughing hard. Hanover wasn't standing over me anymore, probably confident I wouldn't be able to get up. Pain in my ribs kept me from sitting, so he was right. I coughed hard and tasted blood in my mouth, like an old penny. I could no longer taste Tracy's kiss.

Where the hell did he go?

The click of my CD player—a sound I've heard a few times— changing CDs answered my question. The Kinks, a CD I'd picked up years ago in a bargain bin, started up. The song was "Sunny After-noon." I had forgotten I owned it. Hanover strolled back my way, taking his time, examining an ashtray on the coffee table. He didn't seem to be in a hurry. That was good, I thought. Probably gave me more time to live.

"Nice collection," he said, the hint of a Mexican accent in his voice. He nodded toward my CD player. "Not many people have the Kinks. At least not many people I talk to."

"What the fuck?" I managed, finally forcing my way into a seated position.

He grabbed me by the shirt and pulled me up, left-handed. He found the Glock under my jacket. Pulled it from the holster and popped the clip. Then he jacked the barrel and popped out the round. Spun the gun in his hand so the barrel faced downward. He did it cleanly, smoothly, like he'd done it a million times before. He kept his eyes on me. He cocked his arm back, and I knew what was going to happen. I tried to force my way out of his grip, but the gun caught me right on the cheekbone. I felt like I was floating toward the ground, my brain exploding in pain and light. I hit the carpet hard, felt like I bounced three feet in the air, and hit again.

I rolled onto my stomach, forced my eyes open. Hanover was wearing Doc Martens, shoes I thought had gone out of style at the end of the century. All I knew at the moment was they caused my ribs to hurt like hell. Hanover gave me another kick. Somewhere in the ether, I prayed the bones didn't crack. And I prayed they wouldn't puncture a lung, worst-case scenario.

The CD player must have been on random, and the music changed. Oasis, "Talk Tonight."

"Shit," Hanover said. "Ain't this appropriate? We need to talk."

"Could have fooled me," I mumbled.

"Don't think you're in any position to talk shit."

"Yeah," I said. "You're probably right."

I put my hands flat against the ground in push-up position.

"You get up, I'll put you down again."

I stopped where I was, letting air out between my teeth. My head spun and blood rushed in my ears.

"Why were you following me outside of Drew?"

This was bad. He knew I was following him that night and he wanted to know why. I wanted to tell him. I wanted to say, "Your wife hired me. She wanted me to find out if you were cheating on her." But if I said that, he'd bolt out of here, probably go right after her. And I was in no shape to stop him. Better to keep quiet.

One of the Gallagher brothers pleaded with someone to talk. I didn't say a word. Hanover was pacing, his Doc Martens leaving imprints in the carpet.

"Don't make me hit you again. I don't have time for this shit. You know I can hurt you. Why were you there that night?"

I didn't speak. I didn't move. I didn't do anything.

Hanover squatted over me and slapped my cheek. "Wake up, *maricon*. I'm talking to you."

If I stayed quiet any longer, he'd either hit me or give something away. I could stand the pain for a while, and assuming I made it until tomorrow, maybe I could make his visit useful. And if I bought enough time, maybe I'd find a way to take him down.

"You're not with the cops. I see that. Private investigator, but it looks like you do pretty well for yourself."

That made me chuckle despite the situation.

"So, who are you working for? Someone who can afford you."

"Yeah, you should see my hourly fees," I managed. My face hurt like hell from the gun.

Hanover laughed. He walked my way, stepped on my back to step over me.

"All right. You're not going to tell me who it is. Tell me what you know about me."

"Nothing."

He smiled. "Yeah, right."

"Fuck you."

He grabbed me by the collar again, pulling me onto my knees. We probably looked like something out of a *Flintstones* cartoon, a caveman dragging his would-be bride. Pulled me toward one of the closed windows.

"Listen," he said, stopping in front of the window. He unlocked it and pushed it open. He yanked me to my feet. "I'll kill you if I have to. I just want to know what I'm up against here. Who are you working for?"

I took a step and made a halfhearted attempt to hit him. I still couldn't see straight, my face throbbing, my ribs aching. Attempting to throw a punch didn't help. He stepped out of the way. As my momentum carried me past him, he hit me in the jaw, and I tumbled out the open window.

Gravity took hold and I felt my stomach drop, like riding a huge roller coaster. I think I reached for the windowsill. My hands couldn't find a catch and slipped away, momentum taking my body. I may have tried to scream. I may have prayed.

Then, suddenly, I stopped. I felt the blood rush toward my head, and the feeling made me light-headed. I couldn't catch my breath. The pain in my ribs stabbed through my chest.

There was pressure at the waist of my pants. Hanover had me, caught my belt, and hung on. The CDs switched again. Now it was a Stones song, the muffled beat reminded me of "Miss Amanda Jones."

"I'll pull you up if you tell me who you've spoken to and why you're following me."

"I can't."

I felt my ass slip off the windowsill. Jesus Christ, he was going to drop me. I clawed at the brick wall of my apartment building. My nails split and my skin tore. I kicked my legs as well. I shook my head back and forth looking for something.

"Hey, asshole. You struggle like that, I'm not going to be able to pull you up."

I took air in through my nose. Willed myself to calm down, to think things through. On the ground I saw someone staring up at me, a woman who had her mouth covered, the other hand in her pocketbook. I hoped she was searching for her cell phone. Maybe she'd call 911. Though I'd hit the floor as soon as Hanover heard the sirens.

"How do I know you won't drop me?" I said.

I slipped further as Hanover readjusted his grip. "Because I don't do business that way," he said.

"I can't tell you who hired me," I said, trying to figure out the best line of bullshit I could. "They'd kill me." It sounded like the biggest cliché ever, but hanging upside down above Somerset Street, I thought I did pretty well for myself.

"You're not in a position to be worried about someone else killing you."

He let me hang there. Below, the woman was speaking into a phone rapidly. She wasn't even looking up at me anymore, just staring at the oncoming traffic. Finally, I felt my body being dragged back into the apartment.

Once inside, I dropped into a seated position. Rex Hanover crouched over me, his face hovering over mine. As he spoke his breath smelled distinctly of ham. "Kill you, huh? Thanks for answering my question."

I nodded, still trying to catch my breath. Half-conscious, I wiped at my face with my wrist.

"I want you to give Burgess a message," he said. "Tell him to leave me alone. And if the rest of his goons are half the pussy you are, I'll kill them without breaking a sweat."

I didn't even see the punch coming this time. I felt it, though. My neck snapped to the right. Then the room around me swirled, faded, and went black.

＊　＊

The room was dark and empty. I didn't hear sirens, I didn't hear music, I didn't hear anything.

Taking my time, I forced myself to my feet. I had a strong sense of vertigo, but regained my balance. Everything ached. I lifted my arms over my head and tried to stretch out.

My digital clock read four A.M. Making my way to the bathroom, I took a long hot shower. My brain started to reset itself; I realized I'd learned a lot. I'd taken a beating, but learned things in the process. The name Burgess sounded familiar. I was going to have to do a little research when I got to my office. Hanover also said something that clicked, seemed out of place. "I don't do business that way." What kind of business? What was he talking about? The warm water washed over me, searing the cuts and scratches on my hands, but massaging the soreness out of the bruises. I couldn't think about all of this now. My body craved sleep, and I was intent on giving in.

I put on a pair of boxers, pulled the covers back, and lay down. I shut my eyes and felt like I was falling again, my stomach twisting, panic firing up my nerve endings. I sat bolt upright, which didn't do much for the pain. I felt exhausted, but I wasn't going to sleep. I sat staring, adjusting my eyes, trying to focus on nothing, allowing the minutes of the night to pass by. They did, but too slowly for me. I got out of bed and edged my way to the living room.

I grabbed a bottle of Jack from the kitchen and drank myself to sleep.

CHAPTER 26

My HEAD THROBBED, AND I WASN'T SURE IF IT WAS from the beating or the Jack Daniel's. Swimming through the haze back to consciousness, the pain in my temples was the first thing I noticed. The second was the man in the room.

"Jesus!" I said, jumping back in my seat.

"Come on now," he said evenly, "that's not how you say my name."

Wiry and thin, long legs up on my coffee table, Jesus Sanchez relaxed on my couch. He wore a black nylon running suit, Nikes, and had a pencil-thin line of hair across his jawline. Tan skin, dark hair pushed back, he was probably in his midthirties.

Jesus Sanchez, wiseass, drug dealer, and Bill Martin's number-one informant when I was a narc. I'd only met him once or twice when I was Martin's partner. Martin liked to keep his informants to himself.

"Jesus, what are you doing here?" I said his name correctly this time. H*ey-zeus*. "How did you get in?"

"You and me, son, we need to talk." He leaned back, smiling, cradled the back of his head in his hands.

"Don't call me son," I said, getting up. I went down the hallway to my bathroom. Popped a couple of Advil. "How did you get in?" I yelled back to him.

"You left your door unlocked."

"Martin send you?" I asked.

As I made my way back to the living room, I heard Jesus pull open the refrigerator. "Damn, yo. You ain't got shit to eat."

I wiped my face and sat back down. "What do you want to talk about?"

"Word's out about you."

"What do you mean?"

He came back into the room and sat down. Relaxed again, hands cradling his head.

"You looking into that dead teacher thing, right?"

"How do you know that?"

"Word is you took some money from some bad people."

The five thousand dollars. How did Jesus know about that? Word gets around quick. "Who told you about this?"

"Yo, just the word on the street. This teacher thing is bad news. You got some powerful people mad at you."

"Burgess?"

"You know him? Big-time man, I compete with him and he's got me beat."

"He deals drugs?"

"More like supplies them. He's like a distributor or some shit, I don't know. He got dealers on the streets, gives them shit to sell."

"But how do you know about the teacher?"

"Shit, she was a dealer, yo! Sub teachin'. Dealin'."

"What are you saying? I'm not following here."

Maybe it was the headache and the way the words spilled from Jesus's mouth quicker than I could drive. I felt like I was missing something that I'd normally pick up easily. It was frustrating, and I could feel my body grow tense again. I wanted to punch something.

"The sub teacher, she was on Michael Burgess's payroll. And now she's dead."

"That's Burgess's first name? Michael?"

Something was ringing at the back of my neck. I thought of the thugs who came to my office. I thought of the five thousand dollars I'd been spending.

"Yeah, yo. Where you been? When you were a cop, you knew all this shit."

"I'm not a cop anymore."

"You got to talk to me more often." Jesus smiled like he had all the secrets of the world in his head.

"Tell me more about Burgess."

"Whachu want to know, son?"

"Who is he? Where does he live? Can I contact him?"

"I don't know where he lives. Shit, he's tough to talk to. Fuckin' need to go through like three, four different people to even get him to notice."

"You've met him before?"

"Shit," Jesus said, acted like he was thinking. "Once. Couple of years ago. He wanted to do a deal. Bring me in with him."

I rubbed my eyes. My headache still registered on the Richter scale. "Did you work with him?"

"Nah, yo. That would have pissed off the guys who get my stuff. But you never know who could work with him. Maybe people you don't even suspect."

I nodded, wondering who he was talking about. I thought of all the items in Gerry's cabinets.

"Do you think you could get in touch with Burgess now?"

"Shit, I could try. Why?"

"When I call, I get hung up on."

"He knows who you are. Probably not gonna hang up now."

"You're right. But I'm trying to show him a little respect."

Jesus shrugged.

"You know, more polite. Willing to listen."

"A'ight, a'ight. I'll see what I can do."

"Thanks."

"Be careful, yo."

I smiled. "You know anything about the sub?"

"Just that she dead and that she dealt."

"You don't know where she subbed?"

"No."

"Okay. Thanks, Jesus."

He looked at his watch. "I gotta get the hell outta here. Duty calls."

My head hurt too much to ask him again why he came. We didn't know each other well enough for him to help me out. He was Martin's boy. Martin had to have something to do with it.

He left me there, my apartment quiet and dark.

* *

I took another shower. The smell of last night's alcohol still hung in my nose, and I was going to do all I could to get it out. It wasn't easy. I was in the shower for a good ten minutes. When I got out, the smell had faded along with the bar of soap I used. I debated shoving the bar up my nose. Common sense prevailed.

I got dressed and gave Tracy a call. She didn't pick up. It was still early and she was probably still asleep. I left a message on her voice mail and dialed Henry Steir at the *Star-Ledger*. He picked up on the third ring.

"Got a story for me?"

"No, got a question, though."

There was a pause, like he'd taken the phone away from his face. Then, "What's up?"

"Where does Diane Peterson sub teach?"

"Why?"

"Because you said she was a—what was it? You said she was a nobody girl. Nobody knew her, no one talked to her."

"Yeah. And?"

"If she substitute taught, maybe the principal knew her. Maybe some teachers. I want to get a feel for her."

"You trying to solve this murder?"

"No."

"Don't bullshit me."

"I'm not."

"Taft High School in Madison."

"Madison? Isn't that a rich town?"

"Very much. Why do you care about that?"

I could hear car horns and other people talking. He was probably still camped outside Jen Hanover's door. She hadn't called me since yesterday morning, so I was assuming everything was okay. Still, I thought I should probably call her, find out if she knew how Rex was able to find me.

"Because," I said, "I figured you'd say a Newark or Paterson school. You know, the ghettos."

"Ah." I could almost hear the smile in his voice. "Very PC of you, Jackson. What else do you need to know?"

He was trying to get some bits and pieces to craft into an article. I wasn't going to give it to him.

"Thanks, Henry," I said, and hung up.

I dialed information and got the number for Taft High. I talked to the secretary and told her I needed to set up an appointment with the principal. When she asked what it was regarding, I explained I was an investigator looking for information on Diane Peterson.

"The police were here already," she said. Her voice was syrupy.

"Just a follow-up, ma'am," I said.

"Dr. Halberg will be in this afternoon. Is one o'clock good for you?"

27

CHAPTER

BILL MARTIN'S CELL PHONE RANG. He stood in the middle of the convenience store trying to ignore the smell of rotten pears.

"Yo, I just got back from Jackson's place. Tol' him what you want me to," Jesus said, some words broken by a weak signal.

The Chinese guy stood behind the register counting money again. The coffee on the counter was cold. As he spoke on the phone, Martin stared at the register trying to signal the guy to make more.

No reaction. *Fucking rocket scientists at work here.*

"How'd he react?"

"He was askin' all about that sub teacher who got killed last week. But I planted the seed like you say. I could tell it clicked with him."

"Good," Martin said, and turned his phone off.

He strolled to the back room, and the scene was exactly the same as last time. Michael Burgess sat, relaxed. The big man leaned against the wall, tough looking. Josh and Maurice were nowhere to be seen.

"Detective Martin, forgive me if I don't quite trust you, but I'd rather you didn't use your phone in my store."

Martin grinned. "I thought this was a legitimate business."

Just by admitting the man was uncomfortable with a police officer present showed Martin there was more trust than last time. Burgess was willing to admit some semblance of illegal activity.

"Yes, well, please heed my requests."

Martin shrugged. *Whatever.*

"Now, Detective, the reason I asked you here again is so I can make the first request in our partnership."

Christ, Martin thought. *How the hell did this guy become a drug lord and not a* CEO? The only thing missing were finger quotes when he said *partnership.*

"What is it?" he asked.

"I'd like my business on this block to be run hassle free."

"I'm not sure what you mean."

"No police should be on this block when I'm trying to do business. No patrol cops, no detectives, nothing. I shouldn't have to worry."

Martin felt the beginnings of a stomach cramp. Maybe this was how he was sucked in the last time. One block at a time.

"And how do you expect me to do that?"

Burgess spread his hands. The big man hardly flinched. "That's why it's your job."

"I'm not sure I have enough power to do that. It's going to take some time to get that to work."

"Just do it."

Bill Martin could work this. He could drag it out until he wasn't involved with this shithead anymore. By the time Burgess expected results, Martin would have taken him down. And Donne, too. And then he'd be a fucking superstar on the force.

He'd have reached his dream.

"Well, Detective, I have an appointment to keep, but before you leave . . ."

Martin arched his eyebrows to show he was listening.

"I asked around about that man who died the other day. The case you were looking into?"

"What case?" Martin asked.

"Gerry Figuroa." Burgess frowned. "There's nothing on the street about him. No word."

"Oh," Martin said, "yeah. Thanks."

Gerry Figuroa. Martin had forgotten about him. Just some old man, dead in a hit-and-run. No one cared about old men.

Ruining Jackson Donne was important.

Taking down Michael Burgess from the inside, that was important.

And, if he could swing it, killing both birds with one stone would just be icing on the cake.

CHAPTER 28

I FOUND AN OPEN VISITOR'S SPOT IN THE EXPANSIVE lot for Taft High. The building was three stories high and inclined up a hill. Tan bricks surrounded blue metal frames outlining the windows.

Walking toward the front door, I noticed a sign welcoming visitors and noting the mascot was a general. A janitor mopped the tiled floor, a plastic gray trash can on wheels next to him. He whistled to himself and didn't acknowledge me. The main office was across the hall from the lobby. I could see through the wired window a secretary typing on the computer while holding the phone between her shoulder and chin. I walked in and she held up her hand toward me, asking me to wait a minute.

I did, looking at a bulletin board advertising the April break and the prom that would take place at the end of the month.

Behind me, I heard, "May I help you, sir?"

I turned. The secretary had black-framed glasses, a red sweater, and a sweet condescending smile. I returned it.

"Jackson Donne. I called earlier?"

She looked around her desk, which seemed to be a ton of unorganized papers. Sifting through a few, she found a small pink Post-it. "Yes. You're right on time," she said. She was a professional, and ignored my bruises.

I smiled, making sure it was dripping with sweetness.

"Let me buzz Dr. Halberg."

She picked up the phone again and said something I couldn't make out. Then nodded. I continued to smile, hands in my pockets, rocking back and forth on my heels like Carson.

"Okay, sir. You can go in." She motioned to her left, a thick wooden door, open, leading to an office. I wondered if I could still get myself suspended.

Inside, a middle-aged man in a three-piece pin-striped suit stood smiling at me. Graying hair, crow's-feet at the corners of his eyes, gold wedding band, and dirt under his fingernails. I wondered if the only thing the janitors did in the school was mop. This guy was probably a workaholic. Over his shoulder were diplomas from William Paterson University, Rutgers University, and a SUNY college. I couldn't read which one. The lighting was bad.

"Mr. Donne." He held out his hand. I took it and we shook. "Do you mind if I ask for some identification?"

I took out my wallet and showed him my private investigator license. I liked that he and his secretary were more interested in who I was, and not why I looked like I just lost a boxing match. He examined it. He looked at me. Looked back at my wallet. Looked at me again. "I was under the impression you were a policeman."

"I was at one point." I tried the same smile I'd given the secretary. "I told your assistant on the phone that I was an investigator."

"And she took it to mean you were an investigator for the police."

I shrugged.

"Very clever. Why are you here?"

His desk was a lot neater than his secretary's. You could see the wooden finish. There was a computer resting on the corner—its screen saver running—two framed pictures, a telephone, and a small calendar.

"I'm working a case and Ms. Peterson's name came up. I did a little research and saw what happened on the news. I would like to know more about her. See how she related to my client."

"I see." He handed back my wallet. Went back to his desk and sat. Held out his right hand, offering me a chair on the other side.

I took it.

"Well, Mr. Donne, why should I talk to you?"

"Because of my undying urge to fight for truth, justice, and the American way?"

He smiled. "Christ. You're worse than the kids."

I shrugged. "I walked in here and got nothing but an attitude. If I was a real cop, I would have arrested your secretary."

He leaned back in his chair. "On what charge?"

"Annoying me with a condescending smile," I said. "Listen, I just want to ask you a few questions, get a feel for who Ms. Peterson was, take my ball, and go home. Maybe bring my client some good information."

"I apologize for the attitude. It's been a rough few days. Teachers don't usually die on us, never mind get murdered. I was finally able to chase the press out of here this morning. The kids are taking it hard. The rest of the staff is taking it hard."

"I'm sorry for that," I said. "I lost a friend in the past week as well."

"It's been a busy week in New Jersey, hasn't it?"

"You referred to Ms. Peterson as a teacher. I was under the impression she was a substitute."

"She was, but she was good. She was working on getting her master's degree and her teaching degree, but she came here every day and subbed. When a teacher was going to be absent long-term, we trusted Ms. Peterson to come in and take over. We considered her a member of the faculty."

"What about the students? Did they like her?"

"Most of them loved her. She knew their names, said hi to them. She came to the school play. She would stay late and help the students if they asked. She was dedicated. As soon as she got her certification, I was going to hire her."

"Did she have any enemies? Any teachers dislike her? Students threaten her?"

Halburg took some air in audibly. Closed his eyes for a moment and rubbed his temples. "If a student had threatened her, I'm sure she would have reported it to one of our vice-principals. As for the teachers, I try to stay out of that. The teachers sometimes need time to vent, so I don't know all that goes on in the faculty rooms. No one has ever brought any problems of that kind to my attention."

Perfect teacher, I thought. Just the kind that could slide under the radar, dealing drugs in the parking lot, finding moments to sneak marijuana or cocaine or crystal meth to a student when no one was looking. Giving assignments and guidance when everyone was watching. Still, kids talk, and someone must have known something.

"I appreciate your time, Dr. Halburg, but I have one more favor to ask."

"What's that?"

"I was hoping to get your permission to talk to some of your faculty."

Halburg shook his head. "I don't know."

I had to be careful, play it just right. "It might help with the case."

"Are you trying to solve her murder?" He rubbed his eyes. "Jesus, who would murder Diane?"

"My case might coincide with the murder. I'm not trying to solve it, but if I somehow cross wires with the actual murder investigation, I will turn the information over to the right authorities."

Halburg leaned across the desk and smiled. This was a genuine smile. "You're good. Let me show you where our faculty cafeteria is."

*   *

The faculty cafeteria was small, adjacent to the students' cafeteria. Halburg knocked on the frosted window of the wooden door. Behind him the cafeteria was quiet, another janitor lifting plastic chairs on top of tables. There were scraps of leftover lunch, spilled milk cartons, and a few empty trays on the floor. The janitor had a mop next to him.

"Knocking?" I asked.

Halburg nodded. "I don't usually come in here. Sometimes teachers need to vent. This is the place for that. I have an office."

I nodded as a small woman in a short skirt and tight white sweater opened the door. She was probably in her thirties, and her eyes opened wide looking at Halburg.

"Yes, Dr. Halburg?"

"Ah, Reggie, this is Mr. Donne. He's an investigator looking into the case of Diane's murder."

"Oh, um . . ." She trailed off.

"Mr. Donne is going to ask some questions, if you don't mind." He peeked his head into the room. "That okay with you guys?"

I heard a mumbling of "Okay"s. Halburg turned to me, said, "They're all yours."

He turned around and walked away. I found a seat at a round plastic table in the middle of the room. It was quiet, as if I'd just walked in on a bunch of people talking about me behind my back.

I looked around the room, eyeing each of the five teachers: one guy grading papers, not making eye contact; two women sitting at another round table, legs crossed, eyeing me up and down; Reggie, still standing by the door; and another man leaning on the arm of a couch. I tried to look intimidating.

"So," I said. "Who wants to start?"

No one answered. Blank faces trained their gazes on me, and two teachers looked down at notebooks. This was going to be fun. Part of me wanted to say, "I know one of you is the killer, and I've gathered you all here to share that." But I didn't. I wanted to wait them out, but if the bell rang and they had to move on, I'd be out of luck.

"All right, listen, I know most of you knew Ms. Peterson, so why don't you help me out. Tell me a little about her."

Nothing. Then one of the crossed-legged women, a younger lady with auburn hair, black pants, and a blue button-down blouse, said, "Jesus Christ. They can't fix the clocks, but they can get someone in here to keep us from doing our job? Shouldn't you be out trying to solve her murder?"

"Excuse me?" I looked up at the clock hanging over a bulletin board, saw that it was an hour off.

"Shut up, Nancy," the teacher across from her said. She had blonde hair, with dark roots, and wore a yellow pullover and a khaki skirt. "I'm sorry, Mr.—what did you say your name was?"

"Donne."

"I'm sorry, Mr. Donne. We're all a little stressed."

I nodded.

Nancy said, "Yeah. I'm sorry. It's been a rough time. And I'm flipping out about little things."

"Did you know her?" I asked.

"Yeah. She was nice."

"Nice?"

"She—I don't know—she was tough to explain. She was always smiling, always positive about the kids. Didn't seem to get down if she had a bad day."

"Yeah," the guy doing the grading said. "So fucking positive."

"Why do you say that like it's a bad thing?" I asked.

"I don't know. She didn't want to be a teacher. She came in every day and subbed, talked about how great the kids were, like she knew everything about teaching, but it wasn't like she ever talked about being a teacher."

"I'm sorry," I said. "What's your name?"

"Charlie Phillips."

I made a note of it. "Dr. Halberg said she was going to school to get her teacher's degree."

"I think she just told him that to keep him happy."

"How do you think she'd have been as a teacher?"

Keep asking questions, I told myself. Try to get a flow for this conversation. I didn't want to ask tough questions too early, and I didn't want to send people running from the room. If I could get them talking to each other as well as me, I might be able to get to something deeper. When people get comfortable and start a real conversation, they're more willing to let things slip.

"I never saw her in the classroom," Phillips said, "but the kids always said hi to her in the halls, slapped her five. But if she had to discipline them they'd listen. They liked her, they respected her. But I don't know how she actually taught. Couldn't say if she'd make a good teacher."

Reggie stepped away from the door. Showed me she was getting a little more comfortable. "I think she would have made a good teacher."

"Why do you say that?" Nancy asked.

"She was an aide in my class a few times. You know, when Janet took one of her many sick days." Reggie made quote marks with her fingers. "And she was always willing to work with the kids, help them, but not give them the answers. She really knew how to guide the kids. Let them build their own knowledge."

"Ah, those buzzwords," Phillips said.

Reggie glanced at him, giving him half a smile. The kind of glance that told me there was more going on between them than just kidding around.

I, however, was more curious about the one man who wasn't talking, the guy leaning on the couch. He was stoic. His face didn't change, he just stared at me. Didn't even appear to be listening. I wondered if he resented my being here.

"Did anyone ever talk to her privately? Like in here?" I asked.

There were a few murmurs. Each teacher looked at the others, waiting for someone to speak.

Finally Reggie said, "She never came in here."

"What do you mean?"

Nancy jumped in. "She didn't like to. She liked to keep to herself. She didn't take a prep period, they would always find a place for her to cover. And at lunchtime, she'd go out. By herself, as far as I could tell."

"Yeah, I'm gonna agree on that one. I have hall duty sixth period. One of the lunch periods, and I'd see her leaving by herself," Phillips said. "She'd always say good-bye to me, though."

"She was a recluse," Reggie said, chuckling. Then, as if remembering Peterson was dead, she stopped. "She, uh, didn't talk to anyone unless she had to. What time is it?"

I looked at my watch. "One-forty."

"Shit," Nancy and Phillips said. They started gathering up their stuff.

"I hope we helped," Reggie said.

All but one cleared their stuff and moved out. The intercom buzzed, which I assumed was the bell. I sat there for a few moments. The guy on the edge of the couch stood up and walked over to my table.

"Why do you care about Diane?"

I looked him over. Not a big guy. Not intimidating. His face was pale and flaccid.

"It's my job." I sat back in the chair, put my hands behind my head. "Why didn't you say anything before?"

"Because I didn't want to talk about Diane in front of the rest of them."

I nodded. "And you are?"

"Paul Rockford. I teach freshman math."

"You sound like you spoke with Diane."

"A little. She kept to herself."

"So they said. What did you talk about?"

"Oh, where she lived, what she wanted to do with her life."

"What was that?"

"She said she wanted to do nothing. She wanted to be a nobody. To disappear."

There it was again, that idea of a "nobody girl."

"She say why?"

"Nope."

I took a breath. Thought for a second. "You know anything else about her?"

Rockford tapped his fingers on the table. Smiled. "I know what kind of car she drove."

"Yeah?"

"Yeah. A black Beamer. Stylish. The kids loved it. They always came up to her window to slap her five or shake her hand at the end of the day or early in the morning. Take a few minutes to talk to her about it, I guess." He looked at his watch. "Listen. I just don't like talking about people in front of others. Feels wrong. Even though she's— well—even though she's dead, it feels like we're talking behind her back. Enough gossip goes on in this place, we don't need that. I have to get to class. Good luck."

I shook his hand. Probably not the same kind of handshake that Diane gave the students when they came to see her Beamer. I didn't pass anything to Rockford. I figured that's how Diane was dealing drugs. I wanted to talk to the students about it, but I didn't know which ones.

Rockford was opening the door to leave.

"Mr. Rockford?" I asked.

"Yeah?" he said, stopping.

"What time does the day end here?"

He checked his watch again. "Two-thirty. After this period."

"Thanks."

The door clicked shut, and I sat in the empty teachers' room, listening to the sounds of student footsteps and conversation in the hallway.

CHAPTER

tHE BELL FOR DISMISSAL MUST HAVE RUNG, BECAUSE
suddenly students were streaming out of the doors like ants escaping a
smashed anthill. I was across the street, sitting in my car trying not to
doze off.

I didn't know exactly what I was looking for. Some sort of ex-
change between students and someone inside a car, a high five between a kid and an adult, anything remotely suspicious. It felt like I
was getting somewhere with this case, had some sort of lead and
didn't want to lose it. Unfortunately, with Diane Peterson being dead,
I wasn't sure that a new dealer had taken over this spot yet. But I
didn't have anywhere else to be.

I watched the crowds ebb and flow, come together in different
groups. All the kids dressed the same, but each group had its own
stereotypical attitude: jocks, nerds, and stoners. The stoners, the ones
I was trying to keep an eye on, circles under their eyes, hunched over,

slouched against the school wall, smoking cigarettes and looking like they were trying to disappear.

My cell phone vibrated in my pocket. The caller ID read: Tracy.

"Hey." She sounded tired.

"How'd it go this morning?"

"Well," she started, "it was a funeral, so it wasn't fun. But it was a good send-off for him. There were some people there that didn't come to the wake. The priest gave a nice sermon. Talked about his acting. Mentioned Korea. It was nice."

"Did you guys go to the tavern for lunch?"

"Sort of."

"What do you mean?"

A car pulled up. It was a silver Mercedes, and it was wrong. This neighborhood, the Mercedes would be shiny, clean, but down to earth. The one that pulled up to the curb had fancy hubcaps, the kind that spin the opposite way of the wheel. The windows were tinted and the music was loud.

"I mean, Artie, he had caterers in, but they had it at the bar. He didn't cook."

"He drank, though."

The Benz idled at the curb and a few of the students glanced at it. Yet they didn't go toward it. I could hear Tracy in my ear, but I was starting to lose what she was saying.

"What did you say?" I asked.

"I said, I know he's giving you a hard time, but you have to give him a break. He lost a friend. A close friend."

"And his best customer."

All the members of the stoner group turned their heads toward the car. Casually, they turned back toward their group. A few of them dropped their cigarettes. They didn't want to look interested in the Benz, but years of experience told me they were. Be cool, they were probably telling each other. Make sure the fuzz ain't around. Or the cops. Or the pigs. Or whatever the hell the current lingo was.

"Why do you have to say that? What's wrong with you?"

"Nothing. I'm sorry."

She exhaled. "What are you doing?"

"Working."

"Gerry?"

"Yeah," I lied.

A few of the stoners made their way off the wall, checking over their shoulders. They strolled, hands in their pockets, toward the Benz. Bingo.

"About last night," she said. "I can't do it, Jackson. I had too much to drink. The wake, everything. I just slipped."

"It's okay."

"I just wanted to be clear."

"Crystal." It sounded like she was trying to convince herself.

One of the taller stoners, a guy with long greasy brown hair, made his way to the driver's-side window. The window rolled down and I made out the shadow of a profile. A hand came out of the window to slap five. Just slow enough that money and drugs could change hands.

If they knew cops were watching, they never would have done it that way. They would have taken the money and made the kid go somewhere else nearby to pick up his stuff. But this was small-time. Who was going to catch them? A janitor?

"I'm going to stay in New Brunswick a few more days. I need a short getaway anyway, and Gerry has a few more things that need to be taken care of. Are we cool?"

"Sure."

I clicked my cell phone shut, got my gun out of the glove compartment, tucked it in my pants, got out of my car, and headed toward the Benz.

As I moved across the street, I heard a voice from inside the car. I still couldn't make out a face.

"Oh shit, look who it is," the driver said. The doors of the car unlocked.

Through the window, I finally could see my old friend and his bald buddy Maurice. They smiled and nodded at me. Like they were glad to see me. I made sure my jacket hung open so they could see the gun. I pulled the back door open and slid into the backseat.

"Gentlemen," I said.

"Mr. Donne, how are you?" the model said.

"Fuck it, Josh, he broke our deal. Let's kill him," Maurice said.

I pulled the gun from my waistband, laid it on my lap. "Yeah," I said. "In front of three hundred teenagers. Where'd you learn murder? The School for Eyewitnesses?"

"Hysterical. Didn't we pay you five thousand dollars?" Josh adjusted the rearview mirror.

"I used it to buy bullets."

Josh nodded. "Good idea."

"You saying I'm going to need them?"

Josh shrugged.

Maurice had been watching, slack jawed, and finally said, "Would you two shut the fuck up?"

Josh turned toward him. Then back to the rearview mirror. "So what do you want, pal?"

"I want to talk to your boss."

"We don't have a boss."

I scratched my head. "Then who paid me?" I wanted to add "moron."

Maurice and Josh moved their attention to some passing teens, ignoring me.

"All right, let me put it this way," I said. "I want to see Burgess. I'd like you to take me to him."

"Why should we do that? Why don't we just drive the fuck out of here and put a bullet in your head?"

No real reason, I thought. "The fact that I'd take at least one of you with me?"

Maurice smiled. "Motherfucker, think you're tough?"

I shrugged, glanced out the window. Most of the kids had cleared the area, and there were only a few still milling around away from the car.

"Get out of the car," Josh said. "Let this go. We take you to see Burgess, you are going to be in a shitload of trouble."

Again, I shrugged. Didn't move toward the door.

Josh shrugged as well. "Guess we'll take you."

Maurice smiled. "Your funeral."

* *

It was about a forty-minute drive from Madison to New Brunswick. Josh pushed it in thirty-five. I had no idea where we were going, but we were up north on Easton Ave. North of Rutgers, north of my office, north of the tavern, more like Highland Park. We were on the outskirts, where the houses were nicer.

We turned onto a side street, Hazel, and pulled up to a small convenience store. Josh parked in front of a hydrant, left the car idling. Maurice rolled his window down and yelled at two guys playing dice by the side of the building.

"Hey. Mike inside?"

One guy in a hooded 76ers sweatshirt, caramel skin, and thin mustache looked up. "Nah, he just left."

"Where'd he go?"

"I don't know. He don't tell us." He went back to dice.

Josh's eyes reflected at me in the rearview mirror.

Maurice said, "I guess you're fucked." He turned toward me, revolver in his hand. "Give me the gun. I don't see any kids around. Now I can kill you."

They say the best defense is a good offense.

I picked up the gun like I was going to give it to him, my scraped hand still hurting from the night before. He was stupid, didn't realize I was holding it the wrong way. I hesitated just a second like I was balancing the gun, then shot him. The bullet tore through the back of the seat and blood sprayed against the windshield. He didn't die, he just dropped the revolver as his eyes widened. I guessed the bullet slowed as it moved through the fabric. He choked as blood poured from his shoulder. Like he was trying to talk. Finally, he let out a huge scream.

Josh didn't seem to know what to do. He kept looking from the writhing Maurice back to the steering wheel. I opened the back door and stepped out. The air was cool on the layer of sweat forming on my skin.

I yanked Josh's door open, unclicked the seat belt, wrapped my forearm around his neck, and dragged him from the driver's seat. Pushing the barrel of the gun into his temple, I forced him toward the sidewalk. The guys playing dice were staring at us. The dice clattered harmlessly on the ground.

"Oh, shit," one of them said. "Oh, shit. Call the fucking cops."

Time to move.

Josh was choking, trying to catch his breath under my grip. I was cutting off his air supply.

"I will fucking kill you," I whispered to him. "Where does Burgess have an office? Inside this place?"

Josh choked out a yes.

"Take me to where he keeps his records." I pushed him ahead.

The dice players rushed the car behind me. One of them was on his cell phone to 911, telling them a crazy fucker had shot up the street. There was a guy bleeding and, yes, he was still breathing but, oh fuck, there was blood everywhere. I could hear him talking, but the sound was coming to me in slow motion, just like everything else.

Not being able to hear sirens yet, I figured I still had time. Josh was leading me through the front of the convenience store. The clerk thought he was getting robbed and his hands went up in the air. There weren't any customers in the place. It smelled like old cheese and rotted fruit.

"Take the money," the clerk said.

"Shut the fuck up."

Josh led me up the snack-food aisle, knocking Tastykakes off the shelves. We went through a back door into a room, Josh's feet sliding on the wet tile floor. The room was dark with a desk, one lamp, and a whole bunch of food stock—chips, snack foods, soda, juice, fruit—not cooled. The place was a health hazard. Behind the desk was a filing cabinet.

I pushed Josh ahead, letting go of his neck. He stumbled and caught himself against the desk, able to keep his balance. Massaged his neck, tried to catch some air. I trained my gun on him. I could squeeze the trigger and kill him. Easy.

"You are fucking crazy," he said with a hoarse voice.

"I want to see Burgess's files. What does he have to do with the girl? She his dealer? You guys all his dealers?"

Josh said, "Shoot me, I'm not going to say shit. You shoot me, you're back at square one. Now with the fucking cops after you."

"Why did Rex kill her? What does he have to do with all of this?"

"You think he tells me? Who am I? Some thug." Josh smiled.

I stepped forward and hit him in the temple with the butt of my gun. Josh crumpled to the floor. I hit him again. The metal vibrated in my hand.

"What's in the files?"

He grumbled something, and I hit him again. Blood poured from a split lip.

"Talk to me!"

Hitting him one more time, Josh's eyes rolled up into his skull and he passed out. His chest still rose and fell slowly. He was bleeding. He was hurt, but he was alive.

I tugged open the top drawer of the filing cabinet, now trying to ignore the pain in my fingers. Folders filled with papers were stacked neatly, end to end. Pulling a few out, I dropped them on the desk.

I glanced at them. They appeared to be order forms from food distributors. All the shit that was lying around back here. I pulled open another drawer, the same thing. And the bottom one, too.

Now I could hear the sirens, loud, like they were down the block. Seeing Josh prone on the floor, I realized I had no way out. The cops were going to take me in.

CHAPTER **30**

tHe pHoNes weRe RiNʛiNʛ off tHe Hooҟ. His cell phone, the desk phone, nonstop. The police band crackled with reports of gunfire on Easton Avenue. It didn't take much to deduce that some type of shit just hit the fan.

The caller ID on his cell read Michael Burgess. The desk phone was probably some upper-level cop telling him to get his ass to Easton.

He picked up the cell phone.

"Detective, what is going on at my store?"

"I have no idea." His *store*?

"One of my employees just called me. Said there were gun-shots!"

Things were starting to click in Martin's head, just a little, like the pieces of a puzzle coming together.

"I'll look into it."

Burgess hung up without saying anything.

He picked up the desk phone. It was Paul Cramden. He talked about the shooting, too. Again his synapses fired, recognizing a link.

"Thought you'd want to know about it," Cramden said. "Maybe you can catch the case."

"Why the fuck would I want it?"

"Don't you know who's down there? Who did the shooting?"

The entire picture became clear in his head. He reached for his jacket before Cramden was able to confirm the news.

"Jackson Donne," the cop said.

Donne shooting up a bodega? Burgess's bodega? He needed to be on this case. He rushed out the door, down the stairs to the street.

This was it. This was what Martin had been waiting for. He would make sure he got his chance with Donne.

Endgame.

CHAPTER

I STOOD THERE. GUN at my SIDE.

My brain screamed, "Get the fuck out of there." My muscles would not respond in kind.

The sirens were loud now. They were probably right outside. Like they were jolted by electricity, my muscles jerked and I dropped the gun. It clattered but didn't go off, a stroke of luck.

There was screaming—"Get down"s and "Shut up"s and "Move"s—coming from the front of the store. The sirens remained, and I could see quick, flashing red lights coming through the doorway. The cops were here. Instinctively my hands went up.

They came through like Patton's army, four guys, guns drawn, telling me to freeze. I was already frozen. I tried to say my name. I tried to tell them who I was. No sound would come out.

"Turn around! Against the wall, motherfucker!"

I did as I was told. They kicked my feet farther apart, frisked me, and didn't find anything. My arms were pulled behind my back and cuffed. As they dragged me out toward a squad car, I heard one of the cops left in the back giving the address through his radio.

"There are two men down. Requesting an ambulance. Jesus Christ."

✳ ✳

For the second time in three days I was sitting in an interrogation room. The grooves in the wall had gotten a bit deeper, the paint had faded, but I'd been in this room before. Only this time my wrist was cuffed to the table.

The room smelled like old coffee. Realistically I should have been in a holding cell somewhere in the police station, but I wasn't. And I knew whom I had to blame for that. I wasn't sure if I was lucky or about to step in even more shit.

And no matter how hard I tried, all I saw was Josh and Maurice's blood whenever I blinked.

Bill Martin came though the door, cigarette going, coffee in his hand. His tweed jacket was on, but the tie was loosened around his neck and the top button of his shirt was open. He slammed the coffee on the desk so some splashed over his hand. Took a drag off the cigarette, leaned across the table, and let all the smoke out into my face. I did my best not to cough.

"What the fuck, kid?" Martin said. He hadn't called me kid since the first couple of months we were partners.

"Lawyer," I said. It worked in Madison.

"Shut the fuck up. You know I'm not calling your lawyer."

"Lawyer."

"Talk to me. What's going on here? Does this have to do with Gerry Figuroa?"

He wasn't getting answers from me. I sat back, but couldn't cross my arms. I wanted to look like an angry child.

"All right. Let's start from the beginning here, kid. You're looking into Gerry's death, right? So are we. No matter what you might think, we are."

He stood back, took another drag on the cigarette. Eyed me up and down.

"So, where do we find you?" he asked. "In a fucking convenience store that our department has known about for years as a hot spot for drug dealing. And you're there with two guys beaten to shit. The one who was shot is lucky to be alive. One in a car that was filled with marijuana and LSD and a gun. That's the good news.

"The bad news is we find you, gun at your feet, in front of an unarmed guy bleeding from the head. No idea who the fuck he is. And it looks to me, hell, it looks to all of us, like you beat the crap out of him, too. So, why?

"And what does this have to do with the Figuroa case?"

I had a plan. I was going to wait him out. I was going to sit and not say a word until he got so fed up he stormed out. Then they could come in and drag me to Rahway and throw away the key. I wasn't going to give Martin the satisfaction of a response.

But Martin invoked Gerry's name, and instead I said, "This doesn't have to do with Gerry."

Martin took one last drag of his cigarette and flicked it across the room. "You expect me to believe that?"

I nodded.

"Then what does it have to do with?"

"Another case I'm working on."

"And what case is that?"

Time to keep quiet again.

"Come on, kid. I mean, with the shit we've found in Gerry's apartment. You saw it. This whole thing smells like drugs. You know it and I know it. Now we find you shooting some guy in a car. What did Gerry get himself into?"

"This doesn't have to do with Gerry," I said.

"You're not going to tell me shit, are you?"

He wasn't going to get anything more out of me.

"This is a mistake, kid."

He waited.

"Fine. I could have kept you out of prison. Like you did for me. I could have got you out. But you had to play ball. You never wanted to play ball." He stopped to light another cigarette. "Maybe if you spend a night in jail you'll think differently about telling me what you know."

"I've done it before," I said.

"Better you than me." He turned toward the door.

"You should have been in jail a lot longer than just one night," I said as he walked out.

CHAPTER 32

BUT I DIDN'T SPEND THE NIGHT IN PRISON. IN fact, I didn't go anywhere. I remained cuffed to the table for the better part of four hours. No one came in. There was no sign they had even remembered me. My guess? They were trying to sweat me out.

My mouth was dry, my stomach rumbled. No food, no water, that'll do it. My eyes drooped. I fought to stay awake, but found myself dozing off. Every time I drifted away the sight of Maurice and Josh, bloody pulps lying on the ground, fluttered in front of me. The image bolted me awake again.

Martin wanted me to react. He wanted me to call for my lawyer, so he could tell me he wasn't going to call him. He wanted me to get so frustrated I would tell them what I knew and why I shot Maurice and beat the hell out of Josh. He wanted me pissed off. And I was, but I'd be damned if I was going to give Martin the satisfaction. Christ, what I wouldn't give to be like Anthony Perkins in *Psycho*. Not blinking, not moving even with a fly on my cheek. Just sit, show Martin what a crazy fuck I was. Show him how lucky he was I didn't push for him to go down with the rest of the narcs back when.

Goddamn it.

I balled my fists and willed myself to calm down, to focus.

Four hours I sat and hummed to myself. The Stones, the Beatles, Martin's favorite band, the Hollies. Whatever came to mind.

And still Josh and Maurice danced. I was back to square one, no leads, no way to get to Michael Burgess. Rex Hanover was probably in Germany by now. And Gerry was still dead. No leads there either. But Martin thought this was all about Gerry, and it wasn't. Fuck, what did I do?

The door swung open and Martin came back in. No cigarette, no coffee, no jacket, no tie. A little bit more scruff on the chin.

"You going to talk?"

"Lawyer."

He turned and walked out. This was going to be a long night.

* *

Only another two hours this time. I amused myself by counting the paint chips on the wall. Now I was starting to feel a little light-headed. No food, no drink. Jesus, this was capital punishment.

Martin came in, five o'clock shadow rapidly becoming a full beard. The guy could flex and grow hair.

"Feel like telling me what happened today?"

"I could use a burger and something to drink."

Martin looked at me. "You going to talk?"

I shrugged. Which was probably more than he expected.

"I'll see what I can do, kid." He turned and left again.

I went back to the paint chips.

* *

There weren't any more paint chips to count. I had lost track of time, my internal clock shutting down. My stomach was crying. I wanted to stand, but I was afraid if I did my legs would give out and I'd fall. My cuffed wrist ached like hell.

Martin came back in. He had a McDonald's bag. He tossed it on the table. Put a large soda in front of me. He had a soda for himself, too. Took a sip.

"McD's, the best I could do."

"Thanks," I said.

He leaned across and uncuffed me. Again, I balled and unballed my fist, trying to get the circulation going.

Martin unpacked the bag, two Quarter Pounders for me, a box of McNuggets for himself. He put a bag of fries in between us. I opened up a burger.

"Your cell phone rang. Caller ID says Tracy."

I chewed. "Where's the good cop?"

"I sent Bob home. Not much he could do here."

"Didn't feel like playing?"

"Not tonight. So, who's this Tracy?"

"Friend of mine."

The burger tasted like it was made by George Foreman himself. I must have been hungry.

"Friend like Jeanne was a friend? Like girlfriend?" Martin asked.

He was trying to make me comfortable. "How come you aren't out trying to solve Gerry's murder?"

Martin smiled, waved a McNugget in my direction. "Dinner break."

"And you sent your partner home. No leads, huh?"

"I think I have a pretty big lead."

I took a long swig of soda. Tasted like the water had been drowned in sugar. Which was pretty hard to do, if you thought about it.

"I'm going to piss for a week after I finish this."

Martin said, "We have bathrooms."

I finished the first burger, moved on to the second.

"You're not curious about my big lead?" Martin asked.

"Mildly," I said. "Truth is, I'm pretty sure where you're going with this."

"They were dealers, weren't they?"

"Lawyer," I said.

"In a minute. In a minute. You want to know what I think?"

I was going to give him the minute. I wanted to finish my food.

"What do you think?" I asked.

"I think you did what you did because they killed Gerry. I think he was supplying them with crystal meth he made in his apartment. I think maybe he held out or he wanted more money or he pissed them off somehow and they killed him. I think you found out and went for revenge."

"What if Gerry's death was just a simple hit-and-run?" My burger was almost gone.

"You and I both know it wasn't, kid."

"What do you know?" I asked. "Tell me."

"The question is what do you know? What are you hiding, Jackson? For once we both want the same thing. I want to solve this case."

"You want to get back in good standing with the rest of the force. Trying to prove yourself after the demotion?"

"Tell me what happened," Martin said. He rubbed his face. I wondered if he was trying to hide something from me. Hide the fact that maybe I'd hit a nerve.

"This has nothing to do with Gerry."

"Then what does it have to do with?"

My burger was gone. My stomach wasn't rumbling anymore. I was sick of sitting here.

"I want my lawyer," I said.

Martin raised his hands in surrender. "We'll call him right now."

"He's going to be pissed you kept me in here for as long as you did."

"What do you mean?" Martin said innocently. "The paperwork we filled out says we checked you in here forty-five minutes ago. And you just lawyered up now."

He smiled a smile I'd seen many times in my life. He got out of his chair and left the room.

CHAPTER

"aGAIN?" LESTER RUSSELL SAID. "JESUS CHRIST,
you and bodies."

"Listen, Les—"

"This is bad, Jackson. This is really bad. They could get you on
attempted murder. Aggravated assault at the very least. One of them
was unarmed—"

"Yeah, I—"

"No, wait, I don't want to know. If this goes to trial I don't want
to know."

"Trial?"

"It looks like you're up shit creek," he said.

Martin wasn't in the room. It was just Les and me. He was right,
there was no getting around this.

"Get me out of here, Lester."

"All right, slow down. Did you tell them anything?"

I was handcuffed again, and my wrist throbbed.

"Martin was the one who questioned me," I said. "I wouldn't tell him shit."

Russell smiled despite himself. "That guy is an—ah, we might be taped. How long have they had you here? Martin said like two hours?"

Russell looked up at the video camera above us. He knew that somewhere Martin was watching the feed of this conversation. He also knew that everything they had said was on tape. I remembered watching thousands of these lawyer conversations, watching Martin interrogate a witness, even once watching an unsanctioned conjugal visit on those very monitors. It wasn't standard, but we both knew Martin did it all the time.

"More like eight or nine."

"What? What do you mean eight or nine?" Lester was shuffling papers in front of him. "The paperwork says they checked you in—"

"All this went down close to four in the afternoon. They arrested me on the spot."

"And you didn't ask for me immediately?"

"I did."

Now Russell looked directly at me. Like he was making a conscious effort not to look at the camera, not to make a connection with Martin. I knew what he was thinking, and I didn't look at the camera either.

"So what happened?" Russell asked.

"Martin left the room. For about four hours. He was trying to sweat me out."

"And what happened when he came back?"

"I asked for you again."

"And then he was gone for another couple of hours?"

"Yeah."

"Did you two talk at all?"

"A little. Two or three hours later. He brought food."

"He's a saint."

Martin came through the door, smoking, looking calm and collected. A smug smile curved around the cigarette.

"How are you doing? Jackson, has Mr. Russell here talked some sense into you? Are you ready to tell me what happened?"

Russell returned the smug smile. "I'm going to get the tapes in this room, the security tapes of my client being brought in through the front door, every piece of paperwork I can find, and I'm going to use it as evidence. You probably just broke every law in the book. My client has rights. As in 'the right to an attorney' when he asks for it."

Martin looked like he'd swallowed the cigarette. "What are you talking about? We brought him in an hour ago."

"Your paperwork says two hours ago."

"Whatever. Time flies when you're having fun."

"You're in deep shit if this goes to trial. You know that."

"Me?" Martin puffed some smoke, let it out through his nose. "Your client, Mr. Donne, attempted to murder two people. You're lucky they're alive. Who's to say we don't have him on tape?"

Russell sat back. "Give me a minute to talk to my client. And don't listen in."

Martin spread his hands. "Take all night."

When he was gone, Russell said, "I want to make a deal."

"What kind of deal?"

"This goes to trial and he has all that evidence, discrediting a cop is going to be all we have. And even though Martin has a bit of a history, even though he is a dirty cop, you're going to go to jail. You've shot someone before."

"I was cleared of that."

"It's part of a case history. I want to make a deal. But this may hurt. You got into Rutgers, right?"

"Yeah."

"Good. You might need the degree."

I listened to what he had to say.

✳ ✳

Martin came back in. I didn't like where this was going, but Russell was right. This deal might be my only way to stay out of jail.

"I want to make a deal," Russell said.

"What do I look like, the DA? You're going to have to wait for the arraignment and prosecutor for that." Martin was drinking coffee now. The guy didn't look tired at all, but he did need a shave.

"This deal is between you and my client. He told me you said you would have kept him out of jail if he had talked eight hours ago."

"I didn't see him eight hours ago."

"Cut the act, Martin. You're going to like this deal."

Martin took a sip of coffee.

"My client will agree to give up his private investigator's license if you drop the charges," Russell said.

"I'm not authorized to make a deal."

"You are if you drop the charges. It doesn't have to be official."

Martin took a sip of coffee.

"That's the deal. You'll never have to deal with him again."

"Yeah? And what's he going to do for a living?"

Russell looked at me. "He's going back to school."

I thought coffee was going to come out of Martin's nose. "I'll see what I can do," he said. "I'll call the insurance company who bonds you. Tell them to pull your bond, that way we don't have to go through the courts. I can force them to take it away, but it takes time. I'll have to talk to the DA as well."

My stomach ached, not really sure this was going on. I was going to lose my livelihood.

"But you'll let him out, drop the charges?" Russell asked.

"Hold on," Martin said, excusing himself from the room.

I thought I was going to vomit. The McDonald's from earlier rolled around like a medicine ball.

Russell put his hand on my shoulder. "This is the only way," he said. "You'd be in a lot of trouble otherwise."

I nodded. Applying to Rutgers was supposed to help me find direction in my life. To get away from all the blood and violence. From Bill Martin and the narc squad to Jeanne's death to Josh and Maurice, violence permeated my life. I didn't want to go down this way, there was too much still unresolved. But Lester Russell was right. There was nothing I could do.

At this point, I'd probably have to work my way through college at a supermarket.

Martin came back in with my things: my wallet, my keys, my cell phone, and my watch. He unlocked the handcuff and pushed my belongings toward me. I put my watch on first.

As I was picking up my wallet, he said, "Is your license in there?"

"Yeah."

"Let me see it."

Martin held his hand out. Russell nodded at me. I pulled the license, a small laminated piece of paper like a driver's license, and handed it to Martin.

Martin took out a Swiss Army knife and opened the scissors. He smiled at me, enjoying this all too much. "Just in case you get any crazy ideas before we can get this officially revoked," he said.

He snipped the license in half. And then in quarters. The smile never left his face.

I put my wallet away and didn't say a word.

Martin dropped the scraps into a trash can and stood up. He held the door to the interrogation room open. "You guys are free to go."

"Have a nice night, kid. Don't dream too much." As I walked past him, the smile still plastered to his face, he said, "Oh, one more thing."

I turned, unable to ignore him. In retrospect, I should have, but there was something about his voice. Serious, compelling.

"I thought now would be the perfect time to tell you. Remember what I said the last time we talked, kid? That one day I'd blow your mind?"

"Yeah.".

"Good." He put his hand on my shoulder. "When you and Jeanne were on that break. When you were hanging around that cokehead from the bar, Jeanne had no one to turn to."

No.

"Except for the detective who once saved her life. Her boyfriend's old partner."

Not possible.

"Jeanne and I used to fuck every night while you were out getting high and sleeping with whores."

My legs went numb and I had to catch myself on the wall to keep from going to my knees. Static raged in my ears, and my vision clouded.

I balanced myself and looked at Martin. His eyes glittered as he watched me.

"You liar!" I lurched toward Martin.

Martin stepped in and hit me with a right to the stomach.

Two uniformed cops burst through the door and grabbed me, pulling me off the ground.

"You son of a bitch! You were my partner!"

"Let go of him!" Lester screamed.

Martin turned and called to another uniform. The uniform nodded and took the laywer out of the room—not forcefully—shutting the door behind him.

The other two cops pressed me against the wall. I struggled against them. Tears stung my eyes.

Martin stepped in close, right up near my ear.

"You dare bring up that I was your partner?" he said. "That boat sailed away the moment you decided to put half the department on trial. I don't owe you anything."

I spit words through clenched teeth. "I kept your name out of it for a reason."

"No loyalty, asshole. You showed none to your teammates, I show nothing to you."

I tried once again to tear myself away from the cops. Martin hit me in the gut again. I went down to a knee as the air rushed from my lungs.

"You took everything from me," Martin said. "My job, my livelihood. And I had Jeanne. I loved her, too, you know. And she went back to you. All you had to do was go through rehab, clean your act up. I was clean! I could have given her everything! And she still went back to you."

"She . . . didn't . . . love you."

"She did. She would have come back to me. If that car—" Martin crouched, like he had to regain his balance. "Goddamn it."

"You liar! It's not true!"

Martin moved in close again. "She had a mole on the inside of her left thigh. It was small, barely noticeable, but she was self-conscious about it, wasn't she? Didn't want anyone to touch it. I told her it made her who she was. She was beautiful."

"You bastard," I tried, but didn't say it with much force. I could see the mole in my mind's eye.

Standing back up, Bill Martin put his hands in his pockets. "Isn't it funny, Jackson, what can happen when one man dies?"

I struggled to look him in the eye. Every nerve in my body screamed to just ignore him. He was lying. He *had to be*.

"Your friend kicks the bucket and your life goes to hell. And me?" Martin chuckled. "Man, I'm really starting to feel good about myself again. Get him out of here. Give him to his lawyer."

The cops dragged me to my feet and started to escort me out of the interrogation room.

"Wait," Martin said. "On second thought, book him. Put him away."

I went without putting up a fight. I couldn't.

My entire body was numb.

CHAPTER **34**

BILL MARTIN DIDN'T THINK ABOUT JEANNE OFTEN anymore. But now memories of her were everywhere. He could sense her scent, that floral perfume she wore. He heard the lilt of her laugh, saw that half smile.

She said she loved him and Martin had believed her. It was a relationship that shouldn't have worked, but when they were together, they clicked. Everything was right.

Jeanne Baker took Bill Martin's mind off the job.

He exited the interrogation room in search of coffee. He thought about going outside for a smoke. Despite bringing up his own past demons, he felt good. It was time to celebrate.

Jackson Donne was finished.

Heading out the front door, he pulled a cigarette from the pack, smiling.

CHAPTER

35

I spent the night in a holding cell. I didn't sleep. I sat on the metal cot counting the bricks in the wall.

And thinking about Jeanne.

I imagined her with me, smiling over drinks, laughing at some dumb joke, kissing me on the cheek before going to class. And then I thought of Martin. Pictured his arm around her, paying for her dinner, kissing her as deeply as I had. The two of them together poisoned all my good memories.

My stomach clenched, my hands pressed into fists. I tried to get back to counting bricks.

I lost count after ten.

* *

They booked me the next morning, an old judge setting bail at fifty thousand dollars. I glanced across the courtroom to see Martin standing there, a smile plastered on his face. I was reprimanded by the judge when I slammed my fists on the table I was sitting at.

Lester Russell asked me whom to call to pay the bail and I told him. There was only one person I knew with fifty thousand dollars. Then I was transferred back to the holding cell. The bus to the local jail wouldn't leave until late in the afternoon. I hoped my bail was paid by then.

✳ ✳

The guard on duty escorted Leonard Baker to my cell four hours later. He'd aged since the last time I'd seen him, and not well. A few months after Jeanne's funeral we'd sat in a park, him telling me he was going to keep an eye me. Keep me from doing something stupid. At the time he had darker hair and fewer wrinkles. Even after the death of his daughter, he stood up straight. Now his hair was completely gray, wrinkles creased the corners of his eyes and lips, and he hunched a bit as he stood.

"Why did you call me, Jackson?" he asked. "We haven't spoken in years."

I moved to the bars and said, "I missed your witty conversation."

"Bullshit."

The guard unlocked the gate and I stepped through. We followed him down the hall to his desk. He had me sign several sheets of paper, returned my belongings, and told me not to leave the state.

Outside, I asked, "Can you take me to my lawyer's office?"

Leonard nodded, said, "Did you really do the things they say you did?"

"It was either that or die."

"I remember a time a few years back where you would have just given up."

Leonard Baker's car was parked on a side street. I got in the old, blue Buick on the passenger side. Leonard started the car.

"So," he said, pulling out into traffic, "why did you want me to get you out?"

"Bill Martin arrested me."

Leonard didn't react, didn't say anything, didn't take his eyes off the road. He stopped at a red light.

"Does that name mean anything to you?" I asked.

"I don't appreciate your tone."

"He told me some things."

"Like what?"

The light turned green and the car accelerated a little faster than I expected.

I said, "He told me that he and Jeanne had been together."

The lunch crowd was thinning out on the streets, but there was still traffic. People going about their lives unaware that mine had been put on its side.

"Well?" I asked.

Leonard kept his eyes on the road. I punched the dashboard, pain shooting through my hand.

"Talk to me, goddamn it!"

"What would you like me to say, Jackson?"

"Tell me what happened."

"I only met him once. I didn't even know he was your partner at the time."

"You knew?"

"And if I did? How does that change anything?"

We pulled onto Route 18 and picked up speed. Lester Russell's office was in East Brunswick. Without traffic we'd be there in ten minutes.

"You could have told me."

"When? When you and my daughter got back together, she asked that we didn't tell you. And once she passed on, you were such a mess, Sarah and I were too worried about helping you get through the day."

I stared at the taillights ahead of us. "Bill Martin is an asshole."

"You weren't exactly a knight in shining armor."

Leonard hadn't looked at me the entire trip. He took an exit off 18 and stopped at another red light.

"Jeanne and I were good together," I said.

"Yes," Leonard said. "When you were sober. But if I remember correctly, when you were stoned and drunk, you cheated on her."

"I didn't—"

"Jackson, listen. I know you loved my daughter. All women are allowed to make their own choices, aren't they? And eventually she came back to you, when you got your life straightened out."

"That asshole—"

"Just stop. Jeanne's been gone a while now. It's time to let go."

"Every memory I have of her is tainted."

The car stopped and I noticed the familiar sight of Lester Russell's small office. It reminded me of a doctor's office, a gray aluminum-sided house with a sign hanging from a lamppost on the wall. His name and occupation were on the sign.

I started to open the door. "Thanks for getting me, Leonard."

"Jackson, wait," he said. "You're going to do whatever you want with this information. Yes, Jeanne was with Bill Martin. But she picked you."

"I know." I shook my head.

"You're a good man, but not terribly smart. I do you a favor, I bail you out of jail, and how do you repay me? By yelling at me, punching my car. We haven't spoken in years. And you think I'm just going to up and help you out with your problems. You're asking me to crucify my daughter's memory for your own good."

"I—"

He turned toward me. "Get out of my car and don't call me again. After Jeanne's funeral I told you that my wife and I would be there for you. You ignored us. It's too late now."

He reached out his hand and I took it. "Good luck, Jackson."

C H A P T E R

LESTER RUSSELL ASKED, "LAST NIGHT, WHAT DID
he say to you?"

It was a warm afternoon, signaling the beginning of spring's
transition to summer. Russell had the air-conditioning on.

"Nothing," I said.

"You fucked up, Jackson."

I nodded. He was right, but at this point I didn't care about
being a private investigator.

He'd been with Jeanne. Despite my conversation with Leonard, the
image still stuck with me.

Lester Russell stood awkwardly.

"I need to get my car. Can you help? After that, I'll be fine."

"You sure?"

No. "Yeah. I'll be okay."

After getting my car, I drove back to my apartment and tried to sit for a while. I got antsy around midnight and decided to get out.

The Olde Towne Tavern was hopping. The jukebox blared The Clash as I entered. Kids played pool, flirted with other kids, danced, screamed, and drank. The place smelled like old cigars, and a cloud of smoke hung from the rafters. I pushed my way to the front of the bar.

Artie was busy tonight, but his face dropped when he saw me. I must have looked like hell. I tried to ignore the Bud Light sign with the mirror. He finished making a drink and then asked if he could help me.

"Jack Daniel's," I said. "Might as well bring the bottle."

"Jack? You don't drink Jack anymore."

"Pour yourself a shot, too. I see you got other bartenders working tonight. You don't have to do too much."

There was a woman in a black tank top and jeans, long blonde hair, flirting with a couple of guys as she mixed a rum and Coke. There was another guy in a T-shirt and khakis pulling the tap on a Coors Light for two giggling girls. They were all smiling.

"What's the matter?" Artie asked.

"Pour the drink first."

He did, but didn't deliver it to me. Artie cocked his head toward his office behind the bar. I got up and made my way toward him, through the bar into the office. Bare bones, Artie had a desk with papers on it, a small TV, a couch, and a picture of him from his days in the military. Vietnam, if I remembered correctly.

Sitting on the couch, I knocked back the first Jack Daniel's. The liquid burned its way down my throat and calmed my involuntary shiver. It didn't do much for settling my stomach, however.

"What happened?" Artie asked.

I told him most of the story, being arrested, losing my license. I didn't mention Jeanne.

"Did this have to do with Gerry?" he asked.

"I don't know," I said. Truth was, after I listened to Martin speculate, it didn't sound too far off to me. But I was working on Rex Hanover's case when I got arrested. And to believe the two cases to be interlocked sounded way too coincidental. "But I have nothing to do with it anymore."

Artie sat forward. "You're giving up?"

"What choice do I have? I have no license. Nothing." I smiled. "Nothing but my buddy Jack Daniel's."

"Didn't you once tell me you wore a suit with a hole in it to show how dedicated to solving a case you were? That you'd risk everything?" Artie leaned even closer.

"Fuck that."

"Why are you being such a pussy?"

I answered by pouring another glass and knocking it back.

"Why won't you help a friend?"

"Because when you help out a friend, when you look into their lives, you find out you don't actually know them. No one is who you think they are. It's all lies."

Artie poured himself a shot. "That's the way it goes, man. People keep secrets."

"Save it. If I told you what I've found out, you'd understand."

He downed the Jack and said, "Then tell me. I'm your fucking friend. All I know is it looks to me like you haven't been working. Then you come in here and you want to get loaded and tell me that Bill Martin took your license away."

I told him everything. Gerry was probably making drugs. I nearly killed two men. Jeanne slept with Martin.

Artie swore at me, told me that I couldn't give up no matter what, but the night was beginning to fade. The alcohol crept around my brain, around the exhaustion, the tight nerves, and after a few more shots, the evening spun into blackness.

✳ ✳

"What time is it?" I said through a dry mouth.

The lamplights were too bright, and my head throbbed. I had to rub out my eyes before they would focus. I was still in Artie's office, laid out on the couch, empty bottle of Jack next to me. Someone was massaging my shoulder.

"You okay?" Tracy said. "Artie called me. He told me what happened."

I blinked my eyes to adjust to the light. Sitting up made me feel like I was on a boat. "How much did I drink?"

"Artie said he only had two shots. You must have had the rest."

"Shit." I looked at my wrist only to find my watch missing. "What time is it?" I asked again.

Tracy reached over and handed me my watch. "You put it on the table. It's four in the morning."

"Why are you here?" I asked.

"I called you and you never answered. I got worried. I called Artie. It was busy in here, and he didn't get to the phone until I called an hour ago."

"Sorry about that."

She sat back in her seat. "This afternoon, you said whatever you were doing had something to do with Gerry."

"I did?" I couldn't think past the pain in my head.

"Yeah."

"Oh." I rubbed my eyes with the palms of my hands and fought the thought of vomiting. I needed water or Gatorade or something that wasn't alcohol.

Everything that happened came flooding back to me. My vision clouded for a moment, and I shook my head to clear it.

"And when I got here, Artie was pissed off."

"Well—"

"Why won't you look into it?"

I didn't need this now. Not with the headache. Not with all that happened in the last day. "I am looking into it."

"You aren't. Every time we talk you're looking into something else. You're working, but you're not working on finding my uncle's killer."

"I—"

"Are you afraid of something?"

"What do you mean?"

"What are you afraid of?"

"It doesn't matter now."

"Like hell it doesn't." Her face was flushed, burning red.

"I can't look into anything. I'm not a private investigator any-more."

"What do you mean? Artie didn't say—"

I interrupted and told her. I told her what Martin said, how he thought Maurice and Josh were connected with Gerry. And how much I wanted to believe that it wasn't connected, though it *was* too much of a coincidence.

Tracy listened, and as I sat up she put her arm around me. I couldn't see her face, she wasn't looking at me as I talked, and I thought she might be crying. But she didn't shudder or whimper or sniffle.

After I was done talking, she was quiet for a long time.

"You can't look into it anymore?"

"No."

"What are you going to do?"

"Drink."

She glared at me.

"Just a joke. I don't know. I'm going to back to school."

"Bill Martin. Do you trust him?"

"No."

"Why not?"

"I used to be his partner when I was a cop. He was dirty. So was I. But eventually I felt guilty. So I turned our whole division in. I kept his name out of it, but a lot of his friends went down. He got demoted and he blamed me."

"So would I."

I nodded. "Now he's pissed."

"So he took your license."

"Among other things."

I wanted to tell her about Jeanne. About what he took from me. *My past.* But I didn't say anything. When Martin was with my fiancée, I was trying to be with Tracy.

I looked at her. The light from the lamp cast a shadow over her face. She looked tired but focused. Her skin was smooth, her eyes soft. I remembered why I found her so attractive. I tried to hate her for helping me drive Jeanne away. But I couldn't. Tracy and I may not have slept together, but we wanted to.

"Will he solve my uncle's murder?"

"I don't know. I think I was his only lead."

She shook her head. "That not what I meant. Will he work on it? Will he do the best he can?"

"Not if there isn't anything in it for him."

"Is there?"

"I don't know."

She put her hand on my leg, kissed my forehead. I closed my eyes. For a moment the throbbing went away. I didn't want her here. But I couldn't get her to leave. I knew if she left, I'd drink my way into a cocoon. I couldn't deal with Jeanne.

"Don't be scared of him. It's not worth it."

"I'm not." I sounded like the angry, stubborn child I tried to play in the interrogation room.

She shushed me. "Come on. I'll take you home."

It was hard to stand up, but I did. We walked back to my apartment slowly.

CHAPTER

37

BILL MARTIN GOT OFF SHIFT LATE AFTER DONNE was bailed out. He couldn't get the smile off his face. No way was he getting any sleep. Hell, it wasn't even about the kid going to trial. Just the fact that he was put away for the evening and left to stew felt great.

He decided to stop at a coffee shop. The one he used to always stop at. He ordered a large to go and turned toward the counter to fill it with cream and sugar when he finally allowed himself to look at the booth. An empty plastic booth, stained with coffee and covered with crumbs, the corner of it chipped away. One morning, years ago, she'd sat there crying when Martin came in for the first cup of the day.

He sat across from her and offered her a napkin to dry the tears.

"What is it?" he asked. When he worked as a narc, he would have worried about being late, but now who gave a shit?

"Jackson's gone," she said. "I don't even know if he knows what's going on, he's so coked up. But he left with a girl. Another addict. And—oh my God. I can't do this."

"It's okay," he mumbled. Martin reached across and squeezed her hand. He wanted to tell her that Donne wasn't worth it, but somehow he knew she wouldn't believe it. "He's fucked up, Jeanne."

"I know. I don't know what happened. Even after the trial, he doesn't stop. He drinks, smokes, snorts. Goddamn him."

"You need to get away from him. Even if it's just for a while."

She nodded. "I know. But what if I see him tonight? What if he comes home?"

"You won't be there," Martin said. "I'm going to take you out to dinner. We can talk—about anything. Get your mind off this. Keep you away from him."

Jeanne stared at him through her strawberry blonde bangs.

✳ ✳

Most of the night revolved around Donne. Just hearing his name prickled Martin's skin and made Jeanne cry. So he made a rule.

"From here on out, we don't talk about him. He screwed us both over, and he doesn't deserve our attention."

Jeanne agreed.

Then, to brighten the mood, he said, "What's the difference between roast beef and pea soup?"

She shrugged.

"You can roast beef, but you can't pee soup."

She didn't laugh. "I'm leaving. You don't take anything seriously."

Jeanne stood to leave and he grabbed her arm.

"Wait," he said.

Martin didn't expect her to whirl and slap him as hard as she did. His cheek stung, but he didn't let go. Instead, he pulled her closer.

And that's when he noticed her. The glimmer in her eyes wasn't sadness anymore, but anger. She tried to hit him again, screaming at him to let go. The people in the restaurant were staring, but he didn't care. He pulled her even closer, fending off her blows with his free hand.

He leaned in and pressed his lips against hers. She tried to pull away at first, but slowly, he felt her posture change. She relaxed and let him kiss her more passionately.

※ ※

The first time they slept together they'd both had too much to drink. Up until that point Jeanne kept referring to Martin as a good friend. They never talked about Jackson Donne; they never talked about the night Martin shot someone to save her either.

They went out for dinner, and after for drinks at one of the bars on George Street. Afterward he walked her home. Every time he looked at her, all he saw was her eyes. They sparkled, they glittered, they lit up her entire face. "You're beautiful," he said.

Jeanne thanked him.

He leaned in and tried to kiss her, smelling her perfume. She pulled away.

"No. We can't," she said. "The other night was a mistake."

"It's not," Martin said. "This feels right."

She didn't say anything.

"Just give me a shot," Martin said. "If it's wrong, I won't ever call you again."

He leaned in again and she let him. They kissed for a while on the porch. Eventually they made their way to her bedroom.

Martin called in sick the next day and spent it with her.

For the next month, they were together all the time. They had dinner, saw movies, played pool, had sex. They were a couple. Martin loved spending time with her. For the first time in a long time, the job wasn't the most important thing. She was.

In late January, he sat at the bar of Harvest Moon waiting for her. He waited two hours and four beers. She didn't show up. She didn't call.

After another hour, he tried to call her. No answer. He rang the bell at her home. No answer.

There was a message on his answering machine when he got home.

Jeanne's voice sounded tinny and mechanical. "Bill, what we had is over. It wasn't real. It never was. I'm sorry. Don't call me again."

He didn't believe her. It *was* real. It was just a matter of time before she realized it. But he listened to her wishes and didn't try to see her again.

When Bill Martin looked back on it all, sitting in the coffee shop booth, that was what killed him. He never looked for her. Never tried to hold on to her. And with everything that happened, everything he knew, he should have.

He drank the last drops of coffee, then crushed the cup in his hand.

chapter **38**

It'd been a long time since I'd been able to sleep in. When I woke up, the pit of depression returned, and I just wanted to go back to bed. But Tracy was messing around in the kitchen, so I decided to get up. I'd slept on the couch; she took my bedroom. We weren't at the point, yet. In fact, I didn't know what point we were at. I just knew she had been there for me last night.

I needed something to hydrate myself.

"Hey," Tracy said as I opened the fridge, the cool air touching my face.

"Morning."

"Afternoon."

I smiled, pulling out some lemon-lime Gatorade. I took a swig. Tracy gave me a kiss on the cheek.

"How are you feeling?" she asked.

"I've been better."

181

"Rough night?"

"Rough week," I said.

Tracy moved slowly through the cabinets, looking for something. She had Taylor ham and eggs out, so I guessed a frying pan. I couldn't believe I had Taylor ham and eggs in my refrigerator.

"I'm going to start cleaning out my uncle's apartment. What are you going to do?"

I didn't feel like doing anything. "I guess I can help you out."

"You guess?"

"Well, if it's still a crime scene, it might be tough to get in there."

"Why would it still be a crime scene? He didn't die there." She opened two more cabinets. "Do you have a frying pan?"

"Under the sink." I finished off the Gatorade. "The stuff we found in Gerry's house. The batteries, the Sudafed—Martin thinks that's circumstantial evidence. He hasn't bagged it yet, that I know of, but he's not going to let anyone in."

"There's no proof Gerry made that stuff. Maybe he just liked having batteries or Sudafed. Maybe he was obsessive-compulsive."

I nodded, not believing her. "But if they find proof or if they have found traces of crystal meth, they've got more evidence."

"So you believe he was making drugs?"

"I don't know what he was doing."

She found the frying pan and set it on the stove. Cracked two eggs into the pan, listened to the sizzle for a minute.

Tracy took a deep breath. "What do you think? Honestly."

Tossing the Gatorade bottle into the garbage, I turned my back to her. "I don't have an opinion. I didn't look into the case enough. But every time we found something like this when I was on the police force, it led to drugs. We didn't find it often, but we found it enough for me to form an opinion. If Gerry was making drugs, I don't know where he would have done it, but the evidence—"

"Why would he do that?"

Now I turned her way. "Money. He was retired. He didn't have much income. Back in the fall he asked me to find out why his landlord was raising his rent."

"But why wouldn't he ask for help? Why wouldn't he call us?"

"He was a proud guy. He didn't like to talk about his problems. I don't even think he wanted to ask *me* for help."

"So he became a drug maker?"

"It doesn't make sense, you're right. But you never know with people." To me, it did make sense; Gerry could be that type of guy. He would do whatever it took to make his way in life. And if he had a drug background, nothing would surprise me.

The eggs were starting to burn now. Tracy directed her attention toward them. I took note of her ass in the tight jeans she wore.

"Listen," I said. "After lunch we'll go over to Gerry's and see what we can do."

"What if the police are there?"

"We let them do their job."

"Will you get in trouble?"

"If Martin's there, he might give me a hard time."

"Do you think he will be?"

"I don't know."

She put some Taylor ham on the frying pan and found some English muffins to toast.

"It's worth a shot," I said. "It's something you're going to have to get done anyway."

"Cleaning out the house?"

"Yeah."

"That's not the only reason you want to go over there, is it?"

"What do you mean?"

"You want to take another look for yourself."

"There's nothing I can do. I don't have a license anymore. I'm going to be put on trial. I can't look into it."

She smiled. "You want to look anyway."

I didn't. Hell, I didn't even want to risk going over there and seeing Martin. But this wasn't about me; it was about helping Tracy.

Maybe I was getting ahead of myself.

* *

A Taylor ham, egg, and cheese sandwich later, we walked along Easton Ave. Tracy was quiet, and I didn't want to interrupt her thoughts.

The sun was out, a warm spring day, mid-seventies. Leaves were on the trees, wisps of clouds in the air, and tighter clothing on the coeds.

My hands jammed in my pockets, I finally said, "Are you okay?"

"There seems to be a lot of that going around," she said.

"A lot of what?"

"Asking if everyone's okay. You. Artie. Now me."

"I guess you're right," I said.

We crossed at the corner and proceeded onto Hamilton Street. I felt the weight of my gun in my holster. My secondary piece, taken from my bureau when I got dressed. It was force of habit, and I didn't even realize I'd taken it with me until just now.

"Back when we were both coked up," she said, "did you love me?"

I hesitated. "Tracy, I was not a good person then."

"That doesn't answer the question."

"We kissed. We weren't together. I loved the woman who was my fiancée. I cared about you."

A flash of Jeanne with Martin crossed my mind.

"The other night, when we kissed, how did it feel to you?"

"It felt right at the time." Now I felt like everything was wrong.

"I think there's something between us," she said, and looked away.

"But?"

"But, I love my boyfriend. Probably like you felt about your fiancée."

I spread my hands. *What could I do?*

We got to Gerry's house and didn't see any police cars. A good sign. But looking at the front door, there was crime-scene tape covering the doorway. I knocked on James's door.

"What do you want?" he growled through the mesh of the screen door.

"The police letting anyone up there yet?" I asked.

"No," he said. "And I got in a shitload of trouble the last time I let you in."

Tracy said, "What about me?"

"No."

Tracy swore and James said to me, "What's her problem?"

I smiled at him, my best smile. The one I used to use on cases. "She wanted to clean out some of Gerry's stuff."

James looked at her, then back at me, and for a minute, I thought it would work.

"I can't do it, Donne. Sorry."

"No chance?" I knew he was right. Deep down the cops were doing their job, and deep down I didn't want to fuck up whatever evidence was up there. But I still had that itch. It was tough to give up the license that easy.

"Why? So I can end up in prison?"

Through the screen, James looked small, his face shadowed. Martin intimidated him, too. There was no way I could blame James for not letting us upstairs. We had the same motivations. I just wondered if I looked as small and as intimidated as he did. I thanked him and took Tracy by the arm, led her down the steps.

"We're going to leave? Just like that?" Tracy looked over her shoulder at the house.

"I don't want James to get in any more trouble. What were you going to do up there anyway?"

"I told you," she said. "Clean up."

"That can wait," I said, still holding on to her arm. I worried that if I let go she'd run back to the door. "But there's more to it than that, isn't there?"

"What are you talking about?"

"We can go back anytime."

"I have to get this done."

"I know. That's not what I'm saying. What I am asking is why are you so determined to go in there *today*?"

She stopped walking. "I'm not. I—"

"You're tense. You're pissed off. What's the matter?"

"I'm worried about Gerry. I'm worried about what people are going to think about him."

"What do you—" It all clicked suddenly. The batteries, the Sudafed. "You wanted to get rid of it?"

"No, I—"

"Why?"

"I don't want people to think of him that way. And if you're not looking into it, then no one should. The police, they'll ruin him, ruin his memory."

"What do you think I would have done? I would have looked at the whole picture, too."

"No. You would have been careful."

"So you'd rather save his memory than know what happened?" I shook my head and started walking again.

"Please, Jackson," I heard her say. "You can't stop. You promised me. You promised Artie. Please."

I didn't look back.

CHAPTER **39**

My apartment still smelled of fried ham and eggs, although the cooking items had been cleaned and put away. I opened a window, and then sat. I flipped on the TV and couldn't find anything to watch. I couldn't get into a book. I didn't want to call my lawyer.

But I didn't know what to do. I felt much the same as two nights ago, sitting in the interrogation room, nowhere to go, nothing to do. Stir-crazy. I had to do something, get out of the apartment.

Clients. Jen Hanover had to be notified I was no longer on her time. I could close her account, collect my money, and fill out the last of my paperwork. She wouldn't be happy, and I wouldn't be able to tell her the whole story. But it had to be done. I was not getting caught on a technicality because she was still supposed to be paying me. Some-how, I thought, Martin would be checking up on me.

It was finally starting to set in. No longer a private investigator, I left my apartment, leaving my gun at home for the first time in years.

The key to my office slipped in the lock easily, and the door swung open without my having to turn the knob. That was not a good sign. My instinct was to blame the New Brunswick Police Department. Martin had gotten a couple of guys to come and search my office and send a message. But through the small opening between the door and the jamb, I could see nothing had been moved. I tensed.

Pushing the door the rest of the way open with my foot, I paused for a second behind it, waiting to see if someone jumped out. He did, coming around the door and swinging a right hand my direction. I snapped my head out of the way just in time, trying to step inside the arm, but the guy hit me with a left hand directly in the gut. I gasped for air, but remained standing.

I couldn't make out a face, just a shape and clothing. Wide shoulders, dark leather jacket, jeans, muscular. I took a swing at him, feigning a right and jabbing him in the ribs with a left. The guy grunted, but otherwise didn't flinch. I tried to put him down with a hard right, but it was blocked and I took the guy's own right flush on the chin.

I went down to my knees. My legs were jelly as another punch landed on the back of my head. My office circled, spun, and tilted on its side before my eyes like I was on some sick roller coaster. Again I tried to push my way to my feet, almost subconsciously, as if my limbs had a life of their own. This time a foot to my side put me down.

My joints were stiff and my bones ached as I tried to roll over onto my back. A copper taste settled in my mouth, a good sign I was bleeding.

"Oh fuck," I heard myself mumble.

The lights were out in my office, the blinds closed, and I had no idea what time it was. The door opened and closed, and someone was standing over me. Not the same build as the guy who'd beaten the shit out of me. He backed away and sat behind my desk.

"You got the shit kicked out of you," the man said. His voice was gruff, the way someone who'd survived throat cancer would speak.

"You should see the other guy." I managed to sit up.

"I did," he said. "You took a hell of a beating."

I turned my head slowly, trying to get a feel for the room. Other than the man behind the desk, I was the only one in there.

"Where is our huge friend?" I asked.

"Outside. I want to talk to you alone before he finishes the job."

"And you are?" I wanted to stand up, or at least make it to my knees.

"You've been looking for me, I understand. You've certainly got my attention."

"Who are you?"

"Michael Burgess. You injured two of my men, hospitalized. Probably won't ever work for me again. You took five thousand dollars of mine."

His outline in the chair was slim; I could see his face, but not clearly, as it was in shadow. I could see the trim of a goatee and big hair.

"What do you want with me?" he asked.

"Nothing. Not anymore." I spit blood onto my carpet and wiped my mouth.

"And what's that supposed to mean?" he asked.

"I'm not looking into you anymore. I don't care about you or Rex Hanover."

"You've done your homework if you know he's involved with me. What do you know?"

"I know bits and pieces. But it doesn't matter anymore. I've retired."

He laughed and stood up. "Too bad you won't be able to enjoy it."

And with that he left the room. Closed the door. Seconds later it swung open again and Rex Hanover filled the frame.

CHAPTER 40

I WASN'T HURT ENOUGH TO MISS THE CONTRADICTION.
A few days ago Hanover had shown up, beat the shit out of me, and
told me to tell Burgess not to look for him. Now he was here with
Burgess. But before I could get my thoughts in order, a right hook connected with my jaw.

The world tilted again, but I didn't black out. In fact, I found myself getting to my feet.

"Dumb move," Hanover said, stepping inside my stride, catching me with a jab to the stomach.

Gasping for air, it struck me that this wasn't a fight, it was a
boxing match. Or at least Hanover was treating it like one. I decided
it was time to fight dirty, make it a street fight. Already bent over, my
legs pushed as hard as they could and I wrapped Hanover up like a
linebacker. Caught off guard, he toppled over, crashing to the
ground.

I rolled over and tried to connect with a right cross of my own. It worked, knocking Hanover's head back into the paneled floor. He grunted.

I got off him and stepped back, leaning against my desk. I expected him to get up again, but he didn't. He lifted his head up, glared in my direction.

"It's over," I said.

"Fuck you, it's not."

"I mean, I'm not investigating anything anymore. I'm done. I came up here to call my client."

Hanover sat up. "Who is it?"

"You know who it is."

"I know who it isn't," he said. "It's not Burgess."

The world tilted again. I hadn't recovered yet, and needed to find the corner of my desk to brace myself.

"You told me to tell him to stay away from you," I said.

"Things changed."

He found his way to his feet. The way my knees were wobbling, I was pretty sure he'd do me in.

"Your wife," I said. "I was going to call Jen."

"Damn it. You stay away from her."

"It's over. I'm not a private investigator anymore. Get the fuck out of here."

"What do you mean?"

"Exactly what I just said."

"I don't buy it," he said.

"I don't give a shit."

"I could kill you."

"At this point," I said, "I know it."

Running my arm across my lip, I felt blood. Hanover was doing the same. We mirrored each other. He didn't find any blood. My punch wasn't as powerful as I'd thought.

Hanover's teeth were gritted, and he paced back and forth. "What did you tell my wife?"

"Nothing," I said. "Until the other day, I didn't know shit. In fact, I'm not sure I know anything now."

"I'm going to kill you."

I forced a shrug. "You can. I'm in no shape to fight anymore. But I'm done with this case. With all cases."

"You were going to call her tonight?"

"Now," I said.

"Do it. Put it on speakerphone. Tell her you couldn't find me. Tell her you can't work the case anymore. Call her now."

"I have to find the number."

"I know the number," he said, and repeated it to me.

I pressed the speakerphone and dialed. "Mrs. Hanover, this is Jackson Donne. I have to end the investigation."

She didn't respond.

I looked at Hanover. He rolled his hand telling me to go on.

"I am no longer a licensed private investigator. I had some trouble with the police, and it ended with me losing my job."

"Oh, I'm sorry to hear that." Jen sounded like she didn't know what to say.

"You and me both. I'll write up a report and mail it to you with my expenses."

A pause. "Were you able to find Rex?"

I looked at him. He shook his head.

"No," I said. "I'm sorry."

The only response was a click. Jen had hung up.

Hanover smiled. "Good work. If I see you anywhere near her or Burgess, you're a dead man."

"I understand," was the best I could come up with.

※ ※

The Olde Towne Tavern was my next stop. I didn't know where else to go, and I didn't have anyone else to call. Might as well throw a few beers back to go with my likely concussion.

Late afternoon and the bar was empty. Behind the bar, flipping through a *Sports Illustrated*, Artie looked like he'd had a lot of Jack last night as well. Dark circles rested under his eyes, his hair out of place. If I were to guess, I'd say he just woke up. He glanced at me when I opened the door, but didn't say a word, went back to the magazine.

Taking a stool at the bar across from him, I said, "Swimsuit edition?"

"No."

"Baseball preview?"

"Yeah."

"Say anything interesting about the Yankees?"

"Season already started. What does it matter?"

I shrugged. "Just curious."

"Says on paper they're champions. But that you don't win championships on paper."

"Kind of clichéd."

"Guess so."

I sat for ten minutes uncomfortably. Artie didn't ask if I wanted anything. I didn't ask about any other baseball teams.

I looked around the bar, thought about putting some money in the jukebox. Anything to end the icy silence between Artie and me.

Instead of the jukebox, I opted for, "Can I get a beer?"

"You know where they are."

I stared at him. "You serious?"

His turn to shrug.

"Like we're fucking married," I said.

Around the bar, I found a pint glass on ice and pulled the tap on the Sam Adams seasonal. I filled the glass and took a long pull. I topped it off.

Back at my stool, Artie finally glanced up at me. He said, "What happened to your face?" But not like he was really concerned.

I just drank my beer. No need to state the obvious.

After a while, Artie said, "You're really not working anymore?"

I spread my hands, said, "I can't. I want to. I can't."

Artie got himself a Sam Adams from the tap and refilled mine as well. He put the glass down in front of me and said, "Bullshit."

"What is? I don't have a license. I don't want to be arrested."

"That's not what I'm talking about."

"Then what are you talking about?" The beer was smoother this time, the bite of the first one gone. I wondered if it was my body adjusting to the alcohol again or the way Artie poured a beer. I'd never thought about why the second beer always tasted better than the first before.

"That you said 'I want to.' That's bullshit. You don't want to. You haven't wanted to since the beginning. You've avoided the case. Anything you've found, you've found by accident. No matter how much we wanted you to look into it, you weren't around."

"That's not true—that's . . ." I couldn't finish my thought.

"I'm sick of the bullshit excuses. Another case? Why didn't you work on this one? Why did you stay away from it?"

"I don't know," I said.

"Yes you do. It's the same reason you got your ass into all this trouble." He took down the rest of his beer. "Bill Martin."

"What about him?"

"You're scared of him. You tried everything in your power to stay out of his way, and you still got sucked in. You're a pussy."

I didn't speak.

"Tracy said it to you. She told me. I'm going to tell you the same thing. You promised us. That's like promising Gerry."

I finished my beer and got another one. Over the years, the alcohol and the laughter had helped my bruises ache less. I looked at the beer. I couldn't keep my promise to Jeanne. After she died, I never stayed sober. My life was a series of broken promises.

I thought about Gerry's wake. I thought about what I said when I knelt at his coffin. That I would find his killer. I did promise him.

I had a promise to keep.

CHapteR **41**

He DIDN'T sLeep. He DIDN'T ço to woRk tHe Next day, called in sick. All Bill Martin could think about was Jeanne. A guy he knew back when he joined the force twenty years ago once asked him if he was in love with a girl he was dating.

Martin said he didn't know.

"If you think about her all the time, that's how you know. If she's always in your head and won't leave, then you love her."

Bill Martin couldn't stop thinking about Jeanne. He was in love with a dead woman. And she was dead because of Jackson Donne. That was one thing Martin was sure of. If she hadn't gone back to him . . . He shook off the thought.

Martin sat in his apartment, sure he'd done what he'd set out to do. He ruined Jackson Donne. Put him out of commission.

Now it was a matter of taking down Michael Burgess.

That would take his mind off her.

He picked up the phone and dialed the number he'd memo-rized. Burgess was probably pissed off about what happened to his thug buddies. But he needed Burgess to stay out of the way. Donne was probably catatonic now with the news of Jeanne. Getting in Donne's face would only wake him up.

The phone rang and rang. No answer. That made sense. The convenience store was a crime scene. There wasn't any way Burgess was there. He let the phone ring a few more times, anyway.

Surprised, Martin heard, "Hello?"

The voice was heavily accented. Asian. The Chinaman from be-hind the counter.

"Tell Burgess that Bill Martin is looking for him."

"Boss not here."

"When you see him, tell him I'm looking for him."

"Not here. I no see him."

Martin swore. "I know he's not there. But you will see him and you need to deliver a message. Tell him Bill Martin is looking for him."

"Cops here."

"Just fucking tell him."

Martin slammed the phone down and went into his bedroom. If these were the kinds of people Burgess employed, they'd be useless at Donne's trial. And it was all going to depend on witnesses.

He opened the bottom drawer of his dresser and reached under the clothes. Pulling out the picture, he realized he hadn't looked at it in years.

Jeanne stood, beer in hand, smiling at the lens. Her hair dropped to her shoulders; she wore a long wool coat and a scarf hung loosely around her neck. Behind her were the fountains and the the-aters. The good side of New Brunswick. Jeanne was part of that side.

Maybe Donne hadn't suffered enough yet.

CHAPTER **42**

It was a tricky balancing act. Without my license for just over twenty-four hours and already I wanted back in the game. It came down to how I could find out what happened to Gerry and avoid Bill Martin at the same time. One last deal and that was it. Isn't that what they say in the movies, on all the television shows? One last go-around and then I'd hang it up and go back to school. That's what I wanted, why I'd sent the application to Rutgers. Now the opportunity was there.

But I had the itch; I had the promise to fulfill. Where to start? Martin seemed to have pinned his hopes on me. He didn't have anything, which meant I had less. Martin thought it had to do with drugs, and I was inclined to believe the same. But what did Martin know that I didn't? What could Martin have done that I hadn't? And what could I do that he wouldn't?

Walking down Easton Ave., back toward my apartment, I began to check off the investigation tactics Martin and I practiced years ago.

I tried to figure out which ones he would have done first, and what he was left with now. It was tough. The narcotics division acted differently from homicide. But best I could figure it'd be witnesses, evidence, interrogating suspects, and informants.

Informants.

Jesus.

I realized that Jesus Sanchez had yet to call me back to set up a meeting with Burgess. That didn't mean that Jesus hadn't attempted to get a meeting. I felt a pang of panic. Jesus could be lying in a gutter on Church Street, dead. But it didn't make much sense. Why would Burgess take out Jesus?

I kept going on Easton Ave., past the turnoff to my apartment, and turned right on George Street. I vaguely remembered Martin telling me once Jesus worked on George or one of the side streets off it. It was his beat, so to speak. But not just off Easton, that was the area Johnson & Johnson along with Rutgers had earmarked to remake.

Between Easton Ave. and the theater district, as I walked, I noticed the cobblestone sidewalks and roads, extending out from the college like strains of a virus. As I reached the theater district, however, the tenor of the city began to change. A fountain had been knocked down, and a construction site was fenced off, where a convention center would eventually rest. But past that, there were run-down houses, bodegas, and a supermarket. The paint was chipped on the buildings, the roads littered with trash, and the streets now conventional cracked asphalt. The area the city forgot. But Jesus hadn't. Neither had the addicts, the homeless, and the poor.

I saw him from a block away, standing on the curb next to a homeless guy. He watched the campus buses pass by, and I wondered if he was trying to make eye contact with some of the students trying to get to the Douglass campus. Some business venture for him, a night of partying for them.

He didn't see me coming and I got right up next to him before saying, "Jesus, what's up?"

He jumped briefly, but got control. "Hey, Jackson, what's goin' on?" Reached out and slapped me five.

"Not much."

"What happened to your face?"

"I fell," I said, smiling.

He grinned, too. "That's what I tell my bitch to say."

"You get in touch with Burgess?"

"Yo, I tried. Man, I was talking to everybody puttin' out the word, but I ain't never heard from him." He took a look at two kids walking past. They stared at the ground as they passed by. "Hey, I heard some shit about you, though."

"Yeah?"

"No more PI stuff?"

"Word travels fast."

"Man, what you gonna do? I can hook you up."

"And do what, sell for you?"

"Buy, sell, whatever you want, man. I remember back when you were with Martin, wow, you were into the shit. Now's the perfect time to come back."

I tried to smile like it was a joke. "You hear anything about Gerry Figuroa?"

"Who that?"

"Guy got run over outside of Olde Towne about a week ago."

Jesus put a hand on my shoulder. "You ain't got a license, right?"

"Right."

"So, why the fuck should I talk to you?"

"Because you came to me first."

"Fuck no. There ain't anything in it for me. You still owe me for trying to get in touch with Burgess."

"Well, that didn't work out."

"And now that you're not on the case, what you give a shit about the old man?"

I didn't say anything about an old man. Jesus obviously knew something. "He was a friend of mine."

"Who took your license away? The cops?"

"Yeah."

"You put two guys out of the game."

"Two guys that were competitors of yours, I believe."

He laughed. "Hell yeah." Slapped my hand again.

"Help me out."

"I don't know shit."

"You aren't fucking with me, are you, Jesus?"

"Nah, man. The cops really took your license away?"

"Yeah."

"No jail?"

"No."

"Fucking racist, man."

I shrugged.

"Sorry I can't help you out. But it's time for you to retire anyway. Maybe move to Florida."

"I'll think about it."

I turned away. He knew something. I knew he did. But why not tell me? Probably because he was Martin's boy, not mine. He'd come to me. Most likely because Martin sent him.

I walked back toward Easton Ave. Next to me, buses rumbled as the sun began to set.

* *

Tracy's cell phone rang a few times, and then her voice mail picked up. I left a message to call me, but figured she recognized my number and was screening. It wasn't likely she'd call back.

I wanted her to know I was back on the case. I wanted her to know I was going to fulfill my promise. Turned right onto Church Street and walked under the parking deck. Across the street a couple held hands, whispering in each other's ears. They were probably heading to one of the newer restaurants for a romantic evening. It had been a while since I'd taken someone out for more than a drink.

I turned on Albany and made my way toward the Hyatt. Maybe Tracy was in her room. She needed to know.

The Hyatt was a tall white building with a parking deck, green grass, and a fountain. Out front of the lobby, someone was unloading their luggage. I went straight to the elevator, remembering Tracy's room number.

Two minutes later I knocked on her door. She must not have looked through the peephole, because she swung the door open quickly. When she saw me, she tried to shut it again, but I put my arm on the wood to hold it open.

"Wait," I said.

"You're not going to help. Go away."

"We need to talk."

"I said all I have to. You walked away from me."

"I'm sorry. I—"

"Just go away."

"I have to talk to you, about Gerry."

"Why? You're not working anymore."

"Yes, I am," I said.

The air immediately warmed between us. Her shoulders relaxed, and the bags under her eyes seemed to fade just a bit.

"Come in," she said.

Stepping through the door, she wrapped her arms around me, pressing her lips to mine. She kissed me and kicked the door closed. We didn't talk for a while after that.

*   *

I'm not sure how much time passed, but we lay together in bed, Tracy's back to me. Running a finger gently down her spine, I breathed slowly. For the first time in weeks I felt relaxed, away from it all. Tracy snored softly. I listened, and didn't want the moment to end.

Tracy's snoring stopped, and for a while I didn't hear anything. Then she said, "Jackson?"

"Yes?" I whispered.

"Thank you for helping me."

"I haven't done anything yet."

"You will. I know it."

"Well then, Ms. Psychic, you're welcome."

She rolled over to face me and we smiled. She punched me playfully in the arm. Then she kissed me gently.

"What are you going to do first?" Tracy asked.

"I want to establish whether or not Gerry was into drugs."

"How are you going to do that?"

I rolled onto my back, letting my head rest on the pillow. The wallpaper on the ceiling was light beige, a soothing color that made me want to nod off right there. I closed my eyes and let air out through my nose. It was okay to do this now, I thought. Jeanne had been gone long enough.

Despite what Martin had said. Maybe Leonard Baker was right. Maybe it was time to let go. Move on. Tracy felt right.

"I need to know about Gerry's past."

"What don't you know?"

"I know he was in Korea. I know he was an actor. I know he had a son who died of leukemia. And I know he had a wife who disappeared."

"Okay," she said. I felt her hand against my chest.

"I want to find his wife."

For a moment there was silence; the hand slowly moved off my chest. I opened my eyes and rolled on my side. Tracy was propped up on her right arm, looking at me, her left hand covering her mouth.

"I don't know where she is," Tracy said.

I leaned in and moved her hand away. Kissed her lightly. "I didn't say you did. But I want to find her and talk to her."

"Why?"

"Because she knows things about Gerry. There had to be a reason she ran from him, and I want to know what it was."

"She didn't run. She disappeared."

"No one just disappears. It's against the laws of physics." I smiled, but it didn't click with her.

"Don't look for her."

"Why not?"

"It's too late for that."

"You want me to find out what happened to Gerry."

"Yeah, but I don't want you to dig up everything."

I brushed a strand of her hair over her ear. "There's only one way to get answers," I said. "And that's to turn over every rock until I find something. I haven't found anything else."

Tracy kissed my cheek. "There's something I need to know. The other case, the one that was taking all your time away from Gerry. Was it important?"

"You're asking if I was just doing nothing instead of looking for Gerry."

She nodded. I told her about the case. Her eyes went cold when I said Rex Hanover's name.

"What is it?" I asked.

"I knew Rex Hanover. Do you remember when we walked along the boardwalk?"

"Yes."

"I told you I used to date a guy named Pablo. That he was the man you took me away from. His name was Pablo Najera."

I remembered.

"I introduced Pablo to Jen. Just before they met, Pablo decided to change his name to Rex. Something about the police."

I let that sink in. Tracy shifted closer to me.

"I'm involved and I don't want to be. I think Gerry got into drugs when he met Pablo. We didn't see each other much, but Gerry was in the tavern all the time. He got to talking to Pablo one night."

"Pablo was a drug dealer?"

She shook her head. "He works for one."

"Michael Burgess."

"I couldn't tell you. I needed to get away from this. Drugs have been a part of my life forever. My boyfriend—"

I didn't want to hear more. I kissed her to keep her from talking.

Bill Martin trying to link Gerry's investigation to what happened in the bodega yesterday itched at my bones. Everything was connected.

"Can we talk about this in the morning?" Tracy said, finally.

"I'm going to look, whether you want me to or not."

She touched one of my bruises gently, but I still felt a shock of pain.

"I know," she said.

I closed my eyes and let her kiss me.

CHAPTER

It was late when Michael Burgess called. Martin was sleeping and he had to fumble for the handset.

"We need to talk. Boyd Park, half an hour."

❋ ❋

Boyd Park housed the Rutgers crew team dock along the Raritan River. A small red house, the team kept it up pretty well. Even in the dark, it seemed to stand out against the black water backdrop. No paint chipping, very little litter, only the gentle slap of water against the dock. And the sound of traffic from Route 18.

Bill Martin visited the park many times before the demotion. He'd been here once to talk to a hit man, broken up drug dealings and taken the evidence himself, and once to pick up a stoned Donne and get him home to Jeanne.

Now he waited for Michael Burgess. He had enough time to light a cigarette. Burgess and the huge man came from the shadows only a few minutes after Martin got there.

"Not used to seeing you in open air," Martin said.

"We've taken care of Mr. Donne," Burgess said. "Apparently you tried to as well."

"What do you mean?"

"When we saw him, he wasn't steady on his feet. Shaken up, I suppose. Plus he said he didn't have a license anymore. That there wasn't a need for us to put a scare into him."

"But you did anyway."

Burgess pointed to the burly man behind him. "My associate had a point to make."

The big man smiled at Martin. Cracked his knuckles.

"Anyway," Burgess continued, "the store has been compromised for the moment. That doesn't mean we want you to stop what you've been trying to do. Get the cops off our street. Let us run our business."

Martin nodded.

"At the same time, I've some business to take care of. A strategy that I've been working on to increase my own profits. I'd like to ask that you stay away from us for a while."

The traffic on 18 quieted. One of the traffic lights must have turned red. The Raritan continued to flow along.

"Are you saying you're about to do something illegal?" Bill Martin asked.

"Just do as I say, Detective."

"Okay, but let me tell you something about Jackson Donne."

"I told you, we've taken care of him."

Martin shook his head. "I don't think you have. You're right, he was broken. But you should have stayed away."

"He injured two of my men. Shot one of them. They're both lucky to be alive. That can't go unpunished."

"It's going to trial."

"And who would be witnesses for the prosecution? My men? I don't think so."

Martin stepped forward so only Burgess could hear him. "Jackson Donne was beaten. I know him, I worked with him. If anything, you've woken him up again."

"I highly doubt that."

The water rushed alongside them. The traffic had started up again.

"Trust me," Martin said. "But I think we're going to have to take care of him anyway."

"What do you mean?"

Martin closed his eyes and pictured Jeanne. Her smile, her laugh, the last time he spoke with her. How everything was taken from him.

"Jackson Donne needs to die."

CHAPTER

THE NEXT MORNING, I HAD A NAME. ANNE BACKES.
It wasn't much, but enough to begin searching. Tracy hadn't been able
to remember her maiden name, kept calling her Figuroa, but rang her
parents and got the name. She lied and said she'd found some of
Gerry's things and wanted to try and get them to Anne. Tracy's parents
said good luck, they hadn't heard from Anne in years.

After a quick breakfast with Tracy at a local diner, we went our
separate ways. She said she wanted to walk around town, shop and
get her mind off things. I wanted to get back to work. Quietly.

My office door was locked, and I slipped my key in, pushed it
open. Checking the room and finding it clear, I turned my computer on
and let it boot up. The office smelled like it hadn't been used in days,
and there were papers strewn across the floor.

I pulled the window open to let in some air, turned the radio on,
and picked up the papers. The papers weren't anything important—

Jen Hanover's reports that I still had to type up—so I put them on my desk under a paperweight. The Who blared.

Back at my computer, I pulled up one of the search engines I used to find missing people. The keys of the computer were dusty and motes floated through the air between the sunshine and breeze from the open window. I was typing in Anne Backes's name when the phone rang.

"Mr. Donne, it's Blanchett, Madison Police." He sounded tired. But he probably always sounded tired.

"How are you, Detective Blanchett?"

"Listen," he said. "Word's out about you and your license. I want to know what you know about Rex Hanover. We need you to come to the station."

Apparently Blanchett wasn't into small talk.

I took a deep breath. "Sure," I said.

"ASAP." He hung up.

After I hit send on the computer, the cursor turned into a time-piece. The Internet page loaded slowly. The page appeared on-screen, and reported 253 hits for Anne Backes. I saved the page and shut down the computer. The trip to Madison would take me close to forty minutes, and I wanted to know what Blanchett wanted. Curiosity got the better of me.

＊ ＊

The past few days I felt like I'd been all over northern and central New Jersey. The miles put on my car meant it needed an oil change soon. The long interstate and state highways were familiar sights to me, and it was getting easier to predict where the state troopers would be hiding to catch speeders. On 287, trucks hung in the center and right lanes, so I stayed in the left, going about ten miles over the speed limit. It was too early in the day for much traffic, so the trip was relatively easy.

There was a parking space in front of the Madison Police Department. On the front steps, Blanchett was smoking a cigarette, watching the traffic pass. His tie was loose around his neck, and his hair was still out of place. He gave a little nod in my direction when he noticed me.

We shook hands on the steps, and he smiled. "Who'd you piss off?"

"What do you mean?"

"To get your license revoked."

"You don't know?"

"Apparently the cop rumor mill is being selective on the parts of the story it tells this time."

"Oh," I said.

He waited, and when I didn't say anything else, he gave another curt nod.

"All right. Well, thanks for coming in."

"Daniels here, too?"

"She's inside. Come on," he said. He dropped his cigarette, stamping it out under his foot.

We walked down the long hallway I remembered from the night I found the body. To my right were some offices and the cop bull pen, but we didn't turn that way. We kept walking toward the interrogation room.

"Sorry," he said. "Don't really want you talking in public out in the bull pen. One, if somebody starts blabbing in there, everyone would hear, and two, there's more room. Hope you don't mind."

Blanchett was being downright personable.

"I don't give a shit where we talk," I said, just to spice the conversation up.

He smiled and said, "Good."

✳ ✳

We went into the room, bare as before, with just a table and two chairs. I took the chair that was by itself, facing the door.

"You going to record me?" I asked, remembering Daniels playing with the thermostat.

"Not if you don't want me to," he said.

"Who's going to be good cop and bad cop?"

Blanchett smiled again. "You want a cup of coffee?"

"That answers my question," I said. "Sure. Cream and sugar."

He left and for a few minutes I was alone. The room smelled less like coffee this time around. Like someone had taken a can of Febreze and sprayed it around to mask the odor. Maybe there was a deodorizer plugged in somewhere.

How much to tell them? Finding Rex Hanover wasn't my problem anymore. And I knew who he was with. I could just give them Burgess's name and move on. But the connection to Gerry still tugged at my bones, even though I didn't want to believe it. I wasn't going to answer any questions on how I lost my license. They didn't need to know.

Daniels came through the door carrying two Styrofoam cups of coffee. She wore another black business suit, white shirt open at the top, with a wide collar pulled over the lapels of the blazer. Placing one cup in front of me, a smile crossed her face.

"What?" I asked.

"Drink your coffee," she said.

I took a sip, steam rising up my nose. "When you play bad cop, you're not supposed to smile."

Daniels smiled wider. "There is no bad cop today. Come on, drink your coffee."

She sipped at hers. I took another mouthful.

"Laced with truth serum?"

She looked at the ceiling. "Can't just drink it, can you?"

I put the cup down. Some of the coffee sloshed over my fingers and onto the table. "What's going on? I didn't come down here just to drink coffee."

She placed her hands flat on the table. "We'll talk in a few minutes."

"Where's Blanchett?"

She leaned in close to my face. "Stop asking questions. You don't want me to have to be the bad cop, do you?"

A thousand jokes crossed my mind, about half of them repeatable. But I kept my mouth shut, picked the coffee back up, and swirled it. I'd been in enough trouble with the police in the last few days, didn't want to mess with the two who seemed to have some measure of respect for me.

Daniels finished the rest of her coffee and dropped the cup in the small plastic trash can. Crossing her arms, she leaned against the wall next to the door. She didn't say a word. This was the strangest interrogation ever, and I'd been through some odd ones. The past few days alone.

I sipped slowly, letting the coffee cool in my mouth. It wasn't the best coffee. In fact, it was downright awful, but I was savoring it. If only to piss off Daniels. Who was she to tell me how fast to drink?

The door opened and Blanchett stepped through. He looked at Daniels, her arms still crossed, then shifted his gaze to me.

"Jesus Christ," he said, "how long does it take to drink a cup of coffee?"

What the hell was with my coffee? That's it, I decided. I was going to wait them out.

I swirled the coffee and watched as both Blanchett and Daniels's eyes widened, hoping I would finish it. I put the cup back down and gave them a smile.

"Good coffee," I said. "Hate to waste it."

Blanchett's head was going to explode, I was sure of it. On second thought, maybe it was fun to piss off the last two remaining cops with a bit of respect for me.

Daniels looked at her watch. "How long have we been in here?"

"Twenty minutes," Blanchett answered. He looked me over. "Long enough."

Reaching across the table, he grabbed the cup of coffee from my hand and tossed it toward the trash. Brown liquid sprayed across the room and splattered on the floor, narrowly missing Daniels's suit.

"Nice move, smart-ass," she said.

He winked at her and took my forearm. "Come on, you're taking a walk."

"What the hell?" I said.

"Come on," Daniels said, too. She pulled the door open and stepped out into the hallway.

Blanchett waited for me to pass, and then followed me. The three of us were in the hallway, walking at a snail's pace. Two uniforms were headed toward me. They glared at me as if I was the Zodiac Killer.

"Don't say a fucking word," Blanchett whispered as we got closer.

Though they never took their eyes off me, the two uniforms managed to mumble hellos to my escorts as we walked past.

I followed Daniels out the front doors. It was bright compared to the police station, and I had to squint. The sun reflecting off the police cruisers didn't help. And I'd left my sunglasses in my cup holder.

"Where's your car?" she asked.

I pointed across the street.

"Okay," Daniels said. "I'm going to ride with you. Harry's going to follow."

"Harry?"

"Blanchett."

"Oh yeah," I said. "You gonna tell me what the hell's going on?"

Daniels grinned. "Once we're on the road."

We took the stairs and crossed the street. Out of the corner of my eye I saw Blanchett unlocking an unmarked car. It was gray and had a spotlight attached to the sideview mirror, so I guessed he wasn't trying to be too clandestine.

I hit the alarm button and unlocked my Honda Prelude. Daniels slid into the passenger seat and had her seat belt buckled before I opened my door. First thing I did was grab my sunglasses. Able to see again, I turned the ignition. The car stereo popped on, playing the Stones way too loud.

Turning it down, I said, "Where to?"

The street was empty and I pulled out of my parking spot. In the rearview, Blanchett followed.

"Drew University," Daniels said.

"You could have told me that ten minutes ago."

"I like watching you get nervous."

My mind flashed to Diane Peterson rolled in a tight carpet, resting in front of the entrance. I didn't want to go back, and I had no idea why Daniels and Blanchett were taking me there.

"Do I have to call my lawyer?" I asked.

"You should have done that when you were taking your sweet time drinking the coffee."

"Yeah," I said. "I guess you're right."

I made a right turn at the corner and headed toward the campus.

CHAPTER **45**

"PARK IN THE VISITORS' LOT," DANIELS SAID.

"Not on the street?"

"Nah."

I turned the car onto a small drive that led through a gate. A security guard watched us approach. I told him we were just visiting, wanted to take a tour. He handed us a one-day parking pass. Behind us, I noticed Blanchett flash his badge and get in without a pass.

We took the first available parking spot, up against a small bush. Getting out, we watched Blanchett circle the lot for another open spot.

"What happened to your face?" Daniels asked. She wasn't even looking at me.

"Fell down the stairs."

She said, "That's what they all say."

Blanchett parked and made his way across the lot toward us. In one hand he carried a manila folder. He ran the other through his hair and surveyed the surroundings as he walked, like he was expecting to be ambushed. I wasn't sure who worried me more, the cop who was all about the job, expecting anything to happen, or the cop who was too cool for school.

"You guys going to tell me what's up?" I asked when he reached us.

"Walk with us," Daniels said. She was running the show.

They started off toward the campus. I stayed put. When they turned to see why I wasn't walking with them, I said, "No."

Blanchett swore.

Daniels took the classier route, saying, "Excuse me?" Like someone just took a shit on her foot.

For a moment, I didn't say anything. I let them stare at me, see if they could figure it out. Off in the distance I could hear a Dave Matthews song bouncing off the buildings. Commuter campus, dorms, you couldn't get away from the guy no matter what college you went to.

"Walk with us," Daniels said again, a little more *oomph* this time.

"No," I said. Before she could say anything else, I added, "You drag me around like I'm in your dog-and-pony show. I sit in an interrogation room and you watch me drink coffee and don't say a word. Now you have me drive out here, but you won't tell me why? We do this here or I'm leaving."

I had more important things to do. Like find Anne Backes. My earlier curiosity seemed unwarranted.

Blanchett looked at Daniels. Her play. She stared into my eyes, like she was trying to find a poker tell. I wanted her to think I had pocket aces.

She returned Blanchett's glare and nodded her head toward me. Blanchett sighed and they both came back my way.

"We know what happened with you and the incident the other day," Blanchett said. "I know I mentioned it before, but we know the whole story."

"How?"

"We have our ways," Daniels said, unfortunately not attempting a German accent.

I didn't laugh. "So, what does that have to do with anything?"

"Public record, we don't agree with how Detective Martin is handling things," she said. "But we might be able to use it to our advantage."

"You're going to use me?"

"Be nice," Blanchett said, "if you'd cooperate."

"What are you talking about?"

Daniels took the manila folder from Blanchett and passed it to me. I didn't open it.

"Did you know Rex Hanover's name was a fake?" she asked.

I debated my answers. Nothing to lose now. "Pablo Najera," I said.

Her eyes bore into me. *How long have you known? What else have you been hiding?* I knew that look.

"Come on," I said. "With a name like that, it was the first place I looked."

I didn't want them to know about Tracy.

"We see shitty names all the time."

"I'll bet."

"Just look at yours."

I tried to laugh it off. Didn't work too well. But it worked better than breaking his nose.

"What else do you know?" Daniels said, cutting off the pissing match.

"Not much. He's involved with Michael Burgess somehow. A few days ago, it seemed like he was on the run. Now it seems like they're together."

Blanchett said, "You've seen him?"

I pointed to one of my many yellowing bruises.

"Son of a bitch. And you didn't call us?"

I shrugged. "With the concussion and all, I forgot."

"Asshole."

"All right," Daniels said. "You should have told us, Donne."

I shrugged again. "Why am I here?"

"We've come across information from a confidential source. And it might come to light at trial."

"What information?" The folder suddenly felt heavy in my hands.

"Look in the file," she said.

I opened it. There was a picture of Hanover—Najera, though I couldn't bring myself to call him that—on top of a few official-looking papers. He was in an army uniform carrying a machine gun. The uniform wasn't American. I flipped through the papers, but they were written in Spanish.

"What the hell is this?" I asked.

A car pulled into the lot, circled, didn't find a spot, and pulled out. A bird landed on top of my Prelude, checked out its reflection in the chrome, and flew away.

"That is Pablo Najera, when he was a member of the Mexican national army."

"What does that mean?"

"It means," Blanchett barreled in, "that he was a member of the army, but he was discharged."

"Honorably?"

Daniels shook her head. "Not according to our source."

"So, what happened?"

"Well, according to our source—"

"Who is your source?" I asked.

Daniels shook her head. "According to our source, a funny thing happens to disgraced Mexican soldiers. They become hit men for Mexican drug lords."

My blood ran cold. "And Najera?" I said, finally acknowledging the name.

"Became a hit man. But apparently, he got fed up with the Mexican drug lords and came to New York to find work," Blanchett said.

"And he hooked up with Burgess."

They nodded in unison. They looked like marionettes.

"So, what am I supposed to do with this information?" I asked.

Daniels cleared her throat. "You gave it to us."

"When?"

"When you had your cup of coffee," Blanchett said. "If this goes to trial, we can't have our source on the stand. So we need you."

"You're going to fake a witness?"

"It's plausible. You witnessed the murder. You're a private investigator. You got curious, did a background check. Came up with this," Daniels said.

"I don't know."

Daniels frowned. "This is more than you would have ever known. We gave you information on a silver platter. You don't really expect us to give you that for nothing?"

"I need to think about it."

"Take tonight. Otherwise, we won't see what we can do about getting your license back in order, maybe even keeping you out of the courtroom."

"What? I thought the police rumor mill was being selective."

"Ve haff our vays," Blanchett said, this time with the German accent.

"Who's your source? FBI? NSA? CIA?"

"Someone who could cause a bit of a scandal if he were put on the stand and the press caught wind of it," Blanchett said.

"Help us out, Donne."

"Why bring me all the way out here to tell me this?" I asked.

Daniels shrugged. "No one around to see. It's spring break. And I like watching you get nervous."

They left me there, heading back to the unmarked. It wasn't until they pulled out onto the main road that I realized they'd left the file with me.

46

CHAPTER

I walkeᴅ over to the front gate, file in hand. The air was cool and the streets were empty. The silence seemed rare for this area. I stared at nothing, remembering the cold, dark night when Diane Peterson was laid there hanging out of the rolled-up carpet.

I wondered about a lot of things. There was a spot of reddish brown on the sidewalk concrete. Could it be some of Diane's blood? Now that I had more information about Najera, it was clear that this murder wasn't a lovers' spat, but a hit on a drug dealer. So why would Najera take the trouble to drag her body out to the gate? Such a public spectacle. And what could Diane have done to cause a hit to be put out on her?

And was Tracy caught up in this as well? Or was she being honest when she said she had to get out?

A small piece of newspaper blew across the sidewalk in the breeze. It twisted and flipped and found a direction to move in, only to be pulled back by a crosswind. It scraped the concrete, then flew out into the road, and was torn in half by an oncoming car. I thought of Tracy the night before, pulling me into her room, kissing me. I thought of Artie begging me to take the case, and Blanchett and Daniels wanting me to play witness. Martin took my license and Jeanne's memory. I felt like I was going in eight different directions.

Shaking my head, it felt like maybe I needed to get more sleep. Either way, I'd been standing, staring at nothing for too long. Time to get back to New Brunswick.

✳ ✳

The file sat on the passenger seat, closed. A few times I glanced at it, but there wasn't any traffic slowing things down enough for me to get a chance to give it any more attention. For once 287 was empty, and the car was pushing ninety.

Half an hour later, car parked and office unlocked, my computer screen lit my face. I was able to resist the allure of Najera's file in order to look up the Anne Backes information. There were two hundred fifty-three entries on my screen, fifteen of them in New Jersey. I had done an East Coast search to start, just to try and keep the numbers down. Didn't work too well.

Jersey's always a good place to start. I picked up the phone, chose a woman in Hawthorne, and got lucky on the first dial.

"Hello?" a creaky voice said, after three rings.

"Ms. Backes?"

"Who's calling?"

"This is Jackson Donne. I'm a—"

"Ah," she said. "The private investigator. I was wondering when you'd call."

"You're expecting me?" Well, *that was easy.*

"Ever since I heard Gerry died."

"Well, I was wondering—"

"If you could come and see me? Well," she croaked, "I don't see why not."

She gave me an address, which I scribbled on a Post-it note. I didn't know Hawthorne well—it was in northern Jersey—but I was excited enough to rush out of the office without getting directions.

✳ ✳

Union Street was just off Goffle Road in Hawthorne. I didn't know the area, but eventually I made the correct turns and ended on the right street.

The house, one of crumbling black shingles, faded yellow aluminum siding, overgrown grass, and a rusty fence, was not exactly the shining sight on the block. The rest of the block was spotless, two-story, shiny, expensive houses for their moderate size. This area of New Jersey, this close to New York, the houses sold for three hundred grand at a minimum. If you kept the houses in good shape, like most of the block, you could make a mint.

Pushing the gate open, I stepped directly into dog shit. The first sign that this was going to continue being a hell of a day. I scraped my shoe against the sidewalk, hit the porch, and rang the bell. The wind whistled through a hanging mobile. The metal clinked together, breaking an eerie silence. To my left, a window and a curtain moved slightly.

Finally the door creaked open, revealing a short woman with dark hair, standing straight and confident. She had bags under her eyes and crow's-feet at the corners. Her laugh lines were deeply set, and her chin showed some loose skin. She looked me up and down.

"Thought you might be a Jehovah's Witness or one of them kids selling candy again. I hate that," she said. Her voice wasn't as rough as it sounded on the phone. In fact, it had a tinge of sass that seemed to be her holding on to her youth.

"Ms. Backes? I'm Jackson Donne," I said.

"I know who you are," she said. "But I still want to see ID."

I showed my driver's license.

"No PI license?"

"Long story." I hoped I could leave it at that.

Once more she eyed me up and down, taking in every wrinkle in my clothes. She pushed the screen door open farther and stepped out of the way. "Come on in," she muttered.

She wore blue jeans that were loose and a buttonless blouse. The blouse was sleeveless and yellow, as if it went with a blazer. She didn't wear shoes. Her toe- and fingernails were both painted red.

The house didn't smell of mothballs, it didn't smell like steam, it didn't smell at all. I hoped to find pictures, cards, trinkets, anything that would give me an indication of Anne's life that would connect her to Gerry. Anything at all.

The house, however, was threadbare. There were pieces of furniture, cabinets and a TV, dark blue carpet, and a few paintings. However, the place looked hastily cleared of memorabilia; motes of dust rested on the wooden furniture, but there were clean spaces on the mantelpiece like there were missing picture frames. As if they'd been recently moved.

"Can I get you anything?"

"No, thanks."

I took a seat on the couch and nearly sank into the center of the earth. The cushions were fluffy and soft.

Anne must have noticed, because she said, "Comfortable, huh?" She took the easy chair across from me. "I don't know anything about it. Only what I read in the paper."

I waited for her to add "so there," but it never came.

"I'm not interested in last week. I want to know about you and Gerry."

"What do you mean?" She sat back in the chair, but she didn't sink.

"First off, how come no one could find you? Whereas I click your name into a computer and an hour and a half later I'm in your living room."

"Because by the time the computer age came around, no one cared. No one wanted to find me. Before that I wasn't listed, I moved around a lot."

I nodded as if this information was very important. It might have been. I didn't know yet. A dog barked. I looked for it.

"He's in the yard," Anne said.

"Tell me about Gerry."

"I hadn't seen him in years."

"There wasn't much in the paper about it, what happened to him."

"I know. I only saw the obituary."

I smiled. "Short, wasn't it?"

"Yeah. Didn't mention me."

"It didn't mention you because Gerry didn't mention you."

"Did he suffer? Was it quick?"

"He was hit by a car," I said. Let her make her own conclusions. "Didn't you go to the funeral?"

"No," she said, smiling. "Didn't you?"

I shook my head. "Tell me about Gerry."

"I told you, I don't know anything."

"Tell me about when he was in Korea or when he was acting. Or about when you left him."

We were dancing, verbally. Neither of us wanted to give away a weakness. I didn't want to tell her too much, because she might cover up what I wanted to know, using clues from my questions. She didn't want to tell me anything because she was suspicious of me. That led me to believe she knew things. Important things.

So we kept dancing.

"You know a lot about Gerry's past already," she said.

"Not enough."

"I haven't seen him in years. At least twenty. What do you want me to say?"

"Just tell me what you do know."

"That's very broad, isn't it?"

"Okay. Why did you leave Gerry?"

"Because he was a terrible father."

"You left your son with him."

"Maybe I wasn't the best mother, either."

"You weren't there when your son died. You weren't at the funeral."

"How the hell do you know where I was?"

"I was at the funeral. I didn't see you."

She smiled, mirthless. "You didn't see me because I didn't want anyone to see me."

"Why so secretive?"

"Because I didn't want Gerry looking for me."

And Gerry had obviously gotten that message long before he'd met me. He never mentioned Anne. Never said anything. If he'd wanted to find her by the time he'd met me, he'd have asked me to look for her.

We sat silently for a moment. I formulated my next question; she looked at an ashtray on her coffee table. It was the only item on the table.

"Gerry was an addict," she said.

"Drugs?" I asked, surprised she'd volunteered anything.

"Not exactly. I mean he smoked weed, but he was an addict. Anything he did he was addicted to it. The army? He didn't even come home on leave. Acting, at every rehearsal, staying late. Never sitting out, even a matinee. Anything he worked at, he went all the way." She shook her head.

"Is that why you left him?"

She wiped her mouth. Then she picked up the ashtray and looked at the bottom of it. The ashtray didn't look used and the room definitely didn't smell like smoke.

"He never saw our kid . . ." She wiped again, as if trying to catch the words. "Our son. Gerry never saw him. We argued about it all the time, and eventually Gerry got violent. So I left. I wasn't a good mother, I wasn't thinking straight. I left him with our son, so he had no choice but to spend time with him. It seemed right at the time. Now I know it was wrong."

I didn't want to touch that. Sometimes I hated asking questions; you got answers you didn't want. I wanted to know about Gerry's background in drugs. I wanted her to say she left Gerry because he was making crystal meth to support their family.

I should have asked outright. Instead, I said, "Is that why you said you were a bad mother? Because you abandoned your child?"

Anne slammed her hand down on the tabletop, palm flat. "I did *not* abandon my children."

"Children?"

She paled. "Child. I did not abandon Steve."

Her hands shook, and I took it as a sign of nervousness and not age. Now was the time to ask, throw the change-up. Catch her off guard.

"How did you and Gerry do on money?"

"We were fine." Her voice was cold and stiff.

"Acting paid well?"

"Why?"

"Because when I knew him, Gerry didn't have too much money. He kept his head above water, but he didn't have to support anyone then. At least until Steve got cancer."

"We were fine."

"Did Gerry have to work two jobs?"

She eyed me again. "What are you getting at?"

Time to lay it out on the table. "You said he was an addict. I want to know if that involved drugs."

"He smoked weed."

"That's it?"

She looked at me and didn't say anything. Her eyes were a pale blue, like a clear sea. Besides the nail polish, she wasn't wearing any makeup.

"I feel like you're trying to lead me somewhere," she said, "but I have no idea where. Why don't you just come out and say it?"

"How deep into drugs was he?"

"He wasn't a person likely to end up in rehab, if that's what you're saying. We smoked weed on the weekends, that's all."

"Did Gerry sell drugs?"

"What?"

"When you knew Gerry, did he know how to make drugs? Did he sell drugs to help your family make money?"

Anne didn't look surprised, and she didn't look away either. Her gaze held mine, didn't even flinch.

"No."

But she did answer too quickly. And she didn't ask what I was talking about. There was no surprise in her answer.

"Did Gerry know how to make drugs?"

"No."

"I don't believe you, Ms. Backes."

"I don't care."

I wasn't going to get any farther with her. Taking one last glance around the room, looking for any sort of visual clue, I stood and shook her hand.

"Thank you for your time, Ms. Backes."

"That's it?"

"That's it."

We walked to the door together. She smiled. "I hope I never have to see you again." At least she said it as sweetly as possible.

I stepped out into the spring air. She started to close the door. Quickly I turned back.

"One more thing, Ms."

"I don't watch *Columbo*." She held the door, and I noticed dark scars on her forearms.

I smiled. "Neither do I. But I do watch the news. And read magazines. I remember seeing a story on the History Channel. Something about soldiers in Vietnam learning how to make drugs and smuggling them in canteens."

Anne squinted. "Your point?"

"Ah," I said. "I think you know. I'm just curious if the same thing could have happened in Korea."

"I have no idea," she said. Closed the door.

I had other questions. Like why—after leaving him and going through a ton of trouble to hide from Gerry—was she protecting him now?

I unlocked my car, figuring those questions would have to be answered later.

CHAPTER

BILL MARTIN SAT IN HIS OFFICE. BURGESS HAD come up with the perfect plan. Martin didn't care whom it involved. All that mattered was that Donne would soon be dead.

CHAPTER **48**

I WAS DRIVING SOUTH ON **287**, ABOUT TEN MILES from New Brunswick, when my cell phone rang.

"Oh, thank God you picked up," Tracy said.

"What's the matter?"

"Can you get to Asbury?"

"When did you go back? I'm like an hour out."

Brake lights were flashing, the first signs of Sunday night traffic clogging up the highway. If that kept up, I'd be more than an hour out. Anyway, I didn't even know what she wanted. No need to say anything more about New Jersey traffic.

"Pablo was here."

"Rex?" Somehow I still couldn't bring myself to call him Pablo. "What happened?"

"I—well, I came home to see my boyfriend."

The words stung more than I expected.

"And well, Pablo came by, just to see if anyone had been asking about him. My boyfriend said to tell Pablo about you. Pablo flipped, he hit me. He took Jesus."

"Took him?"

Her voice cracked, broke, and she spoke through sobs. "He punched me. He took Jesus. He said—oh my God. It doesn't make any sense."

But it was starting to click for me.

"Your boyfriend's name is Jesus?"

There was a pause on the other end. Then, "Yeah. Why?"

"Jesus what?"

"Sanchez." She was still sobbing, but the breaths were coming farther apart. More like she was scared and confused. I thought about her saying she needed to get away from drugs.

Fuck. Why did Rex take Jesus? Still, I wanted to be sure. New Jersey has a high Hispanic population, and there were probably several Jesus Sanchezes around.

"What does Jesus do for a living?" I asked.

"I don't need to answer that."

"He's a drug dealer, isn't he?"

Traffic slowed to a crawl. I wanted to lean on my horn. I wanted to drive in the shoulder. I wanted to scream. Natural feelings for most drivers in traffic now pushed to a fever pitch.

"Can't you help me?"

"Call the police."

"You know what he does. You just said it. The cops aren't going to help."

I thought about facing Rex again. I thought about facing Burgess again, the beating I took the last time. The fact that I had no idea where they were. I wasn't a PI anymore. I was only helping out a friend. But I couldn't resist Tracy.

"I'm on my way," I said. "But traffic's bad. I'll get there when I can."

There were pieces of the events of the past few days lying strewn around my brain, and they were starting to find their connectors. From what Martin said, from what Jesus had said, from what Blanchett and Daniels had shown me, it was all there. And now it was starting to come together.

※ ※

Most of the homes in Asbury Park were falling apart. Paint chipping, long grass, broken fences. Like a line of Anne Backes's house. I pulled in front of a burnt orange home, Tracy Boland sitting on her stoop watching cars pass. She didn't wave when she saw me. She hardly flinched.

Rounding my car, I could see that her front door was knocked off its hinges, leaning against the wall haphazardly. I couldn't see through the frame, couldn't see how much of the house was destroyed, but Tracy had lied to me. Rex Hanover didn't come here nicely, make idle chatter, and flip out at the mention of my name. Things went bad from the start.

Tracy walked toward me, keeping me away from the house. Her eyes were red and puffy, her face flushed.

"Are you okay?" I asked.

She nodded. Her eyes were red and her nose ran a bit. Her face looked a bit sallow. The changes were subtle, but I noticed them. Years of experience.

"You still do a little coke?" I asked.

"Please," she said. "This is hard. It's scary."

Now wasn't the time for a lecture.

I took her by the shoulders and looked her dead in the eye. "Tell me what happened."

"I told you—"

"No," I said. "Not that bullshit. What really happened."

She brushed at her hair.

"Pablo. He wanted to talk to me, but he was scary. Banging on the door. Asking if Jesus was there. I told Jesus to stay quiet. I said why do you want to talk to him? No answer, just wanting to come in. I was scared. Jesus said to go away. Pablo, he knocked the door down."

She was crying again and fell into my arms. I held her for a while. "Please," she whispered between sobs. "Please help me."

"What would you like me to do?"

"You're looking for Pablo, find Jesus. Save him. Help me by saving him."

I held her still, tighter. I thought about the consequences of getting further involved. In too far, if I ran into Martin I was screwed. That was a risk already. "Let's go inside. Get you a glass of water. So you can calm down."

I found the kitchen and poured a glass of water. The room hadn't been disturbed by Pablo or Jesus or Tracy.

Back in the living room, Tracy sipped at the water, clutching the glass with two hands. Unlike earlier in the afternoon at Anne Backes's, there were pictures all over Tracy's room. Tracy playing saxophone at a jazz club. Tracy with some other sax player. Tracy and Jesus at Liberty State Park. Funny, I never placed Jesus as a date kind of guy.

"How long ago were they here?" I asked.

Hands shaking, she checked her watch. "Two hours? I don't know exactly." She wiped her face. Took another sip of water. "Shit. I'm not helping. I'm not."

"Okay. Relax," I said. "Let's take this slow. I need you to think."

"I can't right now. Oh my God. They took him."

She was shaking harder now, and I could tell the enormity of the situation was beginning to sink in. It was beginning to sink in with me as well. Why would Burgess kill Diane and only kidnap Jesus? Something didn't jibe.

Tracy's cell phone rang. She picked it up and looked at the caller ID display. "Pablo," she said.

"He's calling you from his own number?"

"Yeah."

I closed my eyes, thought for a moment. "Answer it. Don't let him know I'm here."

Her eyes filled but she didn't cry. The phone kept ringing. If she didn't pick it up soon, the voice mail would. Tracy took a deep breath. Hit a button.

"Pablo?" she said.

Pause.

"No, no, I—"

She stopped.

"I'm listening."

I couldn't hear Pablo, if that's who it was. Tracy hadn't taken her eyes off me.

"Okay," she said. "Okay."

She put her hand on her head.

"What do you expect me to do?" she said.

Still she stared at me. Her eyes grew wider.

"I'll try," she said. "There's nothing I can do but try."

I thought she was going to break down again. But she kept it together. Listened again briefly, and hung up.

"What did he say?"

"He said Jesus is alive only because of me. Because I helped him—Pablo—out when he came here. Because we used to date. Because he respects me."

Apparently Pablo Najera had more sway with Michael Burgess than I thought. "Did he say anything about Burgess?"

"No."

Okay, Jackson, don't get ahead of yourself. "What did he say about Jesus?"

"He said, he said—" She buried her face in her hands. "He said I could keep him alive."

"How?"

"They want to meet me."

"Who?"

"I don't know. Pablo and someone, he didn't say. They want me to talk Jesus into giving it all up."

"Giving what up?" But I already knew.

"The drug business."

"Where do they want to meet?"

"Jockey Hollow, tonight at midnight. Wick's farm."

"In Bernardsville?"

"Yeah."

Jockey Hollow was huge, an old Revolutionary War encampment. There were old houses, a museum, and lots of dark grassy walkways. It was the perfect place to hide for a hit. I had no doubt that they were only keeping Jesus alive to draw out Tracy on Burgess's orders. No way either Pablo or Burgess wanted to risk a witness coming back to haunt them.

"Okay," I said. "I will be back."

"Where are you going?"

I looked at my watch. We had plenty of time to get there, which was good. I had to clean up some loose ends.

"New Brunswick. I'll pick up you tonight. Don't do anything without me."

"But—"

"Trust me," I said. I wish I felt as confident as I sounded.

CHAPTER 49

my office was cluttered with paperwork. I was going through files, anything I had on Gerry, on Jesus, any drug cases I'd worked as a private investigator. There wasn't much. New Brunswick cops didn't have a tight grip on the drug business because—at least while I was there—they were all junkies themselves. But the cops knew what was going on so no one came to me privately. The one case I worked for Gerry was a favor, and I didn't keep too many notes. I'd never worked for Jesus. There was nothing to back up my theory. But my gut was telling me my worst fears were true.

The phone sat on the desk, taunting me. I knew what I had to do, but I didn't want to pick it up. Taking on Pablo Najera and Michael Burgess on my own, trying to save Jesus and Tracy on my own, was not a good idea. Using Tracy as bait was the only play I had, but I needed backup. Blanchett and Daniels wanted Najera alive.

I picked up the phone, dialed.

"New Brunswick Police Department," a voice said.

I took in air through my nose, then said, "Bill Martin, please." I rubbed my face. "Tell him it's Jackson Donne."

The operator put me on hold. Martin considered Jesus a friend. Jesus was his snitch. Still, he wouldn't hesitate if he needed to shoot someone. The problem was, what would calling Martin cost me. How much more could I lose?

"What the hell do you want?" he grumbled.

"No small talk?"

"Somehow I doubt you're calling me to catch up."

"Have you solved Gerry Figuroa's case yet?"

"What do you care? Believe me, you'll know when it's solved."

"What if I could help you out?"

"I'd say either you lied to me the last few times I talked to you, or you're working the case again. Either one is a no-no."

Christ, this was the point I'd worried about. Whether or not to take the leap. Outside my window two women eyed shoes at the Payless. Kids played Hacky Sack on the corner.

"You were right," I said. "Sort of."

"What do you mean?"

"I think Gerry was selling drugs to try and make his rent. I talked to his ex-wife. She hinted Gerry had done this before. Sold drugs out of his apartment."

"You talked to his ex-wife?" I couldn't tell if he was pissed with me or impressed.

One of the kids playing Hacky Sack kicked the ball into the middle of George Street. He didn't look before running after it. A campus bus almost flattened him. He jumped out of the way just in time. His buddies laughed.

"I talked to her. Here's what I think is happening. Gerry was killed as a warning. He was small-time. But Burgess—"

"Michael Burgess?"

"Yeah. He wasn't big in New Brunswick when I was on the force. Is he now?"

"I don't have my ear to the ground as much as I once did. Rumor has it since Burgess moved into central Jersey, he's become a force."

"I think he's trying to make a move."

"A move to what?"

"Become the most powerful drug dealer in central Jersey."

"And how is he going to do that?"

"Gerry was a warning. Diane, too. I think she tried to leave Burgess, sell drugs on her own. And now, well, who's one of the big fish in the New Brunswick area?"

Martin paused. "Our old friend?"

"Right. Jesus Sanchez."

"He's dead?" Martin swallowed. "No, I would have heard."

"He's not dead yet." I told him what had happened.

"I don't have jurisdiction in that area," he said.

"Since when has that stopped you?"

"You son of a bitch. Are you trying to play me? You get me up there. There's a shoot-out or something, someone dies, I get in a shit-load of trouble."

"I just want to help Jesus."

I pictured him twirling a pencil while trying to decide.

"You will *not* be anywhere near there."

I didn't say anything.

"If I catch you anywhere in Jockey Hollow tonight, you are up shit creek. You broke my rule. You investigated this case. I could put you away for attempted murder. I still might. And if I see you there tonight, I'll have no choice."

"I told Tracy I would drive her."

The Hacky Sack players were walking back toward Rutgers now. The women looking at shoes were long gone.

"I don't give a fuck. Not that it matters. You never listened. Not to me. Not to Jeanne when she needed help. You were the one who pushed her toward me."

What Jeanne's father said was right.

"And I got her back. Even if it was only for two weeks. She came back to me."

He slammed down the phone.

I waited for a dial tone, then rang Tracy. When she picked up, I said, "Stay by the phone. I'm close."

She started to respond, but I said, "I gotta go," and hung up.

In my cabinet I kept a hunting rifle and my second pistol. I took them both and headed to my car.

CHAPTER **50**

SON of a BITCH. tHAT SON of a BITCH. He wasn't
supposed to talk like that. He wasn't even supposed to call.

Bill Martin took a deep breath. This wasn't a big deal. Donne
would still be there tonight.

He'd still die.

But for Donne to remind Martin that Jeanne went back to him.
That son of a bitch.

Martin couldn't wait to see the look on Donne's face as he died.

CHAPTER **51**

We were on 287. It was nearly ten. traffic was light, but I still had to dance in and out between some trucks that were cruising without deadlines.

"Why did we leave so early?" Tracy asked.

Her hands shook. Her eyes darted around the car without a break. She was still high, most likely did some more after I'd left her.

"We have to get there before anyone else." I hadn't mentioned to her that Martin would be there. I hadn't decided how I was going to be involved and still hide from him.

"Najera and Burgess are going to get there early. They want to beat us. So the trick is to get there even earlier. Watch where they set up, look at all the angles."

"I just want to get Jesus back."

She hadn't realized I was using her as bait. I wasn't going to tell her. Sending a woman I'd made love to into the line of fire was wrong. It hurt me to do it, and made me feel like an asshole. She could be dead by the end of the night. Then again, so could I. We pressed on. It was time to end this.

"We will," I said, putting my hand on her knee.

I turned on the radio. Tracy was nervous; she wanted to talk. Maybe she'd sing along. I had to focus. I'd never planned something like this. And definitely not while attempting to hide from someone on my own side. I stepped on the gas.

About twenty minutes into the drive we started seeing orange signs for JOCKEY HOLLOW. New Jersey tried its best to pump up the good things about the state. Unfortunately, most people didn't get the message. Over two hundred years ago, soldiers stayed there on their way to destroy an army. Now there would be more bloodshed.

"Why are you wearing all black?" she asked.

"Because I'm not going to be standing anywhere near you. And I don't want anyone to see me."

"You're . . ." She paused, looked at the roof of the car. "You're not coming with me?"

"If I'm there, they will kill you, me, and Jesus." *And if I'm not, the odds are they'll still kill the both of you.*

"What are you going to do?"

I took Exit 30B off 287 and got onto Route 202. Traffic was light around the windy road, and I was able to take the curves at forty miles per hour. A sign for Jockey Hollow told me to look out on my left.

"Have you ever seen *Lethal Weapon*?" I asked.

"No."

"Here's the plan. I'm going to be as close to you as possible without being seen. There's no light in the park, and not a lot of open spaces. But where Burgess and Najera want to meet with you, that's kind of open. A wooden picket fence surrounds it, if I remember right."

"Okay."

"I'm going to hide there with my hunting rifle."

I hung a right and pulled into the Jockey Hollow site. I ignored the small parking lot. Across from it was a paved trail just wide enough for my Prelude. I took it slow, ten miles an hour.

"If things go wrong, I'll take out Najera and Burgess."

"Jesus Christ," Tracy said. "I'm just going to talk to them. That's what Pablo said."

"And that's what's going to happen," I said. "Think of me as insurance."

The clock on my dashboard said eleven-eighteen. Less than forty-five minutes until the meet. I turned my car up on a grass trail and hit the headlights. I eased about five hundred feet in.

"If I start shooting, if anyone starts shooting, just grab Jesus if you can, and get the hell down. And try to crawl out of the way."

"Oh my God."

Her hand went to her mouth, and I could tell she was shaking. I put my hand on her shoulder and gently squeezed.

"Relax," I said. "It's going to be okay."

Tracy Boland, eyes wide open, sucked in air through her mouth like she was about to hyperventilate. I squeezed the shoulder a little tighter.

"I promise you'll be fine."

"What should I do now?"

I pointed out my back window up a hill to a small wooden house encased in a rotten wooden fence. Surrounding it were trees with leaves that were just beginning to blossom.

"Wick's farm," I said. "That's where your meeting is. Walk toward it slowly. Try to get to the house in about ten minutes."

"It's only about half a mile away."

"I know. Walk slow."

"What are you going to do?"

"Find the best vantage point."

She said Jesus Christ again and opened the car door. She kissed me on the cheek. "Thank you," she whispered. "Good luck."

"You, too."

I counted to a hundred as she walked away, reached into my backseat, and took both of the guns.

The trail led me to the right of the house, up a steep incline. I tried to run and stay low, but in the darkness I couldn't see the rocks

that scattered the ground and I kept stumbling. I found pavement—
the trail we drove up—and followed it close to the wooden gate. The
Wick farmhouse was about five hundred feet away.

The air was clear, cool, and smelled like must, a sign of oncoming rain. Against the sky hung heavy clouds. A thin moon peeked beneath the clouds, giving the pale grass a stream of light. It didn't help
my vision much, but any light at all was nice.

Finding the clearest view, I lay on my stomach and aimed the
rifle. Best I could do at this distance was lay down some cover fire and
scare the hell out of Najera and Burgess. Hopefully Martin would be
there, and I wouldn't have to worry about it too much. Just a few
rounds to get them running. Then the cops could take over and I
would get the hell out of here.

It seemed like a good plan. But something tugged at me, gently
twisting my nerves, making my hands shake. I'd never fired a rifle from
long range. Accidentally hitting someone I didn't want to was a defi-
nite risk. Hell, missing everyone, not even coming close, was a risk. I
didn't know much about this rifle.

Sighting the gun, I could see Tracy making her way toward the
farmhouse. She slipped to one knee. Her arms were wrapped around
herself as if she were cold. Occasionally she looked over her shoulder.

My wristwatch glowed eleven thirty-five. Twenty-five minutes. I
could hear the clicking of the second hand. A lone drop of sweat
curled its way down my forehead. I blinked to keep it out of my eye.
Still I listened to the second hand click.

Finally, at eleven forty-eight, headlights curved around behind
the one-story glass visitors' center. It found the same path I'd rolled
up. My fingers and biceps tensed. I hoped Martin was already here. I
hoped he saw our car pull up and watched Tracy make her way down
the trail. Because the car that parked next to that same trail definitely
wasn't an unmarked.

The interior light of the car went on as the driver's-side door
opened. A burly outline of a man got out. Pablo Najera. He went to the
back door and pulled it open. His thick arms dragged Jesus out. Jesus's

hands were bound behind his back, and his feet dragged in the dirt. From the passenger side, another man exited. Probably Burgess. They looked toward the Wick farmhouse, then back at Jesus. They seemed to be talking to him.

Finally they spun on their heels and moved toward Tracy. I tightened my grip on the rifle and watched.

Showtime.

CHAPTER 52

tHe ButT of tHe RifLe pRessed into my sHouLdeR, its weight causing my arms to ache. My finger was on the trigger guard, my right eye closed as I sighted with my left. The barrel of the gun rested on the wooden fence. The ground was soft and wet and my body sank into the mud a bit. A few drops of rain began to fall, just another distraction if I had to shoot. Between the wind, the rain, the darkness, and the rifle's questionable range, I'd be lucky to hit the side of the farmhouse.

Tracy stood facing the trail Burgess and Najera dragged Jesus along. She was still hugging herself, rocking back on her heels. It seemed she wasn't sure whether or not to go toward Jesus. She would take a step, then stop, hesitate. *Stay there*, I willed, *where I have a sight line*.

I could make out pitches of noise from the trail. It appeared that Jesus was yelling, but I couldn't tell what. Trying to judge what I knew about Jesus, he was more a coward than anything else, probably screaming in fear. He twisted and struggled in Najera's grip, arms knotted behind his back, but Najera wouldn't let go. Jesus went down to one knee; Najera pulled him back up.

Every muscle in my shoulder, my arms, my back, and my legs was tense. I concentrated on watching everyone's movement, trying not to think about the rifle in my hand. But the gun's weight couldn't be ignored, and it got heavier by the minute. I could also feel the spare pistol sticking out of my waistband at the small of my back. I licked my lips, trying to keep them moist, but knowing somehow that they'd be chapped in the morning.

If I made it that far.

I did another scan of the park, and still no sign of Martin. Christ, he'd have to be here already; it was almost midnight. No good cop would come exactly at the meet time. Wick's farmhouse was just at the entrance to the park, too; he couldn't miss it. But there was no sign of the cops, no sign of extra cars, no sign of any life except for the meet and my own tense body.

Tracy went down to one knee, and it looked like she retched. She stayed on the ground. I wanted to tell her to get up, to not show fear or weakness, but then what was that lead ball in the pit of my stomach?

Najera tossed Jesus over the fence, and then climbed it himself. Jesus rolled around on the ground, and Tracy ran to him, cradling his head with her arms. Burgess was the last one over the fence, taking his time, as if enjoying the moment. He glided along the grass. He probably loved this, probably wanted to draw it out. I also wanted it to take as long as possible. I wanted to give Martin every chance to get here.

Tracy rocked Jesus in her arms. Wind blew across my face and sound wasn't carrying as well anymore. I wondered if she was whispering to him. She stroked his hair and rocked back and forth. Burgess's hands were moving; he was talking as if he was explaining something slowly to schoolchildren. He must have said something important, because Tracy's head snapped up from Jesus and she glared his way.

Wait to see a gun, I told myself. Maybe they would let Tracy talk Jesus out of drug dealing and promise to move to a different city, a different state, a different planet.

Hell, even Cleveland.

Najera was pacing. He wasn't speaking, and he didn't look concerned, but he did look like he was scanning his surroundings. I hoped Tracy wasn't giving away my presence with her body language, with her eyes. Or maybe she was a great poker player and Najera was just doing his job and being paranoid.

Army Special Forces would put the blade of a knife under their throats when they were in this position to keep themselves from falling asleep. I could see why. My entire body was tired, the adrenaline rush was gone, and I felt like dropping the gun. I was losing focus; my vision was blurred. The smell of rain and mud clogged my nose. I kept blinking. A knife against my throat would have done a world of good.

Burgess stopped talking. He turned toward Najera, whose attention snapped back. The burly Mexican nodded slowly and reached under his thin jacket. Tracy tossed her head back and screamed.

Here we go.

The gun came out from under Najera's jacket, and he hesitated just an instant. His mouth opened and he spoke. I didn't have time to fuck around. I squeezed the trigger. The gun bucked against my shoulder, lifting me off the ground.

The bullet whizzed through the air and died somewhere around the three-hundred-feet mark, kicking up a cloud of dirt and mud. It came nowhere near the group of people I aimed toward. But the sound echoed around the park, the unmistakable sound of a gunshot, and that did the job. Najera and Burgess scattered, taking cover behind the Wick House. Tracy pulled Jesus close and hit the ground flat.

I fired two more rounds, the bullets whizzing into the air. The sound echoed off the mountains. Najera and Burgess spread out so I couldn't shoot at either of them. Tracy and Jesus hopped to their feet after the third bullet and made a beeline for the fence at the far end from the house. Jesus was hobbled by his bound hands, but he was making good time. Tracy did her best to help him.

I fired one more round, aiming high, giving the bullet a bit of an arc to help it carry. I was going to have to stop shooting and move in an instant, and I didn't want Najera or Burgess realizing they were really in little danger. The bullet rocketed through the air and probably gained another hundred fifty feet or so. The bullet cracked the ground just in front of Najera. He flinched and tried to find the direction of the gunfire, leveling his gun at the horizon.

Feeling the wind at my face, the cool drizzle on the back of my neck, I was moving instinctually. Bent over, staying out of sight, I ran hard to get closer to the farmhouse. At least I was on paved road, so there weren't many rocks or other obstacles to avoid. Breathing in through my nose, out through my mouth, I tried to keep my heart rate down, to stay calm and not let the new rush of adrenaline take over. Easier said than done.

Pop! Pop! Pop! Pop!

Maybe it was the blood pumping in my ears. Maybe it had to do with the speed of sound. Maybe it was the sequence of events. Whatever it was, the sound of gunfire snapped me back to attention before the sound of the car squealing into the park. Looking up, I saw a Honda Accord bounce over a strip of grass and up through the wooden fence toward Tracy and Jesus. I didn't see either of them fall, didn't know how it happened, but they were both on the ground staring at the car. A red bubble flashed light on its roof.

Martin.

Not once that I knew of had Martin called for backup. I don't know if he saw too many cowboy movies as a kid or if he was stubborn and wanted all the credit, but he broke procedure all the time and never caught hell for it. Mostly because he was successful. Corrupt, but successful.

Today was no different. Out of his jurisdiction, riding in like the fucking cavalry. Najera had his gun trained on the Accord now and fired another two rounds. Since there was no gunfire coming from the car, I assumed he'd also fired the first four.

I stood up straight, leveled my rifle, and was able to get off another round. The bullet embedded itself in the wood of the Wick House. Burgess leaned against the building. My shot had the desired effect. Najera gave up trying to take out the Accord and ran, keeping his head low. Burgess was already halfway toward his car.

Martin leaped out of the Honda. Gun drawn, he ran toward Najera screaming, "Freeze! Police."

Martin moved toward Tracy and Jesus. He stayed low. I could hear his voice, and it sounded soothing. Finding out if they were okay. I hoped like hell they were.

Burgess had reached the car, and revved the engine. I was only about one hundred feet from the bumper when he stepped on the gas. I stopped running and aimed my rifle. Squeezed the trigger and felt the report in my shoulder. I noticed a throbbing pain there.

The back windshield of the car exploded, and the car swerved but didn't stop. In fact, it looked like it sped up. Before I could get another shot off, Burgess found pavement and was out into the parking lot heading toward the exit. He was out of sight. My only hope was Martin got a good view of the car and radioed it in.

I looked toward them to see if Najera was around. He wasn't. Martin got Tracy and Jesus into the Accord. None of them saw me. Tracy and Jesus would be caught up telling stories to the cops for hours. I had to get the hell out of there. Make sure I wasn't hanging around when the interrogation started.

Turning on the path, I headed toward my car. I moved quicker than I had before, aware there wasn't any more gunfire and less to worry about. Just didn't want Martin to stop me, didn't want him giving me any more shit than I already had.

Seeing the moon reflecting off the black metal in the distance, I reached into my pocket and hit the lock alarm. I opened the trunk and dropped the rifle in and reached behind me and dropped my handgun as well. Slamming the trunk closed, I turned toward the driver's side. Next thing I knew I was on my back.

"Knew it was you. Laying down that cover fire." The voice was deep and cold.

"Najera," I mumbled.

"Ah, about time." Now the voice's Mexican accent was thick. No reason to try and hide it anymore.

I rubbed my nose where I'd been hurt. I'd no doubt this hulk of a man had made me bleed again. It was starting to rain.

He stood over me, looking down. I couldn't really see his expression because of the shadows, but I could see his mouth move when he spoke.

"So, what the hell are you doing here? This wasn't what you were hired to do. You were just hired to find me and bring me back to Jen. But here you are firing a fucking rifle at me. What if you had hit me? How would you have been paid for your work? Too bad." He shook his head. "Now. Well, now you're going to die."

He aimed his firearm at me.

Before he could fire, I swung my leg and knocked Najera's out from under him. As he went down, I heard his gun go off and clatter off a rock somewhere in the darkness. I got up and ran deeper into the forest on wobbly legs.

The darkness and the rain made it hard to see and even more difficult to get traction on the ground, so I stopped to get my bearings. Stopping didn't help. I had no idea where I was. I took a step and my sneaker sank into mud. I took another step and nearly fell on my face, tripping on a rock. The goal was to keep moving, get as much distance between Najera and me as possible. He'd kicked my ass twice. I was going to have to use the forest, my dark clothes, and the night sky to my advantage. At least he no longer had a gun. Then again, neither did I.

"I'll fucking kill you!" Najera's voice echoed among the trees.

By this point, I'd have expected to hear sirens. I'd have expected to hear an ambulance or more cops, something to break the silence. But I didn't hear anything. Which meant that Martin was taking care of things himself. He would be able to talk his way out of things later.

The trail was getting narrower and the sound of rushing water carried off to my right. I could feel the landscape more than see it, and I hoped Najera was having even more trouble. He was moving in my direction, not caring about being stealthy. The sounds of snapping twigs and tumbling pebbles reached my ears. To my left the land inclined; toward the water was a cliff with a small drop-off toward the stream.

"You motherfucker!" he yelled.

Odds were if I was careful, I'd be able to get the drop on him. I'd intentionally worn black clothes, my footsteps were quiet, and I was a good two minutes ahead of him. Moving slowly, I veered left. There was a thick tree angling off the incline and I leaned against it, shielded from the trail.

Still I could hear Najera rumbling toward me. The key was to be quicker than him. Both times, he had caught me off guard. Now I had him at that edge. Sure my head still ached from his punch, but at this point every little advantage was necessary.

One minute passed. My stomach tensed. The snapping branches grew louder.

Another minute. Any second now he'd come into view. I held my breath. The breaking twigs, the clack of feet on rocks were deafening.

I closed my eyes and tried to clear my mind. The smell of rain, the patter of the drops soaked my wool cap, then my hair. The rain was harder now, the drops combining to roll off the leaves of the trees. My clothes were heavy. But I was faster than he was. I knew I was.

He came around the curve, slowly, as if he sensed he was close to me. No more crackling branches. No more swearing. I wasn't even sure he was breathing. Ten feet and he'd be next to my tree. He kept moving. Five feet. Four.

Three feet.

Two.

One.

I leapt from the back of the tree onto Najera. We both went down hard. On top of him, I swung three quick rights into the center of his face. I pulled back my hand to land another blow when Najera grabbed both my shoulders and tossed me off him.

I was on my back, and he was rolling to his feet. Rain washed over us. I tried to stand, but he caught me in the ribs with the toe of his boot. I gasped and tried to inhale, and he caught me in the cheek with a huge open paw. On my knees, I spat. I could see it land on a rock, and then wash away in the rain. My ears rang.

He hovered over me. "This is it," he said. "I never should have let you live. Never should have taken you at your word. You screwed

Burgess when he paid you. You lied to my wife. You lied to me. You deserve to die."

He cocked his right fist, and quicker than I'd imagined possible he crushed my nose. I was on my back and he was over me. His huge paws wrapped around my throat, pressing on my windpipe. I couldn't breathe. My lungs were empty.

"You fucking asshole," he said.

The world went blurry, a montage of blood and rain and blackness. Still he pressed tighter. My hands flared and I couldn't think. My mouth dropped open, desperately trying to find air.

"You've ruined my life," I think he said, but it just mixed with the white noise.

I flailed my arms, clawed at his hands. My index finger's nail tore off against his skin. Water pooled in my mouth. I saw Jeanne. I saw Gerry. I pawed at Najera's face.

He spat, and liquid from his nose dripped onto me. My fingers felt along his face. My vision was going. The world turned purple, and then completely black. My hands felt something squish under his hairline. I jabbed my thumb at it. Pressed harder. Felt it give under the pressure, felt a warm liquid ooze across my knuckle. Najera screamed. The soft tissue I pressed on popped under my fingers. He released my throat.

"Goddamn it! Shit!" he screamed. "I'll fucking kill you, you fucker!"

I rolled onto my side and massaged my throat, tried to let the air find its way into my lungs. I coughed up liquid. Slowly, like a fade-in on a movie, my vision returned.

Najera was still screaming. He flopped and rolled on the ground. I still had time to recover. I fought my way to my feet. Soaked, dripping, I realized we were on the edge of the precipice. To my right, water rushed.

"I'll fucking kill you," he said again. It must have taken a huge effort to even stay awake, and he fought his way to his feet. He staggered once, then rushed me like a linebacker. Wrapping me around the waist, he pushed us both over the edge. We tumbled along a steep slope, hitting what had to be every jagged branch and every stone until we both landed in a shallow stream.

He was on his feet first. Everything ached on my body, and I didn't think I'd be able to get up ever again. Pieces of his skin, of his eye, hung from his face. His teeth were clenched and blood poured from his face. This wasn't going to end until one of us was dead.

I found a rock the size of a softball with my right hand. I hefted it and he tried to rush me again. The water slowed him and he was unable to gain any speed. Getting to my feet, I clocked him with the rock. He went down in a heap. I hit him again.

And again.

And again.

And again.

I screamed as his skull crushed beneath my hand. I kept screaming until I was sure he wasn't going to get up again. The water rushed around us. I collapsed to the ground, exhausted. I spit blood.

The rain didn't stop.

C H A P T E R

53

Walking up the incline was the most difficult thing I'd ever done. Everything ached. My windpipe wasn't crushed, I didn't think, but it was hard to breathe. The cuts on my fingers had reopened, bled, and ached. I limped and my nose burned. I had to use branches and trees to pull myself up.

Every inch felt like a mile. At one point my left leg was ankle-deep in mud. It took me a good three minutes of wiggling to get it out. Pushing my way, I reached the trail and looked back down. Throughout the adrenaline-fueled fight and my recent climb, it felt like the incline was huge, fifty feet or more. But looking back I saw it was no more than fifteen to twenty feet.

I sprawled on the trail, feeling pebbles in my back. I tried to catch my breath.

Another dead body by my hand.

I pushed myself to my feet and limped back along the trail to my car. Getting there, I remembered my keys were on the ground, where

I'd dropped them after getting hit. But when I went to reach for them, they were gone. After a minute my eye caught them dangling from the lock near my trunk.

I opened the trunk and found that my rifle was there, but my handgun was gone. I shut the trunk and unlocked the driver's-side door. My cell phone was blinking in the cup holder.

Starting the car, I dialed my voice mail.

Bill Martin's voice came on. "You are one lucky son of a bitch. But there's one more thing you need to know. Jeanne didn't pick you. And if she had lived, you would have found out why."

What the hell was he talking about? It didn't matter now. I had to get back.

With my nailless finger throbbing with pain, I put the car into gear and pulled out to find the road back to New Brunswick.

✳ ✳

I picked up the tail within five minutes. I pulled out onto Route 202 to head back to 287 when a Mercury Cougar pulled behind me. In the streetlights I could see clearly that it was the same shape as Burgess's car. He wasn't trying to hide. Which meant that either he had been waiting for Najera to come out, or waiting to see who pulled out shooting at them. Either way, he was following me now, and he probably knew I wasn't Najera.

My car clock read nearly two-thirty. The streets were empty, and it was difficult for Burgess to hang back, so he tailgated. Good idea.

I couldn't go back to New Brunswick yet. I needed allies. I crossed through Morristown and into Madison. Next to a car dealership was an abandoned parking lot. It seemed like as good a place for this as any. I pulled into the lot, took out a business card, and dialed Daniels's number. Left a message.

The Cougar slammed into the passenger door. My head cracked the driver's-side window. My seat belt locked, and I couldn't undo it. The Cougar backed up and rammed my car again. Glass shattered and metal crunched. I couldn't get a hold on where I was anymore. All the pain, all my injuries were slowing me down. I couldn't react. I couldn't get out of my car.

The Cougar backed up and rammed me again. My car had to have been totaled. The Cougar, too. Blinded by its headlights, I saw the silhouette of the driver's door open and Burgess's thin profile get out. I fought with my seat belt; finally got it unclicked. Then I found the door handle.

I got out of the car, stumbled out actually. I saw Burgess stumbling as well.

"I see you ran into Rex," he said. His words were slurred. His body probably took the brunt of driving into my car.

"Najera?" I asked, leaning against the fender of my car. My legs didn't seem to be able to hold me.

"Yeah. He got you good."

"Not as good as I got him."

"You said that the last time you looked like this."

"Yeah, but this time I'm not lying."

Burgess looked over my shoulder.

I nodded. "Listen, it's over. This whole thing is over."

Burgess pulled a long syringe out of his pocket and began to move toward me. "I've been waiting for you. Only one of you would come out of the trees alive. I hoped it was you. I wanted to be the one to kill you. Fuck you for all of this. Three of my best men out of commission. My business is a mess."

"Jesus is still alive. The police know what you're doing. They'd love to take down the leading drug dealer in this area. It was stupid, trying to take out your competition."

"Do you know what this is?" he hissed, nodding at the needle. "It's a fucking concentrated form of heroin. I'm going to fucking overdose you."

"Jesus I can understand. He's held on to New Brunswick for years. And he's in with the cops. You get too close to him, he'd squeal on you and you'd be out of business. Hell, even Diane I can see. She held that school market. Did she ever work for you?"

Burgess didn't answer. But the small twitch in his eye was as good as a yes. "Keep talking, you fucker. You'll be dead before you know it."

"And you had Pablo leave her out on the front gate of Drew as what? A message for anyone thinking of messing with you?"

Another twitch. He stepped closer, and a drop of liquid fell from the needle's point.

"But why Gerry? Was he really a threat? He was small-time. As far as I can tell, he was only making crystal meth and selling it to a few college kids. To make rent. Diane you left wide out in the open as a sign for everyone to see. But you had Najera make Gerry look like an accident."

He pressed his left arm against my shoulder. I tried to get up, push him off me, but my legs still didn't work. I felt the point of the needle against my neck.

"Why Gerry?" I asked again. "I need to know why."

The needle hadn't broken skin yet, and Burgess's eyes narrowed. "I don't know who Gerry is."

His hand stiffened and the syringe penetrated my neck. I tried to push him away, to grab at the syringe, but I kept missing. I waited for the sweet burn of the drugs to take over.

The sound of sirens made him turn. With one final effort, I reached up and swatted the syringe from his grip. It bounced slightly when it hit pavement. Two marked cars and an unmarked sped around the corner. Daniels had gotten my message.

"Hands on your head! Both of you!" a loudspeaker announced.

I did as I was told. So did Burgess. Two uniforms hopped out of the first marked car and grabbed Michael Burgess, handcuffing him and reading him his rights.

Daniels and Blanchett approached me. I slid off the fender and sat on the cold ground.

"Put your hands down," Blanchett said. He pointed at Burgess. "Where's Pablo Najera? He's not with this asshole?"

I just shook my head.

"What happened to you?" Daniels asked.

"I walked into a door." I tried to smile.

"Tough door."

"You have no idea."

"We should get you to a hospital."

I didn't argue.

✳ ✳

We waited in the hospital until morning. Apparently my cuts and bruises and broken nose weren't enough of an emergency to get immediate medical attention. While we sat, Blanchett received word that some cops had found the body of a man matching Najera's description in a ditch in Jockey Hollow. I didn't know anything about it.

The waiting room was just busy enough. A man who had shortness of breath and chest pains. A woman with a bone broken so bad it stuck out of her arm. A kid stabbed in the leg with a nail. Fun stuff.

The antiseptic walls and bright lights hurt my eyes and occasionally I'd close them to try and get some sleep. Daniels wouldn't let me, though. She was afraid I had a concussion. She kept asking me questions. Why was Burgess following me? Did I know anything about Najera's death? Why did they keep getting reports that Jockey Hollow looked like it had been shot up? Was I still willing to testify, even against Burgess if it came to that?

The only one I answered was the last one. Now that I knew what was going on, I was definitely willing to testify.

It bothered me, what Burgess had said. Why would he admit to me about everything else, but claim no knowledge of Gerry's death? Unless he was telling the truth. It bothered me well into my examination.

It bothered me until they reset my nose. The pain was the only thing I was thinking about.

CHAPTER **54**

Over the next few weeks a lot happened and nothing happened at all. I sat around listening to police officers and lawyers talk to me. I thought about what Michael Burgess had said. He didn't know Gerry. I thought about death and mortality. Never liked what I came up with. Over those few weeks my injuries healed.

Eventually what it came down to was a plea bargain. They didn't have any proof that I killed Pablo Najera, and without testing the rifle, they didn't have any proof that those bullets found around Jockey Hollow were mine. But if I refused to testify, Daniels and Blanchett made it clear they'd follow through a lot harder. I told them I would testify that Michael Burgess hired Pablo Najera as a hit man and was directly responsible for the murder of Diane Peterson and Gerry Figuroa.

At the same time, Burgess's men refused to testify about anything, and my own trial was dropped. Lack of evidence.

Daniels and Blanchett fought to get my license renewed. Martin fought against it. Ultimately I'd been involved in too much violence for it to matter; the state of New Jersey would not allow me to be a private investigator anymore.

When Daniels broke the news to me, an early-May morning, she tried to apologize.

"It's okay," I said. "I'm going back to school. In fact, I have my admittance exam this Saturday."

Daniels wished me luck. It sounded like she was trying not to laugh.

Tracy and I went to dinner a few times, but things weren't working. She wanted to talk about the case. I didn't. She still loved her uncle. I didn't want to talk about the drug war. I didn't want to tell her that he wasn't the kindest man I knew. Or the loving man she was beginning to think he was. On a Thursday afternoon in May, she told me she was going back to Jesus.

The day she was supposed to leave, I asked her to take a ride in my new preowned Toyota Celica before we went back to Asbury. I had to share something with her. We drove to Anne Backes's house.

"Where are we?" Tracy asked, as we waited for the old woman to answer the door.

"Visiting someone I think you should meet."

The door opened and Anne stared up at us.

"What the hell are you doing here?" she asked me.

"Ms. Backes, you've heard about your husband?"

"I read the papers."

The afternoon was warm, a contrast to the rainy, bipolar temperatures of April. The sun beat down and the air was still, constant. The weather that day had the feel of stability.

As if registering the name for the first time, I heard Tracy whisper to herself. "Backes?"

"Can we come in?" I asked.

"I don't think so."

To my right, I could feel Tracy shaking. She put her hand on my arm as she put the information together.

"Ms. Backes, let me introduce you to Tracy." I could have said the last name, but I wanted Anne Backes to figure it out on her own.

"Tracy?" She squinted.

"Aunt Anne?" Tracy said. "Oh my God. It's been so long."

Tracy reached in to hug and Anne fell into the embrace. The frail woman shook along with Tracy and they both had tears in their eyes.

"Come in, girl. Come in," Anne said.

We followed Anne in through the house. There were pictures now on all the shelves. Most of them were pictures of Anne in black-and-white. Old pictures. In a few of them I recognized Gerry. In a few of them, there were two children posing, a boy and a girl.

Tracy walked around the room looking at the pictures. Sometimes she'd pick one up and stare at it for a while, tracing an outline with her finger. Anne watched her. They'd both smile at times, shed a few tears at others.

Picking up one of the pictures of the boy and girl playing, Tracy asked, "Is this me and Steven?"

Anne walked over and looked. She said, "Yes."

"Who's this girl?"

She hesitated. "One of Steven's friends."

"I don't remember any of this. I can't even remember you."

"You were young when I left."

"Why did you leave?"

Anne Backes looked at me and seemed to be turning things over in her head. We both knew it was too late to dance again. The truth was out in the papers; there wasn't anything to hide anymore.

"Your uncle. He was a bad father. He'd go out, he'd party. He smoked weed, did drugs. Sold drugs. He was never around for Steven. He wasn't around for me."

"So you left the two of them?"

Anne looked at me again. "I never told anyone I was the smartest woman. I tried to force the issue. The last time I saw Gerry, he came home with a wad of dollars in his hand. Probably a thousand dollars cash from selling drugs. It had been a good week. Steven went to him and asked for a cookie. Gerry barely glanced at the kid. He was drunk. He tossed Steven a twenty and told him to go buy one."

Anne wiped at her eyes. "I told Gerry he needed to shape up. To be a good father. I told him I was leaving him alone with Steven. He had to shape up, clean up. Then I'd come back. I promised him I would, but I promised myself it wouldn't be until we could be a whole family. No more of the drug shit. By the time Gerry cleaned up his act, Steven had grown up. Mostly on his own, I think. Then he got sick and died."

Tracy was crying now. "You never got to see your son?"

"I found ways."

"But Steven, we kept in touch, even when I was out in Ohio. He said he hadn't seen you. He couldn't remember you."

"I loved them both so much. Steven. Gerry. Why couldn't he clean up? Why couldn't we all be together?"

"Aunt Anne—"

"No. I miss him. He ruined my life, but I miss him. I couldn't even go to the funeral. It wasn't right for me to be there. I wanted to be. But I couldn't go."

Anne shook her head, buried her face in her hands. Her shoulders shook, and she didn't say any more. Tracy sat next to her, put her arms around her shoulders.

I looked at the pictures some more, wondering why they weren't out the last time I'd been here. Maybe Anne was about to dust that day and she put the pictures away before doing it.

All of the pictures were old. All were in black-and-white. Except for one. It was tucked away, around the corner nearly behind the TV, where people wouldn't see it unless they looked carefully. I was trying to keep my eyes averted from Tracy and Anne's moment, so I'd glanced around several times. I stepped closer and looked at the picture.

A jolt of adrenaline shot through my body. Anne Backes standing with another woman. It could have been taken yesterday.

There was a reason the pictures weren't out a month ago. Anne Backes didn't want me to see them.

✳　✳

Anne didn't want anyone to know. So while I drove Tracy back to Asbury, I didn't say anything. Maybe Tracy actually did know. Either way,
it wasn't my place to say.

I parked in front of the house and walked Tracy to the front door.
We looked at each other. Tracy's face was still red from crying.

"Thank you, Jackson," she said.

She leaned in to kiss me. I let her. It was a light kiss; none of the
earlier passion, a fire that was lit again for only an evening or two and
burned out quickly after that. I can't say I felt the same as she did. I
wanted to see her again. I wanted to know her again.

And this time remember the entire relationship.

"It's too bad things didn't work out for us," she said.

I gave her a hug. "We both know they wouldn't have," I lied. "Give
Jesus a hug."

We stood for a moment watching each other. An awkward silence rested between us, as if we didn't know the right way to end
things. The right way to say good-bye.

"Any help you need," I said. "I can get you into a rehab."

Tracy said, "Good luck, Jackson."

"Good-bye, Tracy."

I kissed her on the cheek, and turned back to my car.

That seemed as good a way to leave as any.

55

CHAPTER

THINGS WERE LOOKING UP.

At first, his superiors were pissed that Bill Martin went over their heads and out of district on the case. They told him it wasn't a movie, he wasn't Dirty Harry. That if he wanted to be a trusted member of the police, he had to be a team player.

Then the press got hold of the story and ran with it. Martin was a hero, saving a woman from certain death. Running through a hail of bullets, shoving two innocent people into a car, and driving off. Having a hand in taking down the biggest drug dealer in the state. And his superiors had no choice. They promoted him to detective first grade.

Not being able to get the assault charges on Donne to trial was somewhat a disappointment. Though once Martin was considered a hero, there was no way Donne was getting his private investigator license back. No way was Martin going to let that happen. So he fought Daniels and Blanchett and showed all the evidence and he won.

He sat in his office and felt empty. He kept the picture of Jeanne with him all the time now. And he often stared at it. As he did today.

∗　∗

Three weeks after she stopped calling, Jeanne came to visit him in his office. He didn't speak until she did. He stared at her. Tears streaked her face.

"I'm sorry, Bill," she said.

Martin refused to speak.

"Jackson called," she continued. "He went into rehab. He sobered up."

"And you went back to him?" Martin forced the words out.

She nodded and cried, digging through her purse for a tissue. Every instinct in his body screamed for Martin to go to her. To wrap her in his arms and hold her. But he sat at his desk, folded his hands together, and waited.

"I had to, Bill," she said. "I love him. I've always loved him. He just fucked up, that's all. And now—"

"Now what?" He slammed his fists on the desk, and rage filled him. For the first time the rage was directed at her.

She shuddered at the sound. But she wiped her eyes, didn't leave.

"Now he's working as a private investigator. He's making something of himself. I need to be there for him." Tears streamed down her face. She no longer tried to stop them.

"Then why are you here?"

"I had to talk to you."

Something in her voice softened. There wasn't sadness. Martin let instinct take him. He got out of his chair, went around his desk, and put his arms around her. The floral fragrance of her perfume overtook him. He had to fight back his own tears.

"I went to the doctor today," she said. "There was something wrong with me. I was late."

"What?"

"Bill, I had to talk to you." She fiddled through her purse, but didn't come out with anything. "Because the doctor told me I'm pregnant."

"Oh my God." He could no longer fight off the tears. He pulled her closer to him.

"The baby is yours, Bill. Jackson and I, we haven't slept together. Not since I went back."

"Does he know?"

"No. I haven't told him. I don't know that I will. I have to talk to him tonight. I don't know what I'm going to do yet."

Doesn't know what she's going to do? He pulled her close, felt her hands on his back.

"You're going to tell him you love me," Martin said.

"I can't do that, Bill. I don't know what to do."

"I love you, Jeanne."

"I know."

"And you love me."

She said, "Let me have tonight. I want to talk to Jackson when he gets back from his case. I will call you tomorrow."

Jeanne Baker pushed herself away from Martin. She kissed him gently on his cheek, turned his back on him, and walked out the door.

❋　❋

Bill Martin never saw Jeanne again. Hours later a drunk driver collided with her car and killed her.

There was no investigation.

There wasn't an autopsy.

Jackson Donne never knew. And Bill Martin never told him. He put the picture back in his desk. He hadn't thought of that moment in years. He had put it away, hidden it, like he'd hidden the picture.

Maybe it was a mistake to tell Donne about their affair. Because now Martin remembered everything.

And he couldn't put it away.

CHAPTER

Saturday I sat in Scott Hall and took a six-hour test. I hadn't filled in that many circles since my first and only semester at Villanova. I had to write an essay, do complicated math, and answer questions about a Spanish short story. It was a very mundane and mind-numbing way to pass the time. But without a job, and needing to earn some scholarships, I had to deal with it.

When I finished, I took my newly acquired carpal tunnel syndrome and hopped on Route 287. The leaves were fully bloomed now; the sides of the road looked like thick forests. I exited in Morristown and drove to Jen Hanover's house. It had been weeks since I'd seen her, the news vans had since exited, and her story was old news. I, however, had one last piece of business with her.

She let me in wordlessly, as if she'd expected me. We sat in the living room, and I had the familiar sensation of smelling steam. I thought of my mother, and how my father had left her, my sister, and me alone.

Jen looked as if she'd lost about ten pounds. There were dark bags under her eyes, and her cheeks were sunken.

"Have you been sleeping?" I asked without much sympathy.

"It was a mistake to hire you," she said. "But you've been paid what you were owed. Why are you here?"

"I'd like to sort a few things out."

"There's nothing to sort out. If I hadn't hired you, my husband would still be alive."

The living room was a mess. There were dust bunnies floating around the room. Old newspapers and empty coffee cups were left on the kitchen table. A few scraps of paper were strewn across the floor.

"Why did you hire me?"

"To find my husband and bring him back to me before the police got to him," she said evenly.

"That doesn't make much sense."

"What do you mean?"

"Why would you hire me to find the man who killed your father?"

"What?"

I was very slow in answering, letting my words process in my head. Like a lawyer, I wanted to make everything very clear.

"Anne Backes is your mother, isn't she?"

"What? I—no."

"I was at her home two days ago. There were many pictures of Steven and his cousin. There was one color picture. It was of you and Anne sitting in a park."

"You're lying."

"It's time to own up."

She spoke too quickly, not thinking about protecting her identity. "She told me the pictures were put away."

"If," I said slowly, "Anne is your mother, that makes Gerry Figuroa your father. Your husband was a hit man for drug dealers."

"My husband is dead!"

"I know. And that's not what you wanted, is it? I mean, why hire me to follow him after he killed your dad, unless you wanted me to find him?"

"Shut up."

"You asked your husband to kill Gerry. You wanted it to look like an accident. But almost immediately the police didn't buy it. So you were screwed."

She buried her face in her hands.

"I've figured most of it out, Jen. But you have to help me fill in the holes. What happened when you heard it wasn't being looked at as an accident? That was in the papers, wasn't it? Or did Pablo tell you?"

"I don't have to tell you. You'll put me in jail."

This was the tough part, the reason I didn't come here directly after seeing Anne Backes. If I called the police on this, then Burgess's trial would be skewed. My testimony wouldn't be worth anything and there'd be a chance I'd go to jail. And a drug dealer might go free. I wasn't willing to let that happen. As much as it burned me, as much as she was responsible for the death of my friend, she was the lesser of two evils.

I sat back on the couch. "You're not going to jail. I just want to know the truth."

She looked me in the eyes.

"You have my word. I have nothing to gain by putting you in jail, Jen. I just want to know. And I'm sure it's driving you nuts, keeping it bottled up."

"What do you want to know?" she asked.

"What happened? You asked Pablo to kill Gerry. Your own father. Why?"

"He wasn't my father!" She took a deep breath. "My mother and I were the only family I had. He destroyed my mother, made her crazy. She left my brother with him because she couldn't think straight. He had her so hopped up on drugs, she didn't think to take Steven. She only took me when she realized she hit rock-bottom. She went to clean up and she only took me. She started to use the excuse that he had to learn to be a father on his own. Tough love bullshit. He ruined our family, and he couldn't even clean up for it."

I nodded. There wasn't a flow to my questions, I just asked them when they came to mind. "Did you know you married a hit man?"

Jen Hanover shook her head. "At one point, when I was seventeen, a friend went into a tailspin. She slipped up and got back on heroin. She must have gone through Burgess. She met Pablo. She introduced him to me as Rex. I fell in love with Rex. She cleaned up not long after. He helped her. She always seemed scared of Rex. I never knew why, until . . . until . . ."

"When did you find out?"

"When Steven died, I called Gerry. I wanted to talk to him. He told me he was cleaning up. Stopped drinking. Stopped smoking. All that. I was so angry. Why did he have to wait until one of us died to clean up? I was so mad. Rex thought it would pass. That I would get over it. But I didn't. Finally, a few months ago, he said—" She gagged. Caught her breath. "He said he would kill Gerry if I wanted. And I was so mad. I said yes. That's when Rex told me everything."

The room was still and quiet. The enormity of her words hung in the air as she took deep breaths. There were more questions to ask, but sometimes it was better to let people talk. Once she got her breathing back to normal, I was confident she would continue. Jen needed to talk; the words were spilling out of her now.

"I told Rex to make it look like an accident, but he drove off. There were too many witnesses. And the more I thought about it, the more I started to hate him as well. Now that I knew his business, he let me hear everything. I knew when people were going to die. I knew about that woman at Drew."

I nodded. "So you decided to hire me. To find him, to stop the killings?"

"No. I wanted you to catch him for killing Gerry. When I had talked to Gerry, he was mad that I didn't come to Steve's funeral, wanted to know where I was. That even his private investigator friend showed up. I remembered that and looked you up."

Rubbing my chin, I asked, "But what if he was captured. Wouldn't he implicate you?"

"Maybe I didn't think things through. I trusted he loved me, would do anything for me. But by then, I didn't love him. I hated him.

Part of me didn't even care if he did turn me in. Gerry would still be dead."

I thought about the first time I saw Najera, when he hung me out the window. "Did he know what you were doing?"

She shrugged. "I never told him. Never even saw him. Never got to say good-bye."

"I think he did."

"Why?"

I told her about him acting like Burgess had hired me. Pablo Najera put me on Michael Burgess's tail to keep me away from his wife's. Burgess acted surprised when I told him who hired me, but Najera knew all along.

"How far did you go to make sure Gerry's death wasn't your fault?"

"What do you mean?"

"The police found the ingredients of crystal meth all over his apartment, like he was making it to sell. Did you plant it there? Make it look like he was back in the drug business?"

She thought about it for a moment. "No," she said. "I had nothing to do with that."

I wanted her to say yes. Gerry was supposed to be the lovable old guy in the bar, the guy who'd tell jokes and you could laugh with. He wasn't supposed to be making drugs to survive. But Jen had no reason to lie now. She was telling the truth. Gerry was selling again.

Jen gagged some more.

I stood to go. "One last thing. Did your cousin Tracy know you were Gerry's daughter?"

"No. When we became friends, in college, Tracy was already too deep into drugs, she was a mess."

"You met up with her in college?"

"I knew about her long before that. I wanted to know my family, even though my mother didn't. I found out where she went to college and I applied. When I got in, I looked her up and we became friends."

I nodded and moved to the door.

"You're really going to let me be?"

I was afraid that not pinning Gerry's death on Burgess would give the defense a cause to question the entire case.

"A major drug dealer is going to go to prison because of all of this," I said. "You're small-time compared to that."

"So I'm going to be innocent." It was a statement, not a question.

Staring at her, I said, "You're the one who has to live with setting up the death of your father and being involved in the death of your husband."

I walked to the front door.

"Wait," she said.

I turned back.

Her eyes were nearly black, her face flushed. She looked so small in the easy chair she sat in, so alone. Which, I suppose, is what she wanted to be.

"When I married him, Rex promised he'd never hurt me."

"I think he tried his best to keep that promise," I said.

✳ ✳

At six in the evening the Olde Towne Tavern was quiet for a Saturday. A month ago, Gerry would have been sitting at his usual stool in the corner, sipping his coffee, telling some college kid a war story. Or an acting story. Any kind of story. But now the corner seat was empty.

The college kids who'd usually eat up those kind of stories were playing darts. I sat at the bar drinking Amstel, watching Artie wipe the bar down.

"How was the test?" he asked.

I shrugged. "Pointless."

"Gotta do what you gotta do." He smiled. "It's over now? That Burgess guy killed Gerry because he was selling some drugs to make rent?"

I thought about telling him everything. But it was time to let the case die. Time to leave Gerry's memory alone. "Yeah. That's what happened."

"Fucking old man. He could have come to any of us for help, for money. He was our friend."

I finished my beer. The college kids finished playing darts and moved on to the pool table. As they racked them up, I wondered how close they were to each other, what kind of friends they were, how far they'd go for each other. Or if they were only drinking buddies hanging out because they were all free tonight.

Artie got me another. "I never got to say thank you, Jackson. And sorry."

"For what?"

"For thinking you weren't doing your job. For getting you involved in this. You didn't want to, from the start. But I forced you into it. And you lost your license. And found out a bunch of shit we both probably didn't want to know. I'm sorry for being such an asshole."

I took a long drink from the new bottle of Amstel and thought about how far Pablo Najera went for his wife. Thought about how far Anne Backes went to try and get Gerry to clean up. How far she went to make her family whole. I thought about all the promises people made every day, and how far they went to keep them.

Then I thought about how hard I tried to keep away from mine.

"Jackson?" Artie said. He reached out his hand and shook mine.

"Don't worry about it," I said. "I promised."

about the author

Dave White was born in 1979 and currently works as an eighth-grade language arts teacher. He is a winner and multiple-time nominee for the Derringer Award for best short story, and was short-listed for the 2005 *storySouth* Million Writers Award. He is a member of Mystery Writers of America and International Thriller Writers, and has contributed to many anthologies and collections, including *The Adventure of the Missing Detective* and *Damn Near Dead*. He lives in New Jersey.